THE GREAT REBELLION
OF
QUEEN BOUDICCA

THE GREAT REBELLION OF QUEEN BOUDICCA

PATRICK MAN

ATHENA PRESS
LONDON

THE GREAT REBELLION OF QUEEN BOUDICCA
Copyright © Patrick Man 2009

All Rights Reserved

No part of this book may be reproduced in any form
by photocopying or by any electronic or mechanical means,
including information storage or retrieval systems,
without permission in writing from both the copyright
owner and the publisher of this book.

ISBN 978 1 84748 503 8

First published 2009 by
ATHENA PRESS
Queen's House, 2 Holly Road
Twickenham TW1 4EG
United Kingdom

Printed for Athena Press

*In memory of the late Major General PH Man,
and dedicated to all those he loved
and the places where he was happy.*

Boudicca proclaimed that it was victory or death.
That was her resolve as a woman.

Tacitus, Annals XIV

Contents

Introduction	xi
Gweir	21
Myron	48
Sergius	66
Caradoc	87
Corvio	105
Lucius	142
Rufinus	165
Ailis	187
Glossary	215
Bibliography	216
Major General Patrick Man	217

Introduction

This book describes the great rebellion in AD 60 of Boudicca (often but less accurately known as Boadicea), Queen of the Iceni, against the occupying Roman power in Britain. Some authorities favour AD 61 as being the date of this rebellion, but most of the current experts point to the earlier year and I am content to be guided by them. It is a work of historical fiction, but written with due regard to the facts so far as we know them. In the text I have used Roman place names since these, I believe, add something to the atmosphere of the book and serve to heighten the effect of the events portrayed. Their modern equivalents are given in the table on page 215.

In terms of lives lost, Boudicca's rebellion was perhaps the greatest tragedy ever to have occurred in our history. At that time the population of what today is central and southern England is unlikely to have exceeded half a million; of these probably not less than one hundred and fifty thousand died; say one in four of the total population. Most of the killing occurred in a space of three or four months, and the flame of revolt – from the first spark, through holocaust, to cold ashes, probably lasted less than one year.

The aim of this introductory chapter is to sketch the history of the rebellion and so lay the solid foundation upon which are based the stories that follow. These portray events as seen through the eyes of eight very different individuals – seven men and one woman – who played their separate parts in the Great Rebellion. Four are Britons and the other four are either Romans or in the service of Rome; in this way I have made at least some attempt to present a balanced picture.

The first of these individuals is Gweir, a one-time Trinovantes noble, who helped the rebels to obtain the information they needed, so making rebellion possible at the time the spark of revolt was finally struck.

Next comes Myron, a Greek freedman on the staff of Catus Decianus, procurator of Britain, who was among those whose brutality struck the spark.

There follows Caradoc, a horse dealer of the Coritani, who was by chance in Colchester when the town was sacked by Queen Boudicca's army, and who played his part in the horror that ensued.

Next we have Sergius, a section commander of XX Legion (Valeria), who was in the leading wave of the amphibious assault upon the island of Anglesea.

There follows Corvio, one of the bodyguard of Cartimandua, Queen of the Brigantes, who depicts life – and death – at her court, how the IX Legion (Hispana) was ambushed and what took place afterwards.

Then there is Lucius Aemilianus Silvanus, a tribune on the staff of Caius Suetonius Paulinus, Roman governor and commander-in-chief in Britain, who, in a letter, describes events as they may have thrust themselves upon his general and how, in the end, Paulinus mastered them.

Rufinus, orderly to Poenius Postumus, camp prefect of II Legion (Augusta), takes up the narrative by telling us something of his master; he seeks to explain how it was that Poenius Postumus disobeyed his general's order, what followed and the price he paid for his temerity.

Finally Ailis, Boudicca's one-time nurse, and in some degree her foster-mother, tells us something of the queen and sketches her way of life and the manner of her death.

Few of these individuals met or even saw each other, but

when they did the stories they tell do not always agree in every detail. Frankly this is deliberate. Eyewitnesses describing an incident immediately after it has occurred are apt to differ widely in their accounts of it. Most, perhaps all, the witnesses in the book are recounting what happened and what they saw and did years after the events which they describe. Accordingly, that they differ in detail is to be expected; only were their stories precisely to agree should we be sceptical.

At the end of each story there are some notes. These are intended either to explain a term or phrase used by the narrator, or to emphasise some historical connection which could be of interest to the reader.

For background the writer is greatly indebted to a number of books. These are listed in the bibliography.

For our knowledge of what happened we are dependent, in the main, on two Roman historians – Tacitus and Cassius Dio. Tacitus was writing a generation after the events he describes, but his sources certainly included eyewitnesses, for instance Agricola, his father-in-law, who as a young staff officer was serving in Britain at the time of the rebellion. Cassius Dio, who wrote over a century later, no doubt had access to sources now lost to us, some of which may have been semi-contemporary; Tacitus was no doubt among them. Regrettably there is no British account – Celtic was not then a written language – to portray events through British eyes, and so balance the inevitably pro-Roman bias of our two authorities. Indeed, one of the reasons for writing this book is to attempt, however inadequately, to do just that.

The Romans invaded Britain in AD 43. Their army comprised four legions: II Augusta, IX Hispana, XIV Gemina and XX Valeria, together with auxiliaries both infantry and cavalry, with a total strength of some forty thousand men. By the winter of AD 59/60 they had conquered all Britain roughly up to a line running from the mouth of the Humber, along the Trent, across to Chester, and thence to Wroxeter and on south along the Severn to the Bristol Channel. At that time these four legions were probably in garrison as follows:

II Augusta:	Gloucester and in forts in the area mainly along the Severn valley;
IX Hispana:	Lincoln and in forts along the Trent valley;
XIV Gemina:	Wroxeter and in forts in the area;
XX Valeria:	Chester and in forts to the east and south-east.

A number of auxiliary units were stationed in all four of these areas and probably operated under legion command.

The Roman military headquarters of the Governor, Caius Suetonius Paulinus, was probably in Colchester; but the administrative centre, with Catus Decianus as procurator, had, it is believed, moved to London.

The causes of the rebellion lie mainly in Roman misgovernment, greed, naked oppression and overconfidence. This confidence was based on their certainty which, although based on seventeen years' experience was to prove somewhat misplaced: that the numerous British tribes would never sink their differences, forget old enmities and unite against a common enemy. Colchester had become a colonia in which retired soldiers settled with a grant of land. This land was expropriated from the Trinovantes by the new landlords who, to make matters worse, were apt to help themselves by force, seizing more even than was their due. Colchester was also the centre of the new imperial cult dedicated to the worship of the divine spirit of the Emperor Claudius. The cult entailed the construction of a magnificent and very costly temple, as well as continuing ceremony and ritual – all paid for by Britons. These were Trinovantes in the main, who had in addition to meet the costs of Romanisation, such as new towns, country houses, road building and the like. To raise the money to pay for these projects, those concerned had recourse more and more to foreign moneylenders, who charged extortionate rates of interest; accordingly, and increasingly, they began to face financial ruin. In addition, in the aftermath of the AD 43 invasion, Rome had paid subsidies to friendly Britons to buy their friendship. Rome herself, suffering from acute financial difficulty, now pretended to regard these subsidies as loans and not only pressed for the repayment of the principal, but for additional large sums as alleged interest. Finally, it seems that Rome herself began to lose confidence in the political stability of her new province and as a result the moneylenders – the upright Seneca among them – fearing for the security of their loans, also began to press for their repayment.

Accordingly, what had hitherto amounted to increasing financial embarrassment now meant complete and utter ruin.

Against this background two events occurred virtually simultaneously; together they provided the spark which was the direct cause of the explosion. The first was the death, probably at the end of AD 59, of Prasutagus, King of the Iceni. He was a client king allied to Rome by treaty but, having no son, bequeathed his kingdom jointly to the Emperor Nero and his two daughters with his queen, Boudicca, perhaps in the guise of regent. His will was disregarded and his kingdom was incorporated into the province by force. The takeover was effected with savagery and outrage; Boudicca herself was flogged and her daughters raped; the Iceni were brutally treated, much of their property was expropriated, and many were seized as slaves. In the meantime, while the Iceni were being goaded beyond endurance, the Governor, Caius Suetonius Paulinus, attacked Anglesea with the overt intention of destroying the power of the Druids, who were considered subversive. It is probable, moreover, that Anglesea had become a refuge for former rebels and so, in the eyes of the governor, was a source of disaffection which had to be cleaned up. For his campaign he employed the XIV Legion, and perhaps detachments of II and XX, together with auxiliaries. Accordingly, half the garrison of Britain became fully engaged in north-west Wales, while much of the remainder was pinned down watching the ever-restless Silures and the Brigantes, the latter being probably the most powerful tribe in all Britain. It is very likely that all this was known to the rebels who jumped at the opportunity so presented to them.

The rebellion began, perhaps in March or April, with the coming together of Iceni war bands in the remote forest and heathland of Icenia. It does not seem that information of this 'hosting' reached Roman ears, and if it did, the reports seem not to have been believed. We do not know which other tribes joined the Iceni, but it is certain that these included the Trinovantes and probably part, perhaps all, of the Catuvellauni. There may well have been others, but if there were, it is unlikely that they included the Brigantes since not only was Queen Cartimandua, who ruled them, pro-Roman, but she retained her throne for a further eight or nine years, until driven out by the anti-Roman faction of her people led by her ex-husband Venutius.

Probably in May or June the rebel army, under the leadership of Queen Boudicca herself, broke from the forests and struck at Colchester, which they destroyed utterly, butchering the inhabitants of the town and, no doubt, those of the estates, farms and villages surrounding it. Surviving Romans and Romano-Britons sought refuge in the temple of Claudius, where they held out for forty-eight hours before being overwhelmed. The sack of town and temple was characterised by savagery and atrocity remarkable even by the brutal standards of the time.

When news of the rebellion reached Lincoln, part of IX Legion together with auxiliaries marched south for Colchester. Somewhere en route, perhaps near Godmanchester, the force was ambushed; the infantry was cut to pieces and only auxiliary cavalry, together with Quintus Petilius Cerealis, the legate commanding the legion, escaped. What was left of IX Legion seems to have played no further part in the rebellion, so Boudicca could reasonably claim to have knocked out one quarter of the Roman Army which opposed her.

Paulinus had overrun Anglesea by the time he learned of the revolt. Leaving his infantry to concentrate and follow as best they could, he rode with his cavalry to London, ordering II Legion to join him. This the legion did not do; we are not told why, but we do know that for some reason the legate was absent and that command, surprisingly, had not devolved upon the senior tribune but on Poenius Postumus, camp prefect of the legion. Without II Legion, Paulinus realised that he could not hold London so he abandoned the town, taking with him such of the inhabitants as were prepared and able to accompany him. He learned also that the Procurator, Catus Decianus, had lost his nerve and fled by ship to Gaul.

Boudicca and her victorious army sacked London, massacred the inhabitants with the utmost brutality, and then destroyed St Albans where a further massacre ensued, although it is possible that here she found an all but empty town. By now she had destroyed probably the three largest towns in Britain and, according to Tacitus, seventy thousand Romans and Romano-Britons died in their ruins. Assuming that he includes not only the unfortunate townsfolk, but also the inhabitants of outlying farms and villages throughout the area, his figure seems credible.

Some weeks later, probably in August but possibly as late as September, Boudicca met Paulinus in battle. The place is not known; it may have been near Mancetter, some five miles north-west of Nuneaton. We do know that wherever it was, it had an open plain to the front, and that the flanks and rear of the Roman position were protected by woods and hills. Paulinus had with him XIV Legion, part of XX and auxiliaries; not less than ten thousand men and perhaps a thousand or two more. Boudicca's army greatly outnumbered him, Cassius Dio tells us by twenty-three to one, but this is clearly a gross exaggeration: seven or eight to one is probably nearer the mark; odds which would have been intimidating enough from the legionaries' point of view, who had to face them against a background of utter disaster relieved only by the initial success in Anglesea. In any event, Roman training, discipline and greatly superior armament and armour prevailed. Boudicca's army was utterly destroyed. The queen herself and her daughters disappear from the pages of history and it is probable that she took poison. When the news of the victory reached him, Poenius Postumus fell on his sword. XIV Legion, which had borne the brunt of the fighting, was honoured with the title 'Martia Victrix' and it is possible that 'Victrix' may have been added to the designation of XX Legion as its reward for distinguished service.

The defeated Britons paid a bitter price. Rebel territory was devastated, without mercy; many died of starvation, for the timing of the hosting had made spring sowing impossible; survivors were sold into slavery.

Those who did survive and who also escaped capture found an unlikely champion in Julius Alpinus Classicianus, the new procurator. This man, according to Collingwood, 'stood up to Suetonius in his hour of victory as the champion of the British people'.[1]

---

[1] Collingwood, RG and Myers, JNL, *Roman Britain and the English Settlements*, London, Oxford at the Clarendon Press, 1949

Paulinus was recalled and Britain entered upon a long period of wise and relatively humane government. It would seem that the causes and lessons of the Great Rebellion were not lost on the Roman 'masters', and so Boudicca's personal inspiration, brave leadership and high courage, and the endurance and gallantry of those who fought and died with her, were not in vain. Classicianus died in office; his tombstone is in the British Museum and forms, or should form, a very precious part of our national heritage.

Three of our storytellers are Roman soldiers, so a word about the great army to which they belonged is, I believe, important. A legion comprised some 5,500 infantry soldiers, and was organised in ten cohorts. Nine of these comprised six infantry companies, each of ten sections, each of eight men. The 1st Cohort comprised five double strength companies. A legion was commanded by a legate, the cohorts usually by tribunes, and the companies by centurions; nearly all of these latter having begun their military careers as legionaries. Each legion had a camp prefect, promoted from the centurionate, who, as his title implies, approximated to a senior quartermaster rather than a commander. In the absence of the legate, command would not normally devolve upon the camp prefect but upon the senior tribune, one of six who served in the legate's headquarters.

A legionary wore a bronze helmet with an iron skull plate. His body armour comprised either a leather jerkin reinforced with metal shoulder pieces, or a cuirass composed of metal plates and strips. The lower part of the body was protected by a wide belt and a sporran attachment, both metal studded. He carried a rectangular shield curved to fit the body. His weapons comprised two seven-foot javelins, with a killing range of thirty yards or a little more, a short straight sword slung on the right side of the body, and a dagger worn on the left side.

To Romans and Britons alike, religion and superstition played an important, indeed fundamental, part in everyday life. The unseen world was more dangerous and alarming even than the seen. It was the domain of a large number of gods and goddesses, Roman and barbarian, known and unknown. It was peopled by spirits, demons and the ghosts of the dead, these latter being only too prone to return. All these unseen forces were apt to be vengeful and malevolent; a wise man sought to placate them with proper and often complex rituals and sacrifices. It was only too easy to incur their anger; they were not given to mercy and so to avoid the consequent ill luck or worse was always difficult, sometimes impossible. Omens, favourable or otherwise, were a fact of life; magic, or the effects of it, was as commonplace as eating or drinking, although the results were apt to be more serious and could be lethal.

Now our stage is set. Much of the Roman Army in Britain is being committed to a campaign in north-west Wales. The remainder stands sullenly on guard within grim forts and fortresses upon the frontiers of the Province of Britain. The British tribes grow ever more restive beneath the Roman yoke. Ordinary folk, Roman and Briton alike, pursue their lives as best they may, loving, hating, mating, giving birth and dying under the shadow of great events. Now it is for Gweir, Myron, Caradoc and the others to tell us of these events and the part they played in shaping them.

GWEIR

We were riding in the forest. It was early autumn. The path we followed was muddy and lighted here and there with bright shafts of sunshine, blinding in their brilliance; the tall trees towered over us, each standing stiffly like a great column spreading, far above our heads, into a canopy of green splashed with gold. In the cool shade there was no sound other than the muffled beat of our ponies' hooves. We came to a clearing, much of it in gloom, for the sun was already low and cast long shadows.

As we reined in our ponies Clerides, my tutor, turned to me and said: 'You are born out of your time, Master Gweir; had you lived a half century since you would perhaps have feared the Catuvellauni as they looked with greedy eyes upon the land of the Trinovantes, and sent their war bands to take it. Yet, after some bloodletting, life under Cunobelin proved sweet both for Catuvellauni and Trinovantes alike, and for those other tribes which gave allegiance to that great king. All men prospered and all knew peace under the law. A half century hence all Britain will know learning, prosperity and a manner and level of living beyond all understanding, approaching even that enjoyed by Hellenes in my own country. Today, to our sorrow, we know neither the one nor the other.'

I knew forest, path and clearing well. I had ridden there for almost as long as I could remember, but today it was somehow different. There was another presence, or presences, and the smell of evil. I sensed corruption in the dank forest air. Something drew my eyes from the clearing and I felt a sudden, irrational thrill of fear. Almost unwillingly I found myself staring upwards. High under the green and golden glory of the forest canopy swam a huge, white shape, flat faced, pallid as a full moon, a crooked, cruel beak and great yellow eyes which stared at me unblinking. Its wing beat was slow and rhythmic like a smith's bellows, but primeval and scornfully remote from the vain hopes, fears and struggles of us poor mortals. The monstrous bird, assuredly an owl, was flying not in the deepening dusk, nor under the shield of night, but in radiant daylight. The bird flew, moreover from the left, or unlucky, side. I shuddered; my blood was as ice in my veins, my breath hissed through clenched teeth and the sweat froze upon my face. In sheer panic I dropped the reins on to my pony's neck, made the sign of horns and whispered the age-old invocation taught me by my father, 'May the God deny the Omen'; for unless the Great Camulos himself, Skyfather into eternity of all Trinovantes, was pleased to harken to my sudden, desperate plea, violent death must follow as night follows day, death, moreover, accomplished within a hand's breadth of time.

Clerides was a great talker. He was a student of history, fable and such half-truths and traditions as lie between. He spoke our language fluently and with but little accent, had studied rhetoric in Athens and was bewitched by the sound of his own voice. Nevertheless he was a kindly man – if old; he beat me seldom, and we were friends rather than pedagogue and pupil. He continued speaking, comfortably unaware of the horror which I had witnessed and of my terror.

'Our Roman masters are, as yet, unsure of themselves and even of their future in this land; their lack of certainty breeds fear, spawns cruelty and nourishes oppression. Their government, overstretched, fumbles while seeking to control us, and plans yet further conquest; it is, therefore, totally unable, although not I hold unwilling, to control Romans. Even the Roman gods find themselves unwelcome in a land they believe hostile, a land, moreover, filled with stranger gods, older even and held in greater awe than themselves. Because they feel thus mocked they grow angry and we suffer.'

Clerides paused; his voice died suddenly and he, unwillingly sensing some mystery disturbing the sober march of his thesis, looked about him. But, as ever, his mind was stuffed with scrolls, stocked with learning and redolent of the wisdom and teachings of the ancients. In such a world neither forest, nor time, nor life itself were important – if, indeed, they were real. That I, his pupil, was in mortal terror, had he been aware of it, would have astounded him utterly, for in his philosophy, logic cast out fear and life embraced the proper study of logic. He continued, a little querulously perhaps, his train of thought twisted if yet unbroken.

'I smell blood on the earth and smoke on the wind, but when the blood has dried and the fires have burned to nothing, our children and theirs will know wealth, happiness and above all peace. We owe a clear duty to our children and so must do what we may simply to remain alive.'

I was young, just turned sixteen; now I am old and can understand and even perceive the wisdom in his words. At the time, and thanks to the fire and vigour of youth, I began to put aside what had been all-consuming fear as I invoked not Great Camulos, for yet a further plea must smack of sacrilege, but Cernunnos – the Horned One – and Lord of the Wild Hunt, whose haunt is the forest and whose care is for all those who dwell therein. I vowed to him the choicest portion of the next deer we killed and then, with bitterness and only the memory of fear in my heart, joined wordy battle with my tutor.

'Most worthy Clerides, your great learning or perhaps some god has turned your brain. Your tongue clacks like that of a woman. Once we were a free people, now we are but slaves in thrall beneath the Roman boot which grinds us into dust. Our lands are forfeit; for us there is no justice; in Roman eyes we are but cattle awaiting the knife. In fear my father pays his dues and does naught to offend; his lands are but modest, his livelihood may not excite their avarice. We can, perhaps, sleep more lightly for a while than can our wealthier friends; but our turn will come. Now it grows late and we shall scarce be home before night falls and the spirits walk.'

I wheeled my pony and cantered back along the way we had come; at my heels I could hear Clerides' angry mutter.

I am not called Gweir, nor did my tutor answer to Clerides, but these names will serve as well as any others for my tale, since I have good reason for seeking to remain unknown. I am truly of the Trinovantes and can claim descent from one-time kings, but my family was of a younger branch, no longer wealthy, with but little land, few cattle and but a handful of slaves. My father, when advanced in years, took a young woman of good birth for wife. She bore me as her only living child, I a cripple, in that my right arm is withered and I have but little joy of it. It could be that her women were careless when they tended her at my birth, or that the Mother Goddess frowned and so my coming was both untimely and accursed. My father was minded to put me away, but yielded to my mother's pleadings for my life. It is strange how a woman will ever yearn over the stricken, and lavish more love and care upon a poor cripple than upon a well formed child or even beast. In the end I think my father was glad that he had yielded to her entreaties, for he sired no other child that lived, and the anger of the goddess still lay heavily upon us.

Because of my arm and because he yet hoped for a whole

son to inherit, supplanting me, he took Clerides, a Greek slave, into his house as my tutor. I learned from him to speak and write the Latin tongue; he taught me Greek although I never grasped, in full, the written characters; I learned rhetoric, figuring and accountancy; together we read and discussed philosophy and history, much of it Greek, but some Roman. Indeed I owe him much and wish his spirit happiness and all good fortune in the shades.

From my father I learned to use a sword left-handed, and although my right arm could not bear a shield, I learned that a normal man could find himself hard-pressed by one who, although shieldless, was left-handed. Because our tribe and others were not permitted, by our Roman masters, to bear arms, we kept such as we had hidden, and I learned my swordplay in the main with a dummy weapon in my hand, carefully weighted and balanced to resemble a true sword. I learned also that the thrust proved often more effective than the cut because it bit the faster. The life of a man with no shield must hang, in truth, upon the nimbleness of his feet and the speed of his blade, and so it was that I was able, at times, to get the better of my father. This gave him pleasure mixed with dismay for, although he had grown old, he was still rated a good swordsman and would never admit, even to himself, that I, a cripple, could better him.

We came to our house and found it bathed, most fittingly, in the blood-red glare of the dying sun. Two armed and armoured men stood at our gate, the sun glinting on their helmets and harness; they were Romans and I knew fear. As yet they did not see me, for their gaze turned inwards towards our house. As I approached the gate one of them faced about, saw me, shouted and sprang for my pony's head; I drove my heels into his flanks, he swerved, threw up his head, struck the soldier with his shoulder and the man went down. I found myself galloping across the yard. Herded into one corner I saw our slaves; they were in great fear. Most were kneeling, beseeching with uplifted hands; two soldiers, their swords drawn, stood over them. Two bodies lay beside our threshold; one was a soldier and the other was my father, who lay on his back, his left arm flung wide; he had a gaping wound in his throat. His sword was still gripped in his right hand but he bore no shield. Men, some armed, others wearing only tunics, and one a toga in the Roman fashion, stood in a group beside my father's body. I was unarmed but knew that to seek vengeance was my bounden duty.

I urged my pony straight towards my father, leaped from its back, stumbled, almost fell, stooped and attempted to break my father's grip on the sword hilt. I found his fingers set like iron, and one-handed as I was I could not break his hold. A man shouted: 'He is crippled from birth; the gods will destroy his murderer.' Something struck me on the back of the head, and then I was falling into a pit which had no bottom. I bear the scar from that blow until this very day.

When I came to myself I found that I lay in a strange bare room, with a barred and often shuttered window set high in one wall. When the window was covered, an oil lamp set on a bracket gave relief from utter darkness. Shadowy, noiseless figures drifted through the room; from their smell it would seem that most were women. I saw often a man with thick black eyebrows and dark anxious eyes; sometimes his face was shadowy and far distant, often it was very close – almost pressed against my own; his breath was foul but the touch of his fingers, as he swathed my aching head in layer upon layer of bandages, was light. There was another face, stern, dark eyed, thin lipped, with a jutting nose and a tuft of black beard sprouting from his chin; he had a mane of dark hair which fell to his shoulders. He stared at me long and hard and whispered with his black-eyebrowed companion. The pain in my head eased to no more than a dull ache which gave relief from throbbing agony. Suddenly I was fully awake; memory came flooding back. I half sat up and fell back from weakness; a woman sitting on a stool beside me smiled, put her finger to her lips and glided out through the curtained doorway, leaving me alone.

A man was suddenly in the room. He wore a tunic of brown wool, gathered at his waist with a broad leather belt, and white trousers to the ankles cross-gartered in blue. His feet were bare. He was swarthy with a short black beard, piercing black eyes and a mane of dark curly hair. His right cheek was deeply scarred. He stared at me for what seemed an eternity, smiled, and in a harsh voice said: 'I can see you are better; your eyes are clear and you no longer look like the corpse you so nearly were. You are among friends. I have sent for the slave who has attended you, he will give you a draught to induce sleep; this will help the gods, through you, to give you back your strength. In a day or two we will talk of the future.'

I tried to speak but no words came. The room began to wheel and was suddenly dark; I felt a cup pressed to my lips and a warm, sharp taste on my tongue; again it seemed that I was falling.

One morning, it was I believe, two days hence, I awoke to find Black Beard sitting on a stool beside my couch. I sat up and leaned my back against the plastered wall. He said: 'You are now well enough to know what is past; we can then look to the future. A one-time centurion was granted land adjoining that of your father. He considered his grant to be less than his due, and so seized your father's estate to increase his holding. What was done was against the law, but neither you, nor I, nor any of our people can hope for justice in the courts against a Roman citizen. To aid him in his crime he brought legionaries. Your father fought them and fought them well, for although they were armoured and were many, and he was alone with nothing but his sword, he killed one, wounded a second and so died facing his enemies. Your mother too is dead. She was raped on her own couch not once but often. In this I believe she was fortunate, for I doubt that she knew either fear or pain when, having had their fill of her, they cut her throat. Your tutor, Clerides, also is dead but he did you a service, for the soldier who struck you from behind had thought to spit you with his sword. But due, I believe, to Clerides' shouted warning he struck instead with the pommel. Your father's slaves now serve the centurion, all save one, who ran away and told me much of what I have told you.'

He paused, looked at me hard and said: 'I do not wish to tire you, but must now tell you of myself and what I seek of you.' With a sudden smile he continued; 'I am of the Iceni and am as well born as is your family. Perhaps a little better but, over this, we need not tax our minds. I am now a slave dealer and am charged by the centurion, should you live, to sell you as a slave and remit to him your price, less my commission. This I must do for should I not, and my failure become known, my real task in Camulodunum could suffer, and that I could not stomach.'

He stood up, went to the door, drew aside the curtain and looked to right and left. He returned to his stool, leaned forward and with his voice shading to a whisper, continued: 'We plan to overthrow the Roman power. For this we must have information and I am among those who seek, and under the gods, gain it. Dealing in slaves is helpful to my task and furnishes me, moreover, with a cloak against suspicion. I can offer you two choices, Gweir; you can either work for me and I will guide your sale to a good master, whom I know and who will use you well, or you can become a slave like any other, bid for and bought in the market by whoever offers the best price. Should you make this second choice I would not fear your tongue should you disclose what I have told you, for I am well known, respected, largely above suspicion and in no danger from the idle gossip of a slave, who could be thought to bear a grudge against the dealer who sold him.'

He looked at me hard as if attempting to read my thoughts. He went on: 'Think well. I know what you attempted when you saw your father dead, and I hope I would have done as you did, but it is not hard to be bold when your blood is hot. It is much less easy when you are alone and feel yourself hunted, when you sense that the web of suspicion thickens and is closing around you, when death comes not quickly on the point of a sword in the company of others, but horribly and alone, slowly, very slowly, under the hooks, beneath the ropes and from the searing irons of the tormentors.' I saw beads of sweat on his forehead, and there was a flicker, fear perhaps, in his dark eyes. He continued: 'You have a clear duty to avenge your father and this you may achieve alone, in your own time and in such manner as you choose. Should you work for me, and should we succeed, as under the gods we surely shall, you will be avenged most fittingly: for the blood not of one centurion but of thousands of his like will mingle with, and avenge, that of your father.' In truth I had no choice, and this he knew; I saw it in his cold unblinking stare.

My new master owned a wine shop. He came from Lower Gaul. He was a fat and jovial man who treated his slaves well and never beat us. Indeed, his favoured punishment, and this was rare, was to deprive us of food. He was, himself, a glutton, and was perhaps impressed by the effect that such a penalty would have if applied to himself. Nevertheless, we worked hard, for we preferred to serve him rather than risk being sold to a less kindly master. I became his overseer, saw to his accounts and took charge of much of the provisioning side of his business in the shop, for we offered not only wine but food also.

The place was dingy, opening directly on to the street. In the main room, which extended the full width of the building, were two stone-topped serving counters, set at right angles, one for wine and the other for food. A low wooden bench ran along the wall on either side of the door, and on the side wall, where there was no serving counter. A number of small tables and stools filled much of the space before the counters. Cooking was done in a shed at the back of the shop; it was always in turmoil and often dirty; perhaps this added to the flavour of the food we served, which was excellent. I know this for we slaves were sometimes permitted to eat what was left over.

When I was not out buying or working at my master's accounts I stood in the shop, welcoming those who entered and directing our other slaves to ensure quick and willing service. I came to know our more important customers, learned and remembered their names, and so greeted them and saw to them myself despite my miserable right arm. Thus I was able to watch for informers who sought me, and guard myself against those who came to spy. Such informers as came to the shop wore a thumb ring, but since thumb rings are not uncommon, not every man who wore one was an informer. Having observed a man with such a ring, I would go about my duties in such a manner as to pass close to him. Should he give the ring on his thumb two full turns I knew that he had news for me; I would move away, busy myself at some task, return, make as if to serve him and take his spoken message. Such were never longer than one short sentence, were in veiled speech and to me quite meaningless. As a symbol for them I too wore a ring on the thumb of my right hand, but beyond this no sign was required of me, and not one of my master's slaves, save myself, wore such a ring.

When my duties permitted, I would go to the room which held my master's accounts and scribble the message on to a tablet, using Greek characters which I had learned from Clerides. At first I was in fear lest his shade might be angered by the use I made of his teaching but he never troubled me, not even in a dream, so my fears, it seemed were ill-founded. Moreover, in time I trained my mind to memorise the messages, ceased to record them, and slept more easily since I was thus less fearful of discovery.

I was forbidden, unless summoned, to visit the slave dealer. Instead he came to me, being an honoured, respected and most regular customer. Indeed he and a very few others, whom my master deemed important, were specially honoured since we kept two slave women for their pleasure. Both girls served in the shop but each enjoyed the luxury of her own couch in her own small room. They were not ill-favoured – if over fat for my taste – and were even permitted to retain for themselves a part of the customer's fee, and so offered most willing and, it would seem, pleasurable service. Moreover since my master restricted the use of their bodies to a very few, he did not find it necessary to pay for a brothel license, nor meet the tax for which he would then have become subject.

It became normal for me to lead the customer, and light his way, from the shop through the yard to the woman's room, and thus I was able to give my reports without fear of being overheard. On one such evening this proved impossible for my master, himself, acted as guide. When he had returned to the shop, I took a wine jug, set it upon a tray with two cups, bore them to the room, pushed aside the door curtain and entered. The slave dealer had laid aside his tunic and was sitting on the edge of the couch. The woman, who was already naked, was kneeling on the floor unfastening his sandals and cross-gartering. He gave me a broad wink and nodded his head, which I took to mean that I could tell him what I knew without fear of the woman, whom we both considered to be a foolish creature, furnished with a shapely body but an empty head. The words stuck in my throat, for as I looked at him, I saw that through the matted black hair on his chest ran a series of deep, white, jagged scars reaching from shoulders to stomach, like long furrows in a field newly ploughed.

He saw the expression on my face, smiled and said: 'Gweir, my young friend. Her body should excite you more than mine although I grant that, from the doorway, you are perhaps unable to see the more interesting parts of it. In me you have a sample of what torturer's hooks can do to a man. They drive the hook into your flesh and then pull hard, steadily and without pity. The hook is fashioned to ride over bone but drags the flesh with it on its long, cruel journey. Having torn one furrow, seemingly without end, they begin again, a finger's breadth or so first to one side and then the other, and so they continue. I was fortunate to escape before they dug further, for had they done so I should not have been able to serve Enaid,' he ran his fingers caressingly through the girl's long hair, 'as she would wish.' Enaid looked up at him, smiled, and began loosening his trousers; he continued: 'Place the tray on the stool and we will enjoy the wine after our first encounter and before the second. Tell me what you must and then leave us, for we have more pleasurable matters to attend to and Enaid grows impatient.' He gave me another broad wink.

That night I was much troubled by dreams. I felt the slow, tearing, wrenching, agonising hooks as they tore the flesh from my bones. I awoke in a cold sweat, my mouth dry and my heart thumping. For the first time since I came to the wine shop, I was in real fear of my task and of the penalty of discovery. I gripped with frightened fingers the crescent pendant which hung about my neck on a leather thong. It looked like any other charm of its kind, worn to avert the evil eye, but mine was hollow; the hollow contained poison with which I could hope to cheat the torturers. The slave dealer had given this to me before even I came to the wine shop. That evening I had seen, hanging about his neck, the twin to mine. Perhaps he did not have it when his flesh had been so cruelly torn.

When I went about my master's business it seemed that I was followed. I told myself that my fears were ill-founded but they were not thus easily dispelled. Where a shop had two entrances I would enter by one, scan, without seeming to, the faces of those who followed at my heels, go about my business and then leave by the other doorway, watching for another who acted as I did and so was, perhaps, a pursuer. Having turned a corner, I would suddenly stop, seemingly to count the contents of my arm purse, or loosen my belt, whereas in truth my eyes were on the faces of any who hastened as they turned the corner, and came upon me unawares. Among the many faces which I thus gazed upon were one, perhaps two, that were familiar, faces of possible pursuers, but yet I was in doubt. I told myself that when away from the wine shop my business was, in truth, wholly innocent and that to act as I did would arouse rather than allay suspicion; this, no doubt, was true but it brought me scant comfort.

When serving in the shop I studied the faces of all who entered, while seemingly intent only on their service. I marked down two men who came regularly, but never together, who although they drank but little, were prone to dally over their wine, and who spoke to few. Both were keen eyed, hard faced, soberly clad without ornament or distinction. Since they came regularly I took it upon myself to serve them, but never learned the names of either, although I enquired both of my master and of others in the shop. It seemed that no one knew them, but this was also true of others and so I found no certainty but only nagging doubt, with doubt the brother of fear.

One evening I had taken a message from an informer

who had come to the shop before. As ever the message was cryptic – in this case it ran: 'The twins still plague us'.[1] As was my wont, I spoke further with the man, as if he were like any other customer, expressing the hope that his food and wine were to his liking, and enquiring if we could be of further service. He looked up at me and I saw fear in his eyes; he said: 'Have a care, we are being watched by the one in the corner.' I bowed, took his wine jug and replaced it with another, so giving some semblance that I was attending some complaint. I busied myself with other customers for that evening we had many. Then with cold fear in my heart I went to the corner table at which two men sat. They seemed intent on their wine, although both gazed, incuriously it seemed, about the shop. Neither spoke, but the one who sat on the wall bench and who could, therefore, view the whole room, was one of the two whom I doubted. I addressed his fellow, seeking his assurance that he was content, and enquiring if he sought aught else from us. He was a surly fellow with a matted black beard and a tangle of unkempt hair; he smelled like a midden. He growled something into his beard, which in truth I could not catch, and I was about to move away when his fellow looked up. He stared hard at me with cold eyes and said: 'You can do me a service. Tell me the name of the man now leaving the shop.'

I turned my head and saw the informer. My heart leaped in my body and I marvelled at the steadiness of my voice as I replied: 'Master, we have many customers but I know the names of few. It irks me that I cannot answer your question, but I do not know his name nor, indeed, am I so fortunate as to know yours.'

His cold eyes never left my face as he said, very slowly: 'No matter; I must seek other means.' His voice was low but with a hint of menace. He went on: 'I see, Gweir, that you, like that stranger, wear a thumb ring; show it to me.'

I am fool enough still to be ashamed of my miserable right arm, and such is my folly that I wear the sleeves of my tunic longer than is customary, so as to hide the wasted muscles and misshapen, jutting bones. I was shocked, foolishly perhaps, that this now sinister customer knew my name. Others of our customers were so informed, I told myself, so why not he. I believe, however, that his shock was the greater, for it seemed that he had no knowledge of the nature of my arm. I saw astonishment, disgust even, in his eyes as I drew back the sleeve and showed him the chalk-white, wasted flesh below the elbow. With my face a mask, I said: 'Master, I am not proud of my arm and in my shame strive to hide it, I have suffered thus since birth. Before my mother brought me into the world a wise woman told her that she would bear a cripple. She also gave my mother this thumb ring, saying that should I wear it always, it could be that one day the goddess might lift her curse from me, and my arm would be restored. This ring, she said, would be a symbol that I acknowledged my thralldom to the goddess and recognised her power; hopefully this would give her pleasure, earn for me her pity and she would make me a whole man – perhaps. The ring, as you can see, is of twisted copper, and so contrived as to fit a thumb of any size, and so in my case allow for growth from babyhood. I have worn it from birth and never take it off. One day, because of it, I hope to be well. Now, if it pleases you, I will again hide my shame.' I stared at him with hatred in my eyes as I allowed my sleeve to fall back into place. He dropped his gaze, stood, threw some coins on the table and strode from the shop with never a backward glance.

I had half expected that some day I might be questioned as to my ring, and had thought up and practised my story. I doubted whether my questioner could know that the donor of the ring was the slave dealer, and that I had first worn it when I became a slave in the wine shop.

Two evenings later the slave dealer came. He was expected, and Enaid had already gone to her room so as to be washed and perfumed for his pleasure. I told him of the message regarding the twins and of the matter of the ring. He chuckled, clapped me on the shoulder, and his eyes were kindly as he said: 'I understand your hidden shame as to your arm, but there is no profit for you here. Your courage is high, your wit is sharp and you have learned to use your good arm to do the work of two. Your master is well served, and more important so am I; you have no cause to wear your shame as if it were a badge of infamy. You did well and are learning fast. We will change the sign for all save you, who must now wear my ring for all eternity.' He chuckled again and continued: 'Our affairs prosper and I can see an end – at last. Come to me tomorrow night. I will instruct your master to give you leave when you have closed the shop. Come to the side door, which leads into the slave yard, and give three double knocks. You will be admitted with that sign. Be on your guard that you are not followed. Now I am eager for Enaid and she for me.' The curtain which masked the door of Enaid's room fell behind him, and I returned to my tasks.

The night following, having closed and barred the shop, I took a winding route. No man hindered me or asked my business. I tarried on my way and at times doubled back to ensure that I was not followed. I gave the sign, was admitted by a slave, and taken to his master, who received me with a smile and poured, from a silver wine jug, well watered wine for us both. It was mellow and of good quality, better than much of that served by my master.

He said: 'Gweir, my young friend and true comrade, it is my custom to tell those whom I use only as little as I must. The less they know, the less they can impart – if questioned – and so we all enjoy greater safety. Tonight I shall tell you much, for only thus can I bring my task to full success.

'In all of Britain the Romans have four legions and about the same strength in auxiliaries, who are to be feared equally with the legions – say forty thousand men. If we are to overcome them we must ourselves bring not less than twice that number into the field, and so arrange matters that we never face more than half their force in one battle. We can achieve the first of these things only if we start with such success as will show the doubters that Romans are not gods but mortal men, who can be overcome. When this plain truth is shown in Roman blood the doubters will swell our ranks, while those traitors who still cling to Rome will fear for their safety, and so withhold both aid and comfort, hoping thus to save their miserable lives. This first success lies here for, under the gods, we will destroy Camulodunum, town, garrison and people, and with them your centurion.'

He smiled, but his eyes were as opaque as flints; he continued: 'Now for the scattering of their strength. Here Paulinus, himself, will give us aid for we know that he plans a campaign in the far west. I hold that for this he will deploy two full legions and part, perhaps, of another, together with auxiliaries.[2] This will leave one full legion and auxiliaries which lie at Lindum and in frontier fortresses facing the Brigantes, who are ever restless; thus it will be hard for Paulinus to disengage them from their duty and use them against us. There remains part of another and auxiliaries which lie at Glevum and have both Silures and Dobunni at their throats. Should what I believe prove truth, then once we know that Paulinus is well launched on his campaign, beyond recall, we can rise and if it be the will of the gods, will cleanse this island of its Roman plague.

'To further our design two things are needful. First we must be assured that Paulinus' army in the west will not be less than two full legions. Second, we must know when he launches his campaign, since not until he moves, and is committed, dare we begin our hosting, lest he abandon his plan and turn his strength on us.

'Even as I speak Paulinus and his staff snore upon their couches not one mile distant.[3] Spring is now here and good campaigning weather lies ahead. To set his legions moving he must issue written orders, which he will despatch by mounted messenger with an armed escort. We know that it is his custom personally to dictate orders of such import. Moreover, for orders of special secrecy such as these, he will employ one or other, or perhaps both, of two confidential secretaries who work at his headquarters. One of these, a Greek, loves gold and I have bought him. The other is a Gaul and he cannot be bought. I have it from the Greek that the orders were given two nights since, and I know by other means that a messenger and escort left the headquarters yesterday, and headed into the west. The Greek swears that he did not write the order since he was not on duty. That he was not, I have also from another source. It follows that the Gaul knows what I need to know and what I mean to learn.

'Come the morrow this Gaul will lie with a woman in the brothel used by Paulinus' slaves. They are permitted to use only the one. The place, and its women, are under the eye of secret police and its safety, therefore, would seem assured. The woman with whom the Gaul will bed will keep him with her until midnight, when she gives her body to another. You and one of my men, whom you may call Gwilth, will meet the Gaul when he leaves the brothel; he is a small, anxious man with a red beard; it is his custom to wear a brown cloak. You will bring him to me.'

He uncovered a tablet and revealed a sketch of streets and alleys roughly traced on the wax; he pointed with his finger and continued: 'You will meet Gwilth in the yard at the back of this shop. There is a side gate which will not be fastened, so one can await the other hidden. Having met you will enter the shop and, through a gap in the shutter, watch the threshold of the brothel. A light is kept burning over the door so you can recognise the Gaul when he leaves. Gwilth, moreover, knows him. It is, I believe, certain that he will wish to return to the headquarters since his duty starts at sunrise and he will, no doubt, desire sleep having taken so much pleasure with his woman.' He smiled again. 'You and Gwilth will take him, hopefully without noise. A litter with four bearers will be waiting in this alley. See that he enters that litter. Another of my slaves will be within to keep him fast. The litter bearers know whence to carry him. You and Gwilth will follow, but discreetly; I may need your further aid.

'I should warn you that should our man, by some mischance, be not alone when he leaves the brothel, you will attempt nothing against him, since I do not wish it to become known that he was delayed on his way to headquarters. Last, I should say that your master knows that you are again to have leave from the shop. He believes that I enjoy not only women but also young men, and that you are now my favourite.' He laughed at the expression on my face.

'You could need a weapon. Take this dagger; for such work it will serve you better than a sword. It is of the Roman pattern and, if found, could scarce be traced. You would do well to wear your hooded cloak.'[4]

The following evening I arrived early at the shop. I pushed open the gate in the side wall – it creaked horribly – closed it behind me and stood in the silent yard. There was no movement, so I had come first to the place. It was very dark; when my eyes had grown accustomed and I could see again, albeit dimly, I walked to the back of the shop, my naked feet making no sound on the bare earth. I found myself in what I took to be a store room and, through the doorway which led, it seemed, into the shop, there was a glimmer of light which filtered through the shutter, I moved very slowly, one step at a time, testing before me, for the place dealt in pottery which was stacked in piles upon both shelves and floor. I looked through the shutter across the paved street at the stone building opposite. Two torches burned on either side of the threshold; the door stood open and through it I glimpsed movement and could hear faint laughter and snatches of song. Occasional passers-by moved in the street singly or in groups; one such group seemed very drunk, for men shouted and sang as they stumbled, lurching from side to side across the street. I saw no one enter or leave the brothel. Often I moved from the shutter through the shop to the side gate, and thence to the shop, so as to learn the way. When the Gaul left we would need to move fast if we were to take him.

Gwilth did not come. I went to the gate, opened it a little and looked to right and left along the alley which passed beside it; there was no one. I heard the trumpet sound in the headquarters, which lay some two hundred paces along the street to my left.[5] The blast signified midnight. Still Gwilth had not come; time passed but slowly. Through the shutter I saw movement in the brothel entrance; two men came out and stood in the light of the torches. The smaller wore a brown cloak and his beard was ruddy in the glare. They spoke in loud voices. The taller man moved forward; I saw him raise his hand as if in salutation, and move swiftly along the street away from the headquarters. My man remained standing in the ruddy glare, moved as if to follow his companion, hesitated and then turned and slowly walked the other way. There was still no sign of Gwilth, so I reasoned I must attempt the matter unaided and alone. I hastened after him on bare, noiseless feet and was only a pace behind when he turned his head, sensing my approach. I said: 'I have a knife at your back; make no sound. I need your purse and will take it from you in the next alley. Walk;

do not run.' And I pricked him with the point of my dagger. I saw him wince, but he stood without movement. His eyes were on my face and I could see that he was in fear. I said: 'If you do not move I will stab you and so you will lose both your purse and your life. Should you wish to live – walk.' He began to move forwards and I at his heels. I heard the tramp of nailed boots coming down the street from the direction of the headquarters. I said: 'You will stand and face the patrol; I shall be behind your right shoulder with my dagger point in your side; should you move or cry out I shall kill you.' He stood still and faced the street. As the patrol passed I pretended to be somewhat in my cups and swayed on my feet, but held my left hand steady with my dagger point pricking the hollow in his body just beneath the ribs. I sang the chorus of one of the songs I had learned in the wine shop. As they passed the soldiers of the patrol stared at us. I shouted at them in Latin, slurring my words and invoking the protection of the God Mars. At this some of the soldiers laughed and were silenced by their commander, who cursed me roundly for a drunken barbarian.

When they were well passed we continued along the street, turned into the alley and I saw the litter. With my dagger I prodded the Gaul and he moved, albeit slowly, towards it. I said: 'Enter and keep your mouth shut.' From within the litter I saw the curtains drawn aside. I smelled a faint perfume and marvelled as a woman said: 'Come; I am eager for your body.' There was a trembling strangeness in her voice, a note of desire, perhaps of something more; I found that I was shivering at the sound of it. The Gaul turned his head towards me but in the darkness I could not see his face, nor he mine. For an instant he hesitated; then he stepped up into the litter and was gone; the curtains were drawn together with a snap, the bearers lifted their burden and hastened along the alley. I followed at their heels, using the sound of their movement to guide my feet, for away from the street it was very dark.

 The bearers moved at a steady trot, twisting this way and that as they continued through the network of streets, alleys and passages that was Camulodunum. It seemed that they were following a devious route, perhaps to confuse the Gaul should he attempt to remember the way and so determine whence he was taken. At one point I was lost. I found that the litter was no longer in front; in haste I retraced my steps. I explored two narrow alleys and then a passage, between high walls, so narrow as scarcely to accept the litter. I found that it had halted and the darkness was such that I all but blundered against the bearers, and heard their laboured breathing. Suddenly the litter moved away and I was minded to follow, but sensed rather than saw a narrow opening in the wall on my right, and at the end a faint glimmer of light. I made for the light and came upon a low doorway with stone steps descending. At the foot I came upon a blank wall, but light came from the right. I stumbled towards it and found myself in what seemed a burial chamber, for there were niches in the walls, and some held funerary urns.[6] The place was dank and very cold; in the half light the walls glistened with water. There was a smell of death, and again I shivered.

 In front of me, propped at an angle against the wall, was a heavy beam and upon the beam lay the Gaul. He had been stripped naked; his hands were tied to the beam above his head; his legs were spread apart with his feet upon the floor; his ankles were tied together; there was a gag in his mouth. Two lamps, set in niches, burned in the side walls of the chamber and the place was filled with dancing shadows. Two masked men stood by the Gaul. One, whom I recognised by his beard and mane of dark hair, was the slave dealer, the other, it seemed, was a stranger. As I stood the stranger came across the chamber and shut a heavy door behind me, so denying all access to the stairway.

The slave dealer looked at me, put his finger to his lips, looked down at the Gaul and said: 'Three days since you wrote an order directing Romans to go warring in the west. You will tell me what you wrote. Should you do this now no harm will come to you. Your Roman masters will never know that the purport of their order has been revealed, and you will be free to leave here and continue in their service without fear of discovery. Should you not tell me, or should you lie when you speak, I will tear the truth from out of your body.'

There was a long silence. I could see that the Gaul was shivering, his whole body shuddered, but whether from cold or fear I could not tell. The slave dealer was smiling as he continued: 'I do not know how you fared in the litter. Branwen is demanding and can be persuasive even to a man who has passed his evening, as you have, with another woman. Should your body not have satisfied her as you came, she will obtain her true pleasure now. Women make good torturers, they are more subtle in their means, never grow rough and have no shred of pity, especially Branwen, whose skill I hold could make a dead man scream. She is an initiate of the Goddess Andrasta, known to some as 'Queen of Nightmares'.[7] That goddess, as you may know, delights in cruelty, blood and agony and licks her lips to watch her victims suffer. Branwen serves her well and has, moreover, no love for Romans nor their jackals such as you. Before her eyes they burned alive her husband, and in his arms they set her child. Then, when they had used her body for their pleasure, they crucified her, left her for dead. But here they erred for she was not dead, and now takes pleasure in the sobs, screams and twisted agony of those who writhe beneath her woman's hands.'

He paused, raised his head and looked into the shadows over to my left. 'Come, Branwen. I would not wish you to suffer disappointment, nor to incur the anger of your goddess. You may touch him but no more – yet.' I saw a tall, hooded figure move silently out of the shadows and across the chamber. Because of where I stood, and of the hood she wore, I could not see her face. Her cloak was dark red; her feet and arms were bare. Very gently she placed her right hand upon the Gaul's body and, as if she caressed him, she ran her questing fingers through the red and matted hair which grew there. From her left hand hung a hook on a long shank; its tip, crooked but flattened, sparkled in the light of the lamps. Although she had done no more than stroke him, the Gaul's whole body shook as if with fever, the muscles in his arms swelled as he strained on the rope, his eyes stared and his jaws chewed furiously on the gag as if he were choking.

The slave dealer turned to him, still smiling, and said: 'Should you be willing to tell me what I need to know, nod your head and I will loosen your gag. If you do not nod or if, when I loose your tongue, you scream, I shall again gag you and Branwen's hands will start their work upon your body. She will continue until a little time – it will seem longer to you – has passed after your head nods. I should warn you that much of what you will tell me I already know, and so, assuredly, I shall know if you dare to lie.' Even before he finished speaking, the Gaul was nodding his head so vigorously that the heavy beam upon which he lay shook like a tree in a storm.

The slave dealer beckoned me, gave me a tablet and stylus and bade me note what was said. He loosed the gag. I heard the woman's panting breath as she lifted her hand and returned to her place, but I could not bring myself to look upon her.

The Gaul spoke for what seemed a long time. He listed the legions, detachments of legions and auxiliary units which had been ordered to go campaigning. The first to move would march five days hence and all would be committed within ten. When he had finished, the slave dealer, aided by my tablet, cross-questioned him on what he had said; he enquired as to the whereabouts and duties of yet further units of which the Gaul had not spoken. The replies which he received seemed to satisfy him, for he covered the tablet and hid it beneath his tunic. My eyes were drawn, unwillingly, across the chamber to the woman where she crouched in her corner; I saw her hands striking, twisting and dragging with the hook; I saw the gleam of her eyes deep within the shadow of her hood. Her body swayed back and forth and her head lolled sideways to and fro; she sang very softly with the sound rising and falling like a wind in trees. I felt the hair prick on the back of my neck and I shuddered, so great was my horror of her.

We untied the Gaul and watched him dress himself; his hands shook and he drooled at the mouth. The stranger blindfolded him, gagged him, took him by the hand, opened the door and we heard him stumble as he climbed the steps; there was silence.

I said: 'What of Gwilth?' The slave dealer dropped his mask and replied: 'I know no more of him than you, but I have lost two men of late and that he is not here bodes no good for any of us. This tablet,' he tapped his tunic, 'gives me all I need, so Branwen and I will now return to our own people. Our work is done. You cannot remain here nor, because of your arm, would it be to your gain to come with me and meet what must now befall. Accordingly, I shall send you to a friend, who is also a slave dealer and who is to be found beyond the great river upon which Londinium stands, in a place where you will not be known. I had planned this; he is expecting you and, although you will still be a slave, you will be his slave; he will treat you well and of this you may be sure. Should we succeed you will be safe with him, but when the matter is done and Britain is again clean, come to Camulodunum, to Queen Boudicca's hall and ask for "The Slave Dealer"; I am of her council and you will be honoured and rewarded for what you have accomplished for her and for all Britain. Above this place two horses wait; one is for you and the other for my comrade. He will return here, when he has loosed the Gaul, and will guide you on your journey. You may call him Budic which, as you will know, means victory; there is perhaps an omen here.'

We extinguished the lamps and climbed the stairs, the woman at my back. A seemingly cold draught played on me between my shoulder blades; it was as if the pursuers were at my heels. In my haste to escape from that place of death I stumbled up the steps and fear gripped my heart. The night air smelled sweet and clean and my breath came more easily. To this day I never saw Branwen's face, and of this I am glad for, in truth, I shrank from her and from her greedy, twisting, cruel hands. Of the slave dealer I heard no word and know not even his name.

NOTES

[1] The XIV Legion was formed originally from two legions and so was known as Gemina (twin). Perhaps the message given to Gweir was intended to convey the information that XIV Legion was still in garrison at Wroxeter, and thus available to counter rebellion.

[2] The slave dealer was well informed but his assessment was overgenerous. For the attack on Anglesea, Paulinus employed one full legion and detachments of one, perhaps two others, together with auxiliaries.

[3] It is probable that Paulinus' headquarters was in Colchester.

[4] Heavy woollen cloaks, made in Britain and in Gaul, were not only well known throughout the Roman world, but were even exported to Rome itself where they fetched high prices.

[5] Knowing the time must have been a considerable problem. It was, however, customary for the Roman Army, no doubt so as to

facilitate sentry reliefs, to indicate the hours of the night by trumpet blast with the aid, presumably of a water-clock. It is reasonable to assume that both Gweir and the slave dealer knew this and that Gweir was within earshot, so solving his problem.

[6] Burial chambers similar to the one described have been excavated but not, so far as the writer is aware, in England.

[7] The Goddess Andastra is referred to by Cassius Dio as being the goddess to whom Boudicca sacrificed her prisoners.

Myron

I am called Myron. Anyone with but a hint of schooling or glimmer of intelligence would know from this that I am a Hellene which, in the Latin tongue, is Greek. Indeed he would not need to know my name but only to use his eyes and some faint spark of artistic intellect, for my head would be an acceptable model for that immortal whose name I bear, the incomparable Myron, were he to return and fashion anew his Discobolos or Marsyas discovering Athena's discarded flute.

I was born in Athens, the very fount of all Hellenic culture, art, learning and philosophy, the source indeed of everything that raises man above the beasts, the very cradle of civilisation and of all excellence, the antithesis of the ugly barbarity, lust and superstition which plague us mortals. I take much pride in my birthplace and in my breeding, for I have but little else for pride.

I was born free, but owing to misfortune overtaking my family when I was yet a boy, I was sold into slavery. There followed a period of my life which I seek to forget, for to lose freedom is to lose all. As a slave you do not live, you exist, and as you grow to accept your servitude, not only is your body shackled but your intelligence also. It is in truth a living, mindless death.

I was fortunate in my first and only master. He was a Roman but near-Hellene in his character, outlook, interests and whole manner of life. There are few such. He was wealthy and of patrician family, indeed I, a Hellene, confess that I learned much from him, a Roman. He saw to the completion of my schooling and I am ever in his debt. As a reward for good service, and I do not boast when I assert that my service was good, being faithful, devoted and intelligent, he gave me my freedom. Nevertheless I continued to serve him as a freedman in his household, working as his personal secretary. I was almost happy.

Then cruel fate, fittingly in the shape of a woman, again shattered my life. My master's wife, to her everlasting shame, and may she groan in pain and infamy for all eternity, sought to use my body as a tool for her pleasure. Although of good family like her husband, she was a woman past her prime, vicious in the extreme and totally without principle or virtue. Her manner of life was notorious and her lust insatiable. I do not pretend to an understanding of women, and do not believe that any man has this ability. Their minds, should they have such, are as far removed from the minds of men as is the furthest planet from our world; their thoughts, should they think, are totally without logic or reason and governed entirely by emotion. When I was a slave this modern harpy took not the glimmer of an interest in my existence, but once free I became her chosen prey.

To her bitterness and wild fury I resisted, and continued to resist her embraces, and so great was my fear of her and my disgust, that in shame and despair I was driven to confess her wantonness to her husband, my master and my benefactor, to forestall the lies which I was assured she would weave around me. Being unwilling, and I believe totally incapable of controlling his wife's unbridled desires, and to avoid yet further scandal, my master dismissed me, albeit with sorrow, from his service. But he used his influence to secure for me a post as a civil servant; as such I joined the staff of Catus Decianus, procurator designate of the Province of Britain.

Having ridden on mule back with increasing pain and

hardship for well over one thousand miles, we came to Gessoriacum and took ship for Britain. The sea was lively, the ship behaved like a wild ass, the sailors – rough barbarians all – mocked us with rude gestures, uncouth laughter and with words spoken in their outlandish tongue; I wished for death so great was my misery. After some ten hours the sea grew weary, the nightmare journey ended, and I regained my senses in the calm waters of the busy port of Rutupiae. Thence we rode in further anguish and so came to Londinium.

I found a new, raw town, totally lacking in culture, beauty or merit of any kind. There were few paved roads, most were rutted cart tracks deep in mud when it rained and blinded with choking dust when dry. The climate was vile: the sun seldom shone; rain fell unceasingly. Thick mist from the river, which flowed past the town, turned day into night; the prevailing cold and damp consumed the very marrow of men's bones. There was no theatre, no public baths, no decent entertainment. It was a place of mean streets, squalid houses and a stinking river port, thronged with uncouth barbarians, the scum of the Empire. For a man of any culture, taste or schooling it was a place of harshest exile, well beyond the limits of civilisation and the normal decencies of life.

The Procurator's staff worked in three departments. First that of the revenue, responsible, in the main, for taxes, customs dues, the administration of Imperial estates and the proceeds of goods, largely minerals, exported from the province. Then, that of expenditure, and so responsible for the pay and running costs of the Army and the fleet, and for public works. Co-ordinating the work of these two departments was the secretariat, which dealt also with the Imperial Government in Rome to which the Procurator was directly responsible. Additionally the secretariat controlled all matters which were the concern both of the procurator and the governor of Britain. At this time Quintus Veranius was governor; he was a dying man, due, it was said, to the abominable climate which brought death to many.

Lacking, as I did, any civil service experience, I worked in the expenditure department, with an understanding that having become familiar with that side of our affairs, I would be transferred for a time to revenue, and thence achieve my true status in the secretariat.

I was concerned, indignant even, that I worked among slaves, and worse than this, that a slave named Clodius was the head of my department. From time to time I found it necessary to remind him, and the others, of the great gulf between our respective stations in life. Accordingly, although diligent, I was not popular, but no freedman can be expected to seek friendship or even company among slaves, who can scarce be regarded as human. In view of my background my attitude could seem lacking in logic, but in spite of it – more probably because of it – I am so minded.

Catus Decianus, the procurator, was no patrician but a knight. Fittingly, in view of his character, he had served in the Army with, it was said, some distinction. This I can almost believe for as a soldier, no doubt, he was able fittingly to demonstrate his brutality, greed, vice and lack of any scruple. He was a man totally without culture; he was a drunkard and a glutton; he was wont to satisfy the carnal lusts of his body not with women but with young men. This practice, it is true, is not unknown among the Hellenes, but I have always found it utterly abhorrent as indeed do most of my race. Nevertheless those who practise it obtain their delight more from philosophical discussion, a community of intellect and taste and a meeting of minds, than from mere sexual union, which is indulged only to promote a closer intellectual identity. Catus Decianus had no concept of such philosophy and sought only to gratify his bodily lust. After a time his black eyes, which resembled those of a pig, began to dwell uncomfortably and at length upon me.

He was perfectly aware that I found his habits and manner of life utterly revolting; indeed I am sure that my revulsion added to his pleasure. When I would not submit, and twice refused invitations to dine at his house, well knowing their real purport, he summoned me to his office in the secretariat. His secretary, a slave who, as was well known, performed more personal service than that of a secretary, left the office as I entered, looked at me with angry eyes and then leered at me as he passed. Catus Decianus was alone; he sat in a high-backed chair behind a long table on which lay tablets and scrolls heaped in some disorder; the room was airless and smelled of sweat. I said; 'You sent for me, sir.' And stood rigid just inside the doorway.

Catus Decianus stared at me in silence and slowly ran his eyes over my body. I felt as if I was being stripped naked. I saw him lick his lips and I shivered, but not with cold. He said: 'Myron, do not be a fool; you are far too beautiful to be stupid. You know what I seek, and what I seek I always gain. I have you in the hollow of my hand. Unless you come to me you can expect no advancement in the service. Should you dare to leave my staff there is no employment for you in Londinium, nor indeed in all Britain, for should any man consider using you I have the means to see that he will not. I warn you, moreover, that should you still refuse my very reasonable demands, I shall charge you with disaffection. You are a Greek and a former slave; both these things would be held against you. Additionally I should bring sworn testimony to support the charge. Finally, as you know, Veranius is sick. As a freedman your case would be heard by Drusus, his deputy. Drusus is greatly in my debt. He dare not displease me since my foreclosure of his debt would ruin him, and he would, therefore, find you guilty. The penalty is death on the cross, which is a slow, agonising end without dignity. We have both seen men crucified, know how they look and can guess how they feel.' He paused, stared at me and – smiling – said: 'In time I shall tire of your body and seek my pleasure with another. Your advancement will be assured for I know that you are capable and to be trusted. I have not many such. There is much to be done. My duty is to make this province profitable for Rome. You and I can take our share of that profit. I shall leave Britain a rich man, so can you.' He paused again; his smile faded, and he said: 'Think, Myron; I shall expect you at my house for dinner. Now, you may go.' His voice was as smooth as a silken robe, and charged with menace.

I will not dwell on my manner of life during the succeeding months, except to say that I was utterly debauched, felt unclean, hated myself and began to hate everything that was Roman. After a time, as he had said, he tired of me, and to the astonishment of us all took a woman. I was transferred to revenue. I was in my twentieth year, and in my third as a civil servant.

Nearly two years since, Quintus Veranius was dead; in his place Suetonius Paulinus ruled Britain. He was a man arrogant to a high degree and utterly devoid of culture or humanity. As a soldier he was both capable and ruthless. In view of his character, it was inevitable that military expenditure, unmatched by any gains in the revenue, should have risen sharply. The far from cordial relationship between the procurator and governor became open hostility, matching the worsening financial situation within the province.

On a sad, raw day with rain and biting wind, Catus Decianus sent for me. I feared the summons and although, as I entered his office, I strove to keep my face impassive, no doubt my unease was all too readily apparent. He stared at me for a long minute and then said: 'No need to fear,

Myron, I need your head now, not your body. It is strange how a man's desire, once all consuming, can wither and become as if such had never been. Sit and listen. You may make notes should you so wish, but make them in such a way that should they fall into another's hand he would gain no understanding of their content. First – Prasutagus, King of the Iceni, is dead. As you are aware, he has no son. In his will he has bequeathed his kingdom, jointly, to our emperor and his barbarian wife, a veritable slut called Boudicca.[1] As you know, Rome does not accept queens, since being women, they are quite unfitted to rule. Moreover this one is disaffected.'

I broke in: 'I find this strange; what of Queen Cartimandua of the Brigantes?'

He frowned at my interruption. 'You have a point. The Brigantes are more numerous than the Iceni; moreover, Divine Claudius made a treaty with Queen Cartimandua when he took this province, a treaty similar to that made with Prasutagus; he made none with Boudicca. Moreover, Cartimandua's time will come. I will now continue – if you will suffer me.' His voice was heavy with irony. 'Should you have questions save them until I have finished.' His frown deepened as he continued.

'Rome, therefore, does not recognise this will. Second – we shall annex the tribe and its land; it will form part of the province with a status similar to that enjoyed – or perhaps suffered – by the Trinovantes, Cantiaci and the rest.' His voice grew scornful. 'One day, perhaps, they could even become civilised. It follows from this that Prasutagus' estates, property, and possessions are forfeit to Rome in their entirety. Their value is assessed at three million sesterces. Third – when the treaty with the Iceni was made the Divine Claudius made a loan to Prasutagus. In view of the passage of time since the loan was made, it is possible that the Iceni may now believe that the loan was a gift. This belief, should it be held, is false, and with the end of the royal house the loan, and the interest due on it, must now be repaid; it amounts to a little under two million. Fourth – certain of the Iceni nobles are privately and heavily in debt to powerful men in Rome, whom I will not name. I am required to secure repayment, amounting to a further one and a half million. For this recovery I shall hold Boudicca herself responsible since, when the loan was made and the debts incurred, her husband was king. Fifth – to obtain repayment of this large sum at once, and in gold, is clearly not possible; accordingly, I am sending a delegation from revenue to the Iceni to acquaint them of Rome's intent, and of the nature and extent of the debt. This delegation will secure the royal treasure, bring it here, and assess its value. They will bring with them three Iceni nobles, overtly to see that the valuation does not cheat them – as, of course, it will.' Catus Decianus smiled: 'In fact they come as hostages. All three, you will understand, stand high in the list of private debtors. When the value of the treasure is assessed, I will offset this against the total debt and collect the balance, much of it no doubt in corn, cattle and slaves, after the harvest. Sixth – Clodius, who is an experienced debt collector, will be in charge of this important delegation. I do not altogether trust him; some of what he seizes could stick to his fingers. You will accompany him to see that it does not. I need hardly tell you that the overt reason for your presence is for you to gain experience, as part of your continuing training, as a member of my staff. Seventh and last – it is just possible that you could meet trouble. Accordingly the delegation will take a mounted escort of four troops of Asturian auxiliaries, which should serve to show these barbarians that Rome means to secure the return to her of all that is rightfully hers.'[2]

Catus Decianus grinned and rubbed his hands. 'I told

you once that I would make this province pay, and so I shall, to my benefit and even to yours, should you serve me well.'

A week later I stood in the hall of Boudicca's palace. It was timber built with a roof of thatch, twice as long – perhaps forty feet – as it was wide. The roof was supported on two rows of timber uprights which ran the length of the hall, so making three aisles, the central one being perhaps ten feet in width. The floor was of puddled clay beaten hard. At one end of the central aisle was a raised platform, and behind it a doorway leading, it would seem, to the royal apartments. The hall was gloomy and damp; the air was rancid, smelling of sweat, smoke, stale food and dung.

On the platform was a high-backed chair with arms; it was heavily draped with animal skins. In the chair sat the queen. She was a huge woman with massive shoulders, thick wrists and large hands. Her flaming red hair, held by a fillet of gold, fell to her hips. She wore a multicoloured robe to her ankles, gathered at the waist with a heavy gold chain, and over her robe a dark blue mantle clasped at the shoulder with a gold and enamel brooch. A golden torque was about her throat and heavy gold bracelets encircled her wrists. From where I was standing I could just see that her feet were bare. She looked to be a most formidable woman. Clytemnestra who, as will be recalled, murdered her husband with an axe, could well have resembled her closely except that Clytemnestra performed the deed in her husband's bath, and I doubt if Boudicca knew the meaning of the word bath. I felt some sympathy for her dead husband.

Our delegation stood massed in the central aisle; on both sides of us, between and behind the rows of timber uprights, stood fifty or so men whom I took to be Iceni nobles. All were bareheaded, perhaps in deference to the queen, some were naked above long trousers, but most wore tunics and cloaks. Some were heavily painted or perhaps tattooed; all save two were unarmed. These two stood like statues, one on either side of and a little behind, the queen. They wore bronze helmets and mail shirts. Each carried on his left arm a small, round, decorated shield and each gripped with both hands a long straight sword held upright, point between the feet and hilt level with the waist. From their shoulders hung blue mantles matching the colour of that worn by the queen.

Clodius, with an interpreter at his elbow, stood in front of us. I was immediately behind him with, on my right the Asturian decurion commanding our escort, and on my left a trooper. In serried ranks behind us stood a score of troopers; further troopers kept the door. I took pleasure in the fact that all were fully armed and armoured, for I confess that I was uneasy.

Clodius, of course, behaved like an ignorant slave, since that was what he was. His insolence was such that he even stood with one foot on the queen's platform; he offered her not the slightest deference or courtesy, and his voice was pitched in a tone of studied mockery. The interpreter, I learned later, played his part by omitting altogether some of Clodius' more insulting phrases, but to little avail. As Rome's intentions began to be understood I saw the queen's huge body begin to shake with suppressed rage and indignation. I watched her grind her teeth, and saw her huge hands grip the arms of her chair so tightly that her knuckles grew white. An angry murmur broke from the assembled nobles and steadily increased until it almost drowned the voice of the interpreter. Even Clodius, in fear, began to mend his manners for I saw his body shake and he took his foot from the platform. Only the two figures behind the queen remained motionless and utterly impassive, whereas to my right and left were men with angry, bearded, twitching faces and clenched fists, who pawed the ground with naked feet; out of the corner of my eye I saw the decurion's right hand move slowly to his sword hilt.

Clodius stopped speaking; the interpreter translated and was silent. The tumult in the hall rose to a crescendo and died abruptly as the queen rose to her full height; she was taller than most of the men in that hall. She stepped to the front of the platform, looked down at Clodius' upturned face and spat upon it. She said: 'Tell your master that I do not treat with slaves. I am queen of the Iceni. Should he seek aught from me, tell him to come himself and seek my favour of an audience.'

For a long moment there was dead silence and then, at the back of the hall, a man laughed. Immediately the air was filled with a gale of mocking laughter, men gripped their sides, slapped their neighbours' shoulders and looked this way and that with open mouths and dancing feet.

I saw the back of Clodius' neck swell and turn scarlet. He turned his head slightly and, out of the corner of his mouth, said something to the decurion, who bawled at the top of his voice and jumped for the platform. What followed had been well planned and was well performed. Two Asturians attacked each of the queen's guards, and by their speed caught them unawares; one they killed outright and the other they wounded near to death. The decurion was himself wounded in the neck by one of the guards, not seriously, although he bled much.

I was in fear and stood motionless darting quick glances to right and left. I was, indeed, most fortunate, for at least one of the Iceni carried a dagger and he came for me, thinking perhaps that I was Clodius. I saw his blade flash in his uplifted hand as he leaped at me out of the press. As a boy, in a gymnasium in Athens, I had been adjudged a capable wrestler for my age, and I had not altogether lost the art. I jumped forward, half turned and tripped him with my right leg; he struck wildly, tearing my tunic, lost his balance, staggered, and a trooper ran him through the body. For a long moment there was uproar. The Asturians, by now, had formed into a double rank, back to back, extending nearly the length of the central aisle. I myself stood breathless between the two soldiers nearest the platform. Each rank then moved forward, a pace at a time, only helmets and faces showing over the rim of their shields, jabbing with their swords and striking with shield bosses. Thus they cleared the aisle, drove the Iceni back against the walls of the hall, and held them there. Three Iceni lay dead or badly wounded in the aisle. Two more attempted to run out through the door at the end of the hall which faced the platform; both were killed out of hand.

Two troopers seized the queen. She did not struggle; perhaps she felt it beneath her dignity to do so. They led her to one of the timber uprights nearest the stage, and tied her wrists and ankles to it, passing the rope round her waist and securing the end to the timber, so that she could not move her body. A third trooper slid his dagger down her back cutting her garments free, and so stripping her to the waist. Then in turn they flogged her with a knotted length of rope until her back was cut to ribbons, the blood spurting at every blow. There was utter silence in the hall except for the thud of the rope and the heavy breathing of the trooper who wielded it. Although she must have suffered agonies she made no sound. At last her knees buckled beneath her body and she hung insensible, while I watched as if turned to stone.

I heard Clodius say to the decurion, who by now had tied his scarf tightly round his wound and so staunched the bleeding:[3] 'Call your men off. Let me have eight and I will search this dungheap. Keep good watch on that rabble. Check each in turn for hidden weapons; let none escape. Find the three we need and place them under separate guard.' Then he added, almost as an afterthought: 'I do not wish that bitch to die. Release her, strip her of her jewellery, cleanse her wounds and staunch the bleeding, but keep her under guard.' With the eight troopers he made for the doorway beyond the platform, and I went with them.

A trooper pushed the curtain aside and we found ourselves in a large room the width of the hall. It seemed to be an audience chamber, for on the right, on a dais, stood another throne similar to the one in the hall. A bench ran round three sides of the room. There was a hearth, laid but unlighted, in the centre, and above among blackened beams a smoke hole in the roof. Two frightened women stood against a further doorway. Clodius said, in Latin: 'Clear that doorway.' I doubt if the women understood; none of us could speak their tongue and our interpreter was with the decurion. We hesitated and then two troopers shouldered the women aside. One of them began to scream but the sound died in her throat as one of the soldiers struck her across the face, blood running from her cut lips. Clodius said, with a grin: 'You two can take pleasure in guarding them. No doubt you will use them as you wish.'

We went through a further doorway into a smaller room. In one corner was a raised platform upon which lay furs and rumpled covers, which hung down low to the floor. There was a table upon which stood pots, a bronze mirror, a comb and a small iron-bound coffer. Larger chests stood round the walls. Clodius looked at the Asturians and said: 'Which of you is the senior?' A tall soldier stepped forward. 'Set your men to open, break open if you must, those chests but, as you value your life, do not touch what they contain. There may be more, perhaps sunken into the floor beneath the bed, such is their custom. Look well. Two of your men will come with me, there is a further room.' He pointed to a low doorway in the corner furthest from the bed.

We passed through the doorway and came to the last

room. We knew it was the last for there was no other door. In the room stood three women. Two were very young, one indeed was as yet scarce a woman; both had flaming red hair filleted with gold. The third was older and wore no fillet. They looked at us in silence. This room was also furnished as a bedchamber, but with two chests only. Clodius said to the soldiers: 'Myron and I will go through those chests and search the room. Keep the women back from us.' We found nothing beneath the platform which served as a bed, and no sign of anything sunk beneath the clay floor, although Clodius sounded it with his staff. The chests were part filled with women's clothing and a few items of jewellery – these we took – but left the clothes which were dirty and lice ridden. The older woman shouted at us, in anger at what was done. One of the soldiers struck her in the face with his clenched fist; his blow was heavy; her head crashed against the wall behind her and she crumpled to the ground. The older of the two girls attacked the soldier, scratching at his face with her finger nails. Laughing, he warded her off; his comrade kicked her feet from under her, and kicked her again with heavy boots as she lay weeping on the floor.

Clodius said: 'Enough. You can both use the older one but leave the two younger. From the colour of their hair it would seem that they are daughters to the bitch we flogged, and neither are ripe for common soldiers.'

Leaving the women and the soldiers, Clodius and I returned to the queen's bedchamber. Two chests, which had been hidden beneath the bed, now stood in the centre of the room, and the soldiers were forcing the lids. All the other chests stood open. Most contained clothing, both for men and women; the clothing crawled with lice. The coffer which stood upon the table, and the two chests from under the bed, contained treasure in abundance; gold and silver cups, gold torques, gold and enamel bracelets, necklaces, amulets and a dozen small leather sacks which held pearls and coin. There was much else besides, but my memory fades. We took the three chests, roped and sealed by Clodius, and left the others in the room.

I went into the inner bedchamber. The older woman lay in a heap in one corner; the two girls lay on the bed. From the state of their garments, or rather from their lack of them, it was plain that all three had been raped; the younger girl was weeping. In silence I looked at the two Asturians. One said: 'When we raped the one in the corner, the girls sought to hinder us, so we took them after to teach them manners.' He looked hard at me and, with a sneer, added: 'No "common soldier" is ordered by a slave.'

We headed back towards the hall. In the audience chamber the two women lay on the floor naked below the waist. Only their eyes moved. Clodius laughed and the soldiers grinned.

On the platform in the hall both guards lay dead, for the one wounded had choked his life away; blood was already clotting on his lips, while a myriad flies clustered on his wounds and were busy about the body of his comrade. The queen had regained her senses and now sat in her chair leaning forward, her elbows on her knees and her chin cupped in her hands. Her eyes were dulled with pain. Someone, the decurion perhaps, with unaccustomed humanity – maybe he admired her courage – had draped, albeit clumsily, a dead guard's blue cloak over her shoulders and over the back of her chair. This gave some protection to her torn back, about which more flies buzzed hungrily. She had been stripped of her jewellery and ornaments, and an Asturian, his sword drawn, stood behind her as her guard.

The Iceni nobles stood or lounged in groups, herded into one of the side aisles. With studied insolence they turned their backs upon, and totally ignored, the soldiers guarding them; they spoke together in low tones, like a murmur of bees as if about to swarm. Seven bodies lay huddled in the central aisle, each with an attendant cloud of flies. The decurion guarded separately the three we sought.

The chests were too heavy for our pack mules, so we took a wagon, an Iceni as driver, and four of their chariot horses to draw it. We mounted the three Iceni on led horses, tied their hands and headed south the way we had come, through forests and swamps and over barren heathland, making for Londinium. Both Clodius and the Asturians were in high humour, although some of the troopers complained that they had been less fortunate than their comrades. I felt sick.

So started the Great Rebellion, for within a few short weeks the Colonia at Camulodunum had been utterly destroyed, and ten thousand Romans and their lackeys butchered. Much of the blame lies upon the head of the Procurator, and a lesser burden upon that of Clodius – his slave. I am not without guilt for, in fear, I said and did nothing to dissuade them from their plans or thwart their purpose. Of all our delegation I believe that only I, and Catus Decianus, still live, and he an exiled, broken man bereft of all honour and estate.

When news of disaster reached Suetonius Paulinus, who was campaigning in the west, he rode to Londinium but could not hold the town against Boudicca and her angry rebels. When he left, he took with him such of the citizens as were able-bodied and willing to ride; I was among them.[4] I became a clerk in his headquarters and was present, but took no part in, the great battle which destroyed Boudicca's army. I saw the bloody vengeance which Paulinus visited upon the rebel tribes. Men, women and children were butchered or enslaved, without mercy or remorse; cattle were slaughtered, crops destroyed, farmsteads and hamlets burned. Such few as escaped starved in the forests. A full generation must surely pass before any semblance of normal life returns to that ruined and blackened land. I saw the burnt-out fragments of Boudicca's hall; there were bones half buried in the ashes, perhaps hers and those of her ravished daughters lay among them, although men say that she took poison, destroying herself with her own hand, and that she lies in an unmarked grave.

In midwinter, when the harrying still continued, although the screaming had grown muted amid the dying flames, Suetonius Paulinus summoned me and said that I had served him well, which was indeed the truth. He continued: 'Julius Classicianus has come to Britain as our new procurator. He must start from nothing; all records are burned; your fellow clerks – his servants – are scattered and most are dead. I now send you to him; you will be very welcome, so great must be his need.' He looked hard at me and his lip curled; 'I have a further reason, Myron, as you may guess. You know well that I have no love for procurators as a breed, who conspire with Rome behind my back, as jackals prey upon a lion. I have served this province well, and saved your life; you can repay your debt by keeping me informed of the plots your new master hatches to my destruction.' And so it was that I joined the Procurator, and became, in time, his personal secretary and – I do not boast – his confidant.

I served him willingly, faithfully and, indeed, with devotion and deep respect, for he was a man cultured, intelligent, upright and with humanity. He sought to repair rather than destroy, to heal and not to wound; he showed mercy and spared vengeance. Although I feared the governor, I sent no word and was glad, and less fearful, when I learned of his recall.

To the sorrow of all who knew him, my new master died; he was yet a further victim of the vile climate and harsh manner of life which afflict all who live in Britain. But thanks directly to his commendation, I am now in the service of the governor of Achaea, and so at last have returned to the country where I was born. I have neither wife nor child to cherish me, but live free, as a civilised man should, among his own people.

NOTES

[1] Catus Decianus was misinformed, or perhaps Myron's memory has failed him. Prasutagus in his will made the emperor his co-heir together with his two daughters. Boudicca was not mentioned, but would presumably have acted as regent until one or other daughter married, when the husband might well have become king or consort, cf. Cartimandua and Venutius.

[2] A troop of auxiliary cavalry comprised some thirty men commanded by a decurion.

[3] A scarf tied round the neck was standard Roman military equipment and was worn to prevent the wearer's skin being chafed by his armour.

[4] It is certain that Paulinus did enable some of London's citizens to flee the town under the protection of his soldiers. It is equally certain that he had only cavalry with him together, perhaps, with such few infantry soldiers as may have been based in London. It is difficult to believe that when he retreated into hostile, or potentially hostile country, he would take with him a swarm of refugees on foot since these would impair seriously his mobility. It makes better military sense, therefore, to assume that such as were lucky enough to be allowed to accompany him, and so save their lives, had as a prerequisite to provide their own horses.

SERGIUS

It was dark and very cold. A gentle breeze blew steadily from the north-west; wave upon wave of ink-dark water broke against the blunt prow of the barge, lapped along its sides and hissed hungrily upon the beach. Aboard the barge were a score of legionaries, eight rowers and a steersman. They were tightly packed; most knelt for there were benches only for the rowers. The sky was heavily overcast and neither moon nor stars shone through the murk, but away to the east the sky was beginning to lighten, revealing a jagged mountain ridge, jet black against the lighter darkness of the lowering sky.

At the prow of the barge a man stood leaning forward over the dark water. His left hand grasped the gunwale and his left knee was pressed against the planking beneath it. His right hand held two seven-foot javelins – upright – with their iron-shod butts resting on the flat bottom of the barge. He was fully armoured, with his short straight sword slung by a leather baldric on his right side. His body swung back and forth with the gentle rise and fall of the barge; his lips were pursed in a soundless whistle. He lifted his head and stared into the darkness beyond the prow. He could just discern a black and ragged skyline beneath a background which was shading to dark grey. There, he thought, lies the island of Mona. Because it is there, I, Sergius, the five legionaries in my section[1] who are with me, the other two sections of my company, and the Batavians[2] who man the oars and steer, shiver in this leaping barge. Others of our comrades also crouch in countless other barges, strung out along a spirit-haunted beach which fronts a tangle of mountains and valleys – the abode of unknown Gods – standing upon the edge of the world. Only Romans, and legionaries at that, could be so foolish. Sergius spat over the prow and his hands tightened on gunwale and javelins alike; involuntarily he shivered. Whatever the reason which requires us to be on parade, he thought, be it for inspection by the legate, be it in preparation for everyday camp fatigues or to prepare for an attack, we are always ready hours before the time appointed, so that our centurions can be sure of us, so that our tribunes can be sure of them, so that our legate can be at ease with our general, and so we wait, shiver and worst of all, think. What is more, I would wager a month's pay that my thoughts reflect those running through the heads of every legionary in my section, indeed of every legionary and every auxiliary in this whole army. Waiting to go into battle is always the worst kind of waiting; it is as bad for veterans as it is for recruits. Indeed, it is probably worse for us, the veterans. We know what could happen; we know what a man looks like, and sounds like, when his belly gapes open and his guts are tangled round his ankles, or when he has a spear fast in his chest and lies drowning in his own blood. We veterans have seen these things many times before; some of the men whose misery we saw and whose agony we heard were good comrades, now forgotten as if they had never been. Our own good luck is running out; our turn must come – perhaps this day. It is small wonder that a man finds his mouth dry like an eastern desert, that his belly feels empty like a split wineskin and that he has to brace his knees to stop them shaking, which is how I feel. Sergius' jaws worked beneath the cheek pieces of his helmet and his knuckles whitened with the intensity of his grip.

Deliberately he straightened to his full height, released his grip on the gunwale, and steadied himself with the javelins against the movement of the barge. He turned over in his mind the orders for the attack. When the trumpet sounded all barges would weigh anchor, or rather haul on board their bow and stern ropes each with a rock lashed to the end, which served as such. The barges would then row across the narrow strip of water – at most four hundred paces – which separated them from Mona. Keeping proper station was important, but this was primarily the duty of the rowers and steersmen. As soon as the crossing began, onagri,[3] mounted on timber platforms built upon the beach just above the low-water line, would start throwing missiles at the 'reception committee' on the further shore. These were less disturbing thoughts, more fitted to fill the head of a section commander with a task to accomplish, with men's lives in his hands and a battle to win. He smiled, a trifle grimly in the darkness, and his thoughts ran on before him. The range for the onagri was nearly extreme and assuming that the missiles – rocks the size of half a man – reached the further shore, they should be deadly against massed, unprotected savages. In addition, the ballista[4] mounted in the prow of every fourth barge would open up, throwing heavy barbed bolts at the beach. Each of these missiles could pierce no fewer than three barbarians should they be found in line one behind the other.

Better still, whereas the onagri would have to cease throwing when the barges neared the beach, the ballistae could keep at their work until they grounded.

Once ashore Sergius and his section would form up in two ranks immediately in front of the prow of the barge, with the other two sections coming up on his right and left. The front rank legionaries would cast both their javelins. This accomplished, the rear rank would pass through the front rank and cast theirs. Both ranks would then draw swords and move up the beach for twenty full paces and then halt. The second wave of legionaries, having landed from a further flight of barges, would pass through and clear the beach up to the edge of the trees, the first wave moving up on their heels. Thereafter further orders would be issued to meet the situation then obtaining.

He, Sergius, would be the first of his section ashore, and his men would form up on him. Macro, Constans and Julius would stand as the original front rank. Sergius, with Lucius on his right and Victor on his left, would pass through and lead up the beach, the other three two paces in rear. He had explained it all, twice, to his section, had questioned each legionary as to his role and had obtained the proper answers. He had personally checked all weapons; all javelins were ground to razor sharpness, swords were sharp and deadly, shields were solid with straps and buckles secure. Nothing should go wrong.

The auspices, moreover, were more than usually favourable, or so they had been assured by their centurion, who had witnessed General Paulinus take them. Paulinus had made the customary fighting speech that it was fitting for a general to make on the eve of battle. He must have done it well for their centurion, a hard-bitten, cynical veteran and a man of few words, had repeated in some excitement what he could remember of the speech. It seemed also that there was loot in plenty to be had for the taking, and that the act of killing a Druid, because it would give pleasure to the Roman gods, should add to the killer's personal store of good luck. Moreover no Roman, as yet, had dared to invade Mona. Today's attack was the stuff of history, would be remembered until the end of time, and those who took part would be numbered with the heroes of old. Paulinus was a stickler in all such matters, as in everything to do with soldiering. He was a hard man but a good soldier and a fine commander. He could even be right about the good luck invoked by killing a Druid. The Roman gods could have but little love for their barbarian cousins and none at all for those of the Druids; loathsome creatures of blood and fire who took pleasure in human sacrifice, ghastly cruelty and the magic arts. Sergius shivered, but not from cold. May the gods bestow the gift of swift death on any Roman who falls into their bloody hands. No, nothing should go wrong; especially were he able to kill a Druid.

The light was coming up fast now. Sergius turned and his dark eyes flickered over the barge. Macro and Constans were playing at dice with a thwart for a board. Julius was keeping the tally using a stick which he notched with his dagger blade. Lucius, it seemed, was asleep on his knees, leaning against the side of the barge his helmeted head cradled on his arms. Sergius almost envied Lucius his talent of being able to sleep anywhere, under any conditions, which is in truth a most valuable military virtue. Victor, wide awake, was sharpening the blade of his dagger on his personal whetstone, from which he was never separated, although he, like his comrades, was in fighting order and so carried neither cloak nor equipment staff. These, and remaining items of personal equipment, were under the eye of Marcus who, as section muleteer, was still ashore and would not cross until later that day. Sergius doubted whether Cyclops, the one-eyed mule, would enjoy the swim, pictured Marcus' language and methods of encouragement, and grinned at his thoughts.

Most of the legionaries in the other two sections were huddled in the stern of the barge. Their section commanders stood over them, leaning on their shields. A few paces beyond the stern was the prow of another barge, forming part of the second assault wave, and beyond that was the beach – a scene of ordered confusion. At the water's edge was a long line of stakes, which had served as markers for the barges when they were beached prior to embarkation. All barges had been brought by the fleet from Deva. A little to the right reared one of the onager platforms and above it, like a pointing finger, the giant throwing arm soared upwards into the sky. The onager crew, like a disturbed ants' nest, were heaving stone missiles on to the platform. As Sergius watched the throwing arm seemed to shrink and he understood that the crew were winding it back in preparation for loading; he could hear the screech of straining timber in the grip of twisting cords. Behind the onager a dark mass extended the length of the beach, legionaries of the third assault wave who would embark in barges returning empty from their initial crossing. At the top of the beach Sergius sensed rather than saw a further dark smear; auxiliary cavalry, he thought and as if disturbed by his thought a horse neighed harshly. Sergius' face darkened; barbarians all, he thought, toy soldiers who looked impressive on parade with their fluttering lance pennants, gaily coloured harness and capering horses, but no match for the real thing – legionaries. He had all the traditional infantry contempt for cavalry but in his distaste there was, perhaps, a sour taste of envy.

Sergius looked to right and left and saw a line of barges similar to his own stretching seemingly into infinity. That on his right was loaded like his own and contained three sections of his company. The one on his left carried fewer soldiers, one section only, but at the prow crouched the squat outline of a ballista. He heard a gentle but sustained rattle which mingled with a strange vibrant hum, as of a lyre string freshly tightened and there was a heavy snap as of a door bolt being shot; the weapon was now fully wound and lacked only a bolt in the guide for throwing. It must be nearly time, he thought, and an end to the prolonged suspense which was becoming unendurable. His body shivered in the damp and biting cold.

His thoughts turned to Deva and the one-roomed hut built of rough-hewn timber, wattle and daub; little better, if somewhat cleaner, than those used by well-to-do barbarians. Gwynneth, his woman, would be sweeping out the hut and setting the place to rights, her breasts already swollen and her belly distended with his child. Under the gods his son – for Gwynneth was sure that she carried a son – would be safely born before he, Sergius, could see Deva again. She was a Brigantes, tall for a woman, fair skinned with blue eyes, broad hips, full breasted with a tangle of auburn hair which fell to her knees. He was fond of her, she was a good housekeeper and an excellent cook; she had a good body and was responsive – eager indeed – when she lay with him. No other woman had given him greater pleasure. She was obedient also and had given him cause only for two beatings since he had taken her. To his surprise he had found, when he first lay with her, that she was still a virgin. Sergius' face softened and his tight mouth relaxed. Childbirth was a painful and dangerous business. His mother had died giving birth to her fifth child, and he had never forgotten her screaming agony, and the blood-sodden couch. When he returned, and his son was safely born, he would dedicate an altar. Moreover, then she would be eager to lie with him anew. He thought of her body; it was strange to feel desire quicken at the moment of battle.

Suddenly, above the beach, a trumpet sounded urgently, the brazen notes echoing along the shore. For an instant there was silence, broken only by the sweep and surge of the sea and the strident calls of sea birds, surprised and frightened by the clamour which burst upon their solitude. In the distance legionaries began to cheer; the cheering was taken up, was magnified and the sound swelled as it swept along the beach and over the sea like a moorland fire driven before the wind. As Sergius hauled the bow cable aboard, he found that he too was cheering himself hoarse – with relief that the waiting was over. It was full daylight.

The rowers unshipped their oars; their blades dipped into the sea, which boiled as the oarsmen threw their full weight into their work. A long double line of barges began to creep forward away from the beach and towards Mona. Behind them there were a swift series of monstrous thuds as the throwing arms of the onagri, released by their crews, crashed against the thickly padded stop beams; their heavy missiles rose lazily and mightily into the air in huge arcs, attained their separate zeniths, and plunged angrily towards the further shore.

Sergius lifted his shield, slipped his left arm through the straps and rested the lower rim on the gunwales of the barge just behind the stern post. He looked towards Mona; he saw a line of tall trees, at their feet a wide stony beach and upon the beach barbarians massed like a crowd at the circus. A distant clamour as of men shouting came to him on the wind. He flexed his arms and legs, looked up at his javelin points, turned his head and said to no one in particular: 'Soon we shall give that barbarian scum something to shout about.'

Over to his left there was a heavy thump and he watched a ballista bolt skimming over the waves. The aim looked good but he lost the bolt before it reached – if it reached – Mona. He watched the crew reload and discharge their second bolt. This one flew true and he saw a gap suddenly appear, and as suddenly disappear, in the thronged figures upon the beach. To right and left he saw other eddies in the crowd; he could see that there were bodies lying where the waves broke upon the shore. The barbarians were still shouting, leaping and brandishing their weapons but it seemed that the sound, as it came to him on the wind, was higher pitched, almost shrill, with a note more of fear than of defiance. He saw two onager missiles fall just below the trees; both tore ragged holes in the press of bodies. He pictured the effects of the missiles themselves, and the wounds occasioned by the stones of the beach and fragments of rock driven outwards from the impact like a hail of slingshots.

He looked right and left; the line of barges was now ragged but his own craft was well advanced, leading those nearest by perhaps half its length; he thought of a line of water beetles creeping slowly across the surface, and remembered a stream in which he had fished as a boy. It seemed that they were now in midchannel. He turned his head and said: 'We shall soon come within range of their archers,[5] should they have such. Macro, you will come forward to me and rest your shield on the gunwale to my right. Julius, when Macro is come you will come and rest yours on the gunwale to my left, thus we shall afford some protection to the rowers. Macro, move now.' It was done, and the barge crept steadily on towards the beach.

The barbarians were moving back. Until now their foremost men had been standing in the sea, now the shoreline and some ten paces of beach were clear except for a scatter of bodies, some lying still, some crawling up the beach and others twisting and struggling as they lay in their agony. The onagri had ceased throwing but the ballistae still directed their bolts upon the beach. A further fifty paces and the barge would ground. Sergius heard rather than saw an arrow flash past his head, just above the rim of his shield. He heard a shout, looked round, and saw that the steersman's arm, below the shoulder, had been shot through. One of the section commanders grabbed the steering oar, the other drew his dagger, cut off the arrow tip, withdrew the shaft and tightly bandaged the wound. Sergius felt the thud as another arrow struck his shield boss and glanced off into the sea. One of the oarsmen screamed and slumped backwards into the bottom of the barge, his hands plucking at the arrow in his throat. His oar, dragging in the water, slewed the craft over to the left nearly fouling the barge carrying the ballista. Sergius shouted: 'Victor, take that oar and row like great Neptune himself. You can show us that you are a good oarsman and may do with the exercise.'

He grinned, the legionaries laughed and Victor, with a face like thunder, took the oar and, using the dying oarsman's body as a stretcher for his feet, began mightily to row.

Sergius looked towards the beach.[6] The barbarians had moved well back. He saw that many of those who were nearest wore a white mantle and had a mane of long hair hanging unkempt below their shoulders. Of these some leaped in the air and screamed as if demented, some held their arms above their heads invoking, it would seem, the aid of their gods, others were upon their knees with beseeching hands uplifted. Some thrust their arms with fingers spread wide towards the barges, as if warding off the evil eye. These must be Druids, thought Sergius, and they are attempting magic against us. Suddenly the wind which, throughout the crossing, had been blowing steadily from ahead, freshened into a veritable gale and whistled over the barge screaming like a forest demon. Sergius had to use all his strength to hold his shield steady on the gunwales. He heard Macro cursing aloud and calling upon Mars while Julius, his face ashen, spoke of devils. Sergius felt the hair prick on the back of his neck. He turned his head and saw wild eyes and frightened faces. He shouted; 'Keep her head into the wind and row like legionaries; our magic has more power than theirs.' And he flourished his javelins. There was a grinding, shuddering shock as the barge grounded, lifted on a wave, dropped with a crash and held fast. Sergius leaped over the prow and landed up to his waist in water; a stone turned beneath his foot, he stumbled, almost fell, took half-a-dozen staggering paces and found himself clear of the sea. Lucius came up on his right and Victor on his left; with shields held high and steady they stared up the steeply sloping beach into the teeth of the wind which bore down upon them, and drove at their shields like a battering ram screaming past their ears.

Among the white-robed figures Sergius now saw others

in black. These carried flaming torches high above their heads and with hair streaming and mouths agape and screaming they leaped forward down the beach with giant strides. Behind these figures smoke rose above the trees and was swept upon them by the shrieking wind; the air was filled with the unmistakable stench of burning flesh. Macro, Constans and Julius hastened up the beach and formed rank. Sergius said: 'Those devils are burning Roman prisoners; they cry to us for vengeance. First javelin ready – prepare to throw – throw! Second javelin ready – prepare to throw – throw!' He, Lucius and Victor stepped forward through the gaps in the front rank and all three cast their first javelins. Sergius took as his target a dishevelled, black-robed Fury who was running straight at him, hair streaming behind her, her flaming torch held high above her head, her face contorted like a demon mask worn at the theatre. Sergius was proud of his skill with a javelin but to his surprise, and a jab of fear, he missed his throw, the javelin passing over her left shoulder and into the body of a white-robed figure who ran behind her. Leaving his second javelin standing upright among the stones, he drew his sword, just in time, and as her body ran headlong upon his shield he braced himself, threw his body forward against the shock, and stabbed beneath his shield deep into her belly. The shock of her rush drove him back a full pace. She fell in a screaming heap, thrusting at him with her flaming torch; she clawed at his legs with her fingernails and sank her teeth in his right ankle. He smashed the lower rim of his shield down across her head and, as she opened her mouth, drove the point of his sword into her throat. He stepped forward across her body and braced himself to face those who followed. Swords hammered on his shield, a javelin glanced off his helmet, a thrust spear gashed his right knee. Like a machine he stabbed beneath and beyond the right edge of his shield into unprotected bellies and thighs. He drove his shield forward with each hard-won pace, using both shield boss and rim as weapons, and his sword flickered in and out like the tongue of a snake. He counted twenty hard-won paces and halted. Almost breathless he shouted: 'Stand fast.' Suddenly, in front, the beach was clear and he was panting like a long-distance runner. He became aware that the wind had dropped.

He looked to his right and saw Macro, his chest heaving, a smear of blood on his right cheek, and his shield scarred and dinted as if it had been savaged by wild beasts in the arena. Macro gasped: 'Lucius took a flaming torch in the face and a spear in the chest; I think he is dead.'

On his left stood Julius who grinned and said: 'It was hot while it lasted; they fought as if possessed. The bitch devils were the worst, Victor took a sword cut in the leg and is down there,' he pointed down the beach, 'so I took his place. What caused that wind; was it their magic?' He pointed with his sword towards white-robed figures who stood at the edge of the trees.

Sergius turned his head and saw Constans on one knee behind his shield; with his left hand and teeth he was knotting a rough bandage round his right forearm. Constans looked up and with a mouth full of bandage muttered: 'I finished off the ones you wounded; one of those black devils did this with her teeth and hung on like a dog. I threw her off and ran her through the heart but she will not die.' He shuddered and pointed back down the beach to where a huddled black figure writhed, clawing and biting at the stones. Beyond her, legionaries of the second wave were moving slowly forward up the beach stabbing with their swords at anything un-Roman which still moved. Wounded barbarians are apt to be as deadly as those still whole, and it is prudent not to take chances.

To the right and left of Sergius' section stood other legionaries of his company. All were deployed, fronting the barbarians with an unbroken rank of legionaries, one man to each pace. Losses had been such that in the second rank, two paces behind the first, there were more gaps than legionaries. All breathed heavily as if after a forced march. The single rank stood motionless with shields held high. Eyes above shield rims were steady, but tight-lipped mouths gave evidence of strain not lessened by the dull, agonised, throbbing murmur and higher-pitched screaming of wounded and dying men, and women, at their backs; a sound so compelling that it drowned the beat and surge of the restless sea upon the beach.

A voice hailed Sergius; he turned his head and saw his centurion striding over the stones towards him. Sergius answered, 'Sir,' and sprang to attention.

The centurion said: 'Get Constans into line.' Sergius stepped back two paces and Constans moved slowly forward into the gap. Sergius faced his centurion and saw to his surprise that that hard-bitten, humourless officer, a bloodied sword in his hand, was grinning as he said: 'You were the first man ashore when others held back. I saw it. I have spoken to our commander and he will put you up for the Mural Crown. The sea, whipped up by that devil's wind, and that beach of sorcerers and their attendant furies made as formidable a wall as I have ever met, or ever wish to. I hope you get it; it will be a triumph for my company and a credit both to our cohort and XX Valeria. But the fight's not done yet. Watch your front.'

The second wave moving forward up the beach passed through. A legionary said, out of the corner of his mouth: 'Now we will show you what real soldiers can do.' Sergius grinned and was about to reply in the same vein when another said:

'Hold your tongue, Wineskin – you heard the centurion; you speak to the hero of the day.' He gave a mock salute. Sergius laughed, ordered his three legionaries to move forward and followed at their heels. He found that his step was light and that conscious effort was needed to keep his face as impassive as a good soldier should.

To his front there was a confused uproar of shouting and screaming and the clash of weapons. The steady advance stopped dead in its tracks and was resumed a pace at a time. Sergius stepped warily over and between the bodies of dead and wounded barbarians. Most were naked to the waist with faces, chests and arms covered in tattooed – perhaps painted – whirls, spirals and close-packed concentric circles of lines in red, blue and green. Some wore bronze-winged helmets or round iron caps, but most were bare headed. Some of those still living snarled at him like wolves with lips curled back and frenzied hatred in their eyes. Sergius' sword point was busy among them and none moved where he had passed. Among them lay Romans, some silent, some groaning aloud in agony. The shouting died away; the advance quickened and then halted at the head of the beach where the trees began. A trumpet sounded twice; the ranks of legionaries re-formed into company columns. Again the trumpet sounded short, clipped blasts and the steady advance resumed.

Sergius and what remained of his section led their company; their centurion followed twenty paces at their heels and at his back some thirty legionaries.[7] The undergrowth was thick, the pace slow; it grew colder as the light faded beneath tall trees which rose about them and spread into a leafy, dark canopy far above their heads. The silence was broken only by the beat of nailed boots and the crash of breaking branches as the legionaries forced their way ever deeper into the gloom. Lichen hung from the trees like the trailing fingers of men long dead; tree trunks were moss covered and glistened with damp; feet sank into ooze and slime and men in the rearmost ranks sank to their knees. The air smelled of rotting leaves and the stink of corruption was all about them. Smoke hung among the trees, catching parched throats and causing eyes to stream; in the smoke hung the pungent, sickly smell of burned flesh. The legionaries eyed each other uneasily in the gloom and looked warily about them. This was an evil place, the abode of spirits and unknown sinister forces, against which neither sword nor shield nor the presence of comrades could offer comfort. The rate of advance slowed to a crawl.

There was a lightening in the trees; suddenly Sergius found himself on the edge of a clearing. He saw the grass was trampled as by many feet. Two huge fires had burned here and their embers still glowed darkly red and streaked with grey ash; the stench of burned flesh was overpowering. On the further side stood three huge oak trees, that in the centre being the greatest tree which Sergius had ever seen. He doubted whether his complete section, standing with arms extended and fingertips touching, could circle the vast trunk. Human skulls hung from the branches of the trees and he could see among the lower leaves the dull glint of gold from torques, necklaces and armlets hanging in abundance. At the base of each tree lay a large flat stone heaped with brushwood, and on the top of each a long low cage of plaited withies about the length of a man. In front of each stone stood two motionless figures. One was white robed, bearded, wearing a gold torque at the throat and gold armlets, hair to the shoulders with a wreath of oak leaves worn as a fillet; the other was robed in black with matted hair to the waist. Sergius thought: more Druids and their attendant she-devils. He saw that each Druid held in his right hand a golden sickle, and that each devil, or perhaps witch, bore a flaming torch above her head.

Sergius looked to right and left and saw that his men had halted as if suddenly turned to stone. Macro balanced on one leg too fearful, it seemed, to complete his pace; Constans leaned forward, in the act of marching, his weight on his left foot and his right heel raised. It seemed as if an invisible wall was built about the clearing, a wall which could neither be climbed nor breached. His mind felt numb; the silence was absolute; it seemed that time stood still and that here he must stand frozen for ever. He watched the three Druids slowly, very slowly, raise their golden sickles at arm's length, directing the sickle points towards him and his soldiers. He heard Constans whimper. Suddenly, with a swift movement, the three witches thrust their torches into the brushwood and he saw the wood crackle into bright flame. He thought, there are men, Romans perhaps, in those cages who will burn alive before our eyes. This is not magic but an abomination which, should I suffer it, would render me accursed for all eternity. He forced his body forwards and the invisible wall was gone. He raced into the clearing shouting his legion's battle cry: 'Valeria – Valeria', and found comfort and reassurance in the familiar sound. He made for the centre stone of the three and became conscious of the Druid's eyes, which were fixed upon him, and seemed to grow luminous and larger under his own. He blinked, and as he did so, raised his shield in front of his face and drove it forward with all his strength, the thrust of his legs and his headlong rush, against the Druid's body. He heard a clash of metal as his shield boss struck the sickle and felt a shock as if he had run at speed upon a rock. He stumbled over something at his feet, the lower part of his shield struck the edge of the flat stone, wheeled forward over it and he fell in a heap upon his shield. He was aware of swift movement to his right, thrust instinctively with his sword, heard an ear-splitting, half-human howl and felt a burning pain on his face. He staggered backwards and regained his feet; he found that he still grasped his shield although his left arm was in agony, as if it were broken. The Druid lay on the ground, his sickle snapped in two and his head doubled unnaturally beneath his body. On his right the witch lay in a crumpled heap with blood welling from a deep wound in her breast. Her eyes were open, staring at him, but without expression like those of a snake. She still grasped her flaming torch which Sergius now understood she had thrust into his face, singeing his hair beneath his helmet and scorching cheek and chin. The pain was all but unbearable. The brushwood on the altar was burning fiercely, but the thrust of his shield had dislodged the wicker cage, which lay smouldering at the foot of the oak tree. He could see a figure twisting within it with open screaming mouth.

It came to him that the clearing was filled with legionaries. To his right and left brushwood flamed, but where there had been wicker cages he glimpsed white and black-robed figures, which writhed and jerked, held in the fires on legionary sword points. There was a roaring in his ears as of an angry sea, the trees began to spin in some monstrous dance and he crumpled like a filled grain sack suddenly split. Everywhere there was darkness except for two close-set discs of searing flame, which he knew were the eyes of the Druid he had killed; they bored ever deeper into his head.

I am called Cleon and am the senior medical officer of XX Valeria. I am in charge of the legion's hospital in the fortress of Deva. Although not given to boasting, I am a good doctor, of wide experience, and know that I enjoy not only the confidence of the legion but also that of my legate, whose personal physician I am.

I admitted Sergius Tullius Flaccus as a patient three days after the assault on Mona. His was one of the strangest cases which I have ever known. It seemed that he was totally blinded and yet his eyes were undamaged; he babbled in delirium but he had no fever; he was dead in twenty days but suffered neither mortal injury nor bodily sickness, at least no sickness which lay within the parameters of my expert knowledge and experience. The hurt, if hurt there was, could have lain in his mind, but for such a malady it is gods, rather than doctors, who must prescribe. His overt injuries were but trifling and comprised a broken bone in his left arm; this I, myself, set and the bone was beginning to knit without complication or undue distress. He suffered burns covering the whole of the right side of his head, or rather those parts of it unprotected by his helmet; he had sustained a gash on his right knee, inflicted by a spear and a deep bite on his right ankle, which I first took to have been inflicted by a dog or some other beast, but which I later learned were the teeth marks of a Druid priestess. This same harpy, with her nails, had torn deep furrows in both legs. All these wounds had, of course, become infected but such would not challenge the skills of even my youngest orderly, and all were either healed or healing when the man died.

You may find it strange that I, the senior medical officer, should be so much concerned with the fate of one section commander in a legion which held six hundred such. It seemed that this man had shown outstanding bravery upon Mona, winning the award of the Mural Crown. He was, moreover, the first soldier in XX Valeria to have gained this distinction in many years. In addition, it seemed that he had even been recommended for the award of the Oak Leaves, for saving the life of a comrade under conditions of great danger. It is not the duty of a doctor, however distinguished, to question military awards, nevertheless it seemed to me that the man had faced only a woman and a Druid, and he armed only with an ornamental but unwarlike sickle, and I could not wholly justify, to myself, the basis for so prized a decoration. His officers, therefore, even the legate himself, were personally and continuously concerned with the affair, so much so that, in truth, I neglected much of my other duty to oversee his case and ensure the proper and most devoted treatment.

Believing, as I still do, that his sickness lay in his mind and not in his body, I arranged for a rota of clerks on my staff to attend the man day and night. I bade them encourage him, when he was in command of his senses, to speak of all that had passed and to record his words. This was done most faithfully in pursuance of my orders. I myself would study each written record, and after some days we were able to set down the passage of events, as they occurred, and with them disclose even the thoughts and impressions which had come to him at the time. I myself, sitting beside his couch, would run through with him this record, hoping that by surveying the facts and the nature of his injuries rationally and dispassionately, I should restore his confidence, banish his fears and awaken his will to live.

When I learned of her existence I traced his barbarian woman and had her brought to my hospital. I was with her when she entered his ward, in which he lay alone, saw fear grow in her stupid, sheep's eyes, heard her babble of the power of the Druids and of danger to her unborn son. Despite her swollen belly she ran from the hospital, it would seem into thin air for we could find no further trace of her despite most thorough and diligent searching.

He died in the early morning of the day on which we received word of Boudicca's rebellion. He babbled of two scorching suns which had destroyed his sight and burned their way into his head. I reported the death to the legate, newly returned from Mona. He stared at me and then asked at what time the man's spirit had left his body. I replied: 'Sir, it was at sunrise. I was with him. I saw the first sun's ray touch his forehead; he gave a little sigh and I saw his jaw drop.' The legate rose from his table, paced his office to and fro like a beast in a cage, then, without even a glance at me, as if talking to himself, he said: 'Strange, on two counts.

First, the Druids worship the sun both as the life-giver and as the taker away of life. Second, it was at sunrise that Sergius Tullius Flaccus leaped on to the beach at Mona. May his brave spirit have a safe journey and find honour and comfort among the shades.' His voice was steady, but it was clear to me that his mind was unquiet.

The legionaries of XX Valeria, and I believe many, perhaps all, the officers ascribed his death to magic arts. For this I am not displeased, since in their eyes my own high reputation remains untarnished and the legate, with no loss of confidence, continues to lean upon my services.

NOTES

[1] The normal strength of a section was eight men. Sergius, including himself and the section muleteer, had seven and so was below strength. Since XX Legion probably had to fight its way from Chester, before assaulting Anglesea, this seems a reasonable assumption. In any event legions seem seldom to have been up to strength; sickness must have been a constant drain on manpower.

[2] There were eight auxiliary cohorts of Batavians in Britain – all attached to XIV Legion. They certainly crewed ships on the lower Rhine and may well have performed duty as rowers and coxswains in the attack on Anglesea.

[3] An onager (onagri is the plural word) performed for the Romans the task of heavy artillery. It could throw a one-hundred-weight stone missile some three or four hundred yards. They were extensively used in siege operations and may have been employed in the attack on Anglesea, although I know of no evidence of this.

[4] A ballista (ballistae is the plural word) acted as light artillery. It resembled a giant crossbow and discharged either stones or heavy barbed bolts. The range was similar to that of the onager. They were light enough to be carried individually on a cart and may have been allocated on a scale of one per company.

[5] It does not seem that bows and arrows were widely used in Britain. Nevertheless, they are certainly mentioned by Strabo who refers also to slingers. These latter are further attested by sling

stones in large numbers excavated in hill forts – notably Maiden Castle – in southern England.

[6] Tacitus describes the scene: 'The shore was lined by a motley battle array. There were warriors with their arms, and women rushing to and fro among their ranks, dressed in black, like Furies, their hair dishevelled, brandishing torches, and Druids with their arms raised to heaven and calling down terrible curses. The soldiers, paralysed by this strange spectacle, stood still...'

[7] A company at full strength comprised 80 legionaries. The writer has allowed for casualties occurring prior to and during the landing. In addition, of course, ten muleteers – one for each section – were still to make the crossing.

Caradoc

The lock-up in Camulodunum is a poor place. The condemned cell, fittingly perhaps, is the worst part. You go down a steep flight of twenty or so stone steps into a barrel vault, some four feet wide and perhaps ten long, very like a burial chamber. This too is fitting, I suppose, since it is death's anteroom. The stink is scarcely to be believed. When I was down there it was flooded, but I do not believe that it is always like that – only after heavy rain. They chained my wrists and ankles to the wall, my arms stretched sideways and my feet spread wide, resembling a man crucified. The door slammed shut behind them and there I stood, naked as I was born and already shivering in the black and icy darkness. After a time it seemed that things moved in the water, certainly I heard faint splashes and there was a regular drip which began to beat on my brain like a smith's hammer. I even fancied, after what seemed a very long time, that I could hear the beat of Charon's[1] oars as he rowed his boat upon the waters, looking for me, but I grow impatient.

My name is Caradoc; it is Latinised now but I prefer the Celtic form and use it whenever I am so able. I am of the Coritani tribe, and a horse dealer. For several years past, like my father before me, I have brought horses to Camulodunum, sold them to the Trinovantes and returned to my people. On occasion I have sold to Romans but not directly, since they would have been too important, in their own eyes that is, to bargain with a barbarian like me. Sometimes they would watch the sales standing on the edge of the crowd, hard-faced, clean-shaven men with disdain in their eyes, wrinkling their noses at us, and with scorn writ large on tight-lipped mouths. A slave or a freedman, as they call their one-time slaves, would bid on their behalf. I would rather deal with slaves since freedmen are apt to be even more haughty than their masters; it is often thus when a man has risen above his proper station in life. I despise freedmen who are neither hare nor raven and who, to justify themselves to the world, and in truth to themselves, often put on the most insufferable airs. Some of the horses I sell are mine; most are not and for these I take commission. So as to see that I do not cheat, those others who give me their horses to sell send with me either a trusted slave or more usually a member of their family. Such men I need, moreover, to help me drive or lead the horses, tend and guard them until sold.

We came to Camulodunum in the spring to find the citizens fearful and prey to much wild rumour. Men spoke of a rain of blood; some said that the statue of the Winged Victory, which stood before the temple of Claudius the God, had been found tumbled from its pedestal and lying face downwards, shattered to fragments; distant farms, it was said, had been burned and their owners with their beasts and households butchered. None had seen such things but most, it seemed, believed them. A number of the more wealthy citizens had already left for Londinium and the south, and some shops were closed. This I could see for myself and so believe. I was glad of these rumours for I obtained good prices for my horses, since a man mounted can flee more quickly from his fears than can his fellow on foot. I have never sold so many horses for so much gold in so short a time.

As on former occasions, when the sales were done I went to a certain wine shop to celebrate my good fortune, intending to leave Camulodunum next morning. My companions, who heeded the rumours more than I did, hastened from the city in fear leaving me alone. I found the wine shop I sought, and serving there a woman I had known before, for the place not only served wine but offered an even older, and at times more desirable, form of entertainment; this I was seeking. After we had drunk wine together she took me to her room. She stripped, lay back on her couch, smiled at me and held out her arms; she said she was fearful for her life, that she loved me but would deny her body unless I swore to take her with me when I left the city. I was very young and like a fool became angry – perhaps it was the wine. I told her that she had a fine body but was a common harlot, no less and certainly no more; that as was fitting I would pay her for her service, but that she could expect no more of me; then I lay with her. She wept and entreated me but was not altogether unwilling. When I had taken my pleasure, and she also was pleasured, she slipped from the couch, threw her cloak about her body and ran back into the shop screaming that she had been raped. I was astonished. Most of the customers laughed for they knew her trade, but a fool of a soldier believed, or feigned to believe, her story and arrested me.

Next morning I appeared before the magistrate. She gave evidence and proved herself an incomparable actress, dressed in a white mantle, freshly laundered, with her hair modestly veiled, her hands entwined most prettily, and her cheeks blushing and unpainted; with tears in her eyes she bewailed my violence and her lost virginity. I laughed out loud and was reproved by the magistrate who, to my sorrow I later learned, owned the shop and saw his reputation in some danger, for he had neglected to pay for a brothel licence. The landlord also spoke, swearing that his shop was just a wine shop, and that the woman was of as unblemished a reputation as was his disreputable establishment. I was a stranger quite without friends or influence, lacked the opportunity if not the means of bribery, and so stood no chance at all. I was found guilty and sentenced to death by fire.

No rational man fears death, only the manner of it. When the Destroyer comes for me I hope that he – or perhaps it is she – will be quick about it and will not play with my body like a cat for his pleasure and to my agony. I have a horror of cats, although men say that they are worshipped in Egypt; this I find extraordinary. Fire is a cruel death and I have watched men, and women too, die in the flames. The wood is often damp and so it takes longer. I remember a woman who clung to life for nearly one whole hour and never once did she cease screaming. I was very frightened but was able horribly to curse both the woman and the landlord before they stopped my mouth and dragged me from the courtroom. I heard the woman cry aloud and hope she was in fear because of my curse, perhaps she had good reason to weep – as you will hear. So I hung on the wall, hoped that the wood would be dry and that they would fire the top and not the base of the heap, since that way seems to bring death more quickly.

My body grew colder and I lost all feeling in my legs, becoming unaware even of the water which lapped my knees. It was strange to hear the water splashing but not to feel it, for I could move body and feet a little to one side or the other and so disturb the water. After a while I ceased even to shiver and became stiff: indeed I was set like a statue. The Destroyer was very near although I did not see him, and so still do not know if that god be shaped like man or woman. I began almost to welcome the thought of the fire, I was so cold.

Time passed and then in my tomb I became aware that someone was shouting; the sound, it seemed, came from a long way off, stopped and was resumed. With the sound it seemed that a gong was being well beaten. Why must they hammer on the door, I asked of myself; surely they have the key, could they not leave me in peace to die in the dark. A light hurt my eyes and I blinked to ease the pain. I thought of the fire. I heard splashing and loud voices. A man laughed. A voice said: 'He lives but is shackled; bring a hammer.' When my senses returned to me, I knew that I lay on a stone floor, and I looked up upon a ring of bearded faces which hung above me. Most were half naked; some wore ragged tunics; all wore long trousers and were armed, most with spears or swords, but some carried only knives or sharpened stakes, and one a heavy club clumsily fashioned from a tree root; there was blood on the club. One, who seemed to be the leader, wore a helmet of bronze, a bronze torque was about his neck and a dark blue woollen cloak, secured with a heavy bronze clasp, fell from his shoulders. My legs were in agony, they were torturing me; I screamed with the pain and tried to rise. Two men were rubbing and slapping my legs, which were the colour of dirty chalk; the returning blood was causing the pain. I was ashamed, clenched my teeth and bit my lips until the blood ran. The pain began to ease and I staggered to my feet swaying like a tree in a storm.

The leader said: 'Well met, my friend; I do not know who you are but, thanks to Roman hospitality, you would not have lasted much longer.' He grinned, spat on the floor and continued: 'Now we have more pressing business to attend to. There is much plunder in the town but many hands to be satisfied, including ours. There are garments on the bench and a sword. There are still live Romans and their jackals in their temple. When you can walk join us there. Like us, it is plain that you have old scores to settle.' They went away and I was alone.

There was a smell of smoke in the room. I staggered to the door, which hung drunkenly from one hinge, and looked out. The row of shops opposite was burning, there were corpses heaped untidily in the street, a dog limped past on three legs howling. The slave in charge of the prison lay on his back, stark naked, with his head beaten in. I remembered the man with the club. Above the roar of the flames I could hear shouts and screams, the crash of doors beaten in and the rumble of falling buildings. On the bench were two filthy tunics and a pair of dirty trousers which had once been white but now were bloodstained. Beneath the tunics lay a short sword of the Roman pattern hanging from a leather baldric. I found I was shivering like a man with fever. I put on the clothes and was glad of their rough warmth and even of the lice they carried. I slung the sword over my shoulder and staggered into the street, coughing as the acrid smoke caught my chest and stung my eyes.

I made for the house which served as my lodging. It lay on the edge of the town, and had been looted but not burned; it was deserted, there was no sign of my horse. In the corner of a room was a loose brick; I pulled it out, put my hand into the cavity and revealed and drew out a small leather bag which contained the gold from the sale of my horses. I had contrived this hiding place and used it on previous visits. I cut a strip from the hem of what now served as my under-tunic, put the bag into it and tied the ends of the strip round my waist. I was now a man again and my legs had, at last, become part of me. I knew that I was very thirsty and went to the well in the yard at the back of the house. Rope and leather bucket stood in the shed. The well was narrow but not deep and looking in there was much weed on the surface of the water. Holding the end of the rope, I let the bucket fall free and leaned over to haul it up. A face glimmered in the deep shadow; what I had seen was not weed but a woman's long hair. The water tasted sweet; a thirsty man will take what he can find. When I had drunk my fill I headed for the temple of Claudius the God.

I have engaged in tribal raiding, have myself been raided,

and have played my part in the dirty business of cleaning up and getting life going again after the raiders have left. My father often told me stories of raiding and being raided in his day, for since the Romans came peace has become near normal. Nasty things can happen and sometimes do – my mother died in a raid – but on the whole you raid with loot rather than killing in your mind; in the main you kill enough, you do not over-kill. Women you rape as a matter of course, this is expected of you, and they expect it too; should you need more women for work or for breeding you take them as slaves, and often they bring you more sorrow than joy. Seldom do you kill women, still less do you kill children. You burn the village, of course, but it is easily rebuilt. You take the cattle. Should you be raided, you expect them, the raiders, to do the same to you – no better, no worse. It is almost as if there were a set of rules, not set down in writing since we do not write,[2] but well understood and generally well observed. There is always greed in raiding, sometimes vengeance; seldom in my experience is there real hatred.

Camulodunum was different; plunder was to be had, of course, in plenty, but blind, black hatred was the driving force. You could almost smell it in the smoke-filled air, and hear it in the crackling flames.

I watched a mob, in the main I think they were Iceni, breaking up with stones a cluster of funerary monuments. They foamed at the mouth like rabid dogs, and even tore at the earth with bare hands to get at the ashes buried there. I felt sick. I watched another group with ropes pulling down a marble portico which fronted a large, perhaps governmental, building. The building had been fired, and when the roof fell in the portico would probably have fallen with it, but this would not satisfy them. When the pillars, as they crashed, broke up into large stone drums, they even set upon the drums and carved capitals as they lay in the dust.

I came upon the naked trunk of a man lying outside a fine house. Perhaps he had been the master of it. Where his arms and legs had been there were mere bloody sockets. At the side of the road lay a rope tied to the ankle of a leg. He had been pulled apart and even then I am not certain he was dead, so I cut his throat to make sure. I hate mindless cruelty to men or beasts – especially to horses. I saw a woman spitted on a stake; it had been driven into her body between her thighs and the sharpened tip projected from her right shoulder. The stake had been set fast in the ground so that her feet were level with my chest. She was still alive for I saw her lips moving in a soundless, continuing scream. Three men were pelting her with stones and filth. They were a little drunk and did not look very dangerous, so I levered the stake out of the ground with my hands, (it was slimy with blood and filth), lowered it as gently as I could, felt for the space between her ribs beneath her left breast and with my sword ran her through the heart. Perhaps her shade thanked me for my service before it departed on its long, dark journey. The men were angry, of course, but I threatened them with my sword and they staggered away cursing me for spoiling their sport.

I came to the temple of Claudius. It was, and still is, the most magnificent building I have ever seen. The temple stood on a stone plinth fifteen feet high with sheer sides. The height to the tip of the roof was at least seventy feet and perhaps more. The front was approached by a long flight of steps which extended the width of the plinth – say ninety feet. The whole building was faced with shining, multi-hued marble, and the roof tiles were gilded. It was almost beyond belief and must have cost a fortune to build. This fortune had, of course, been raised largely by the Trinovantes with aid from the Iceni and Catuvellauni; they had been largely beggared in the process. It was small wonder, I suppose, that they hated that temple, hated also the town which spawned it, and hated all who lived in the town who, as they saw it, waxed fat on their stolen livelihood.

The temple now served as a fortress. From where I stood, I could see along the top of the steps a barricade built of stone blocks, loose timber and carts. Indeed, the defenders had used anything readily to hand which would serve as an obstacle. So far it had served them well for the whole of the upper part of the steps was a tangle of heaped bodies, the wrack of repeated assaults. Just appearing above the top of the barricade I could see the helmets of the defenders, and knew that there were soldiers there, not just frightened citizens. Along both sides of the temple ran a colonnade, and on the side which faced me, I could see that the spaces between the great marble columns – there were ten or perhaps twelve – had been blocked with timber and stone, and in each space were more helmets, and below of course a fifteen foot drop.

The temple stood in a huge courtyard bounded by a low wall. Thronging behind the wall was the greatest crowd I have ever seen, thousand upon thousand of men looking very like the band which had freed me from my prison. In the main they seemed to be Iceni, Trinovantes and Catuvellauni; you can tell them apart by differences in the way they paint their arms, faces and bodies. All were staring at the temple, some in silence, but many were shouting, cursing and screaming. The menace, anger and hatred in the eyes and on the faces of that mob was terrifying and the noise deafened me.

As I watched, an untidy rabble of perhaps two hundred broke away from the mob and made yet another attack on the steps. They ploughed up, through and over the heaped bodies. The defenders, behind the barricade, hurled a shower of javelins and then there was hand-to-hand fighting at the top. Just a few, a very few, of the attackers succeeded in climbing over the heaped stone and timber, were silhouetted momentarily against the sky, and were gone. Then it was over, unwounded survivors streamed back across the courtyard, the wounded staggering or crawling at their heels, and the piles of dead on the steps had grown higher. The crowd roared in sullen fury and, above the barricade, there was movement for a time and sword flashes; then all was still and the sentries resumed their silent vigil.

This is madness, I thought. All they have to do is wait. There are certainly hundreds, perhaps thousands, packed into that vast building, with little food and less water. All they must do is wait until hunger and thirst do their work for them. They can then move in and butcher at their leisure, unless, of course, a Roman relief column were to arrive in time. Most of the Roman Army was far away campaigning in the west, or so it was said, but there were garrisons which were nearer at hand – Lindum for instance. If they came and saw what I had seen their vengeance would be terrible. It would be wise to return to my tribe and hope that they had not become too involved, for Romans had a dangerous habit of swift movement and quick and bloody victory. I was frightened and sought reassurance from the feel of the money belt about my waist.

Out of the corner of my eye I saw something fall, apparently out of the sky, on to the temple roof. It left a thin trail of smoke and there was a puff where it landed. I looked to my right and, after a pause, there was another smoke trail and again a puff on the roof. Understanding came; someone with a bow was shooting burning arrows. They are excellent for firing thatch but useless against tiles. A thought came to me. I waited for the third arrow, the flight of which gave me the rough direction of the archer, and struggled through the mob until I found him.

He was standing immediately behind the low wall which

surrounded the temple courtyard; there were a press of people about him in a tight half circle; he had a small fire going. I watched him tear a strip of cloth from what had been a cloak, wind the cloth round the tip of an arrow and tie it, dip the point into a bowl of oil, apply fire and when it was well alight, shoot the arrow upwards in a huge arc so that it fell on to the roof. I stepped forward out of the circle and tapped him on the shoulder. He turned and I saw that he was of the Coritani. My heart leaped and I felt that at last I had found a friend in that huge crowd of strangers. I said: 'Greetings, cousin. Skyfather[3] must have willed us to meet. Are there any more of us here?'

He grinned and replied: 'I have seen none. I was a slave to a one-time Roman soldier. When all this started I ran away but brought my bow with me. I am a good archer and my master graciously permitted me to use it for hunting, provided he had first choice of my game-bag. He was not all that bad, except when drunk; he was often drunk. I shall carry his scars on my back for ever. I believe that he may be in there;' he pointed to the temple.

I said: 'You can fire arrows on to that roof until the end of time but you will never set it afire. I know this temple well; the roof is supported by huge timber rafters; these project outwards over the sides of the building, and the weight is carried on the pillars of the two colonnades. To add to the splendour, there is a wooden ceiling of gilded planks running the length of each colonnade; this hides the rafters. If you can lodge an arrow in that ceiling, you could perhaps start a fire. It would be out of reach of all, save the gods, and so could never be put out. Should your master be inside, in this fashion you could even the score.'

We smiled at each other like friends of long acquaintance and, together, looked at the top of the colonnade. Owing to the overhang of the eaves the ceiling was out of view. To reach it with an arrow would mean moving forward some distance into the courtyard, shooting up at an angle, and directing the arrow between the capitals of two adjacent pillars. If the aim was good, and the arrow lodged firmly, the timber might catch.

He said: 'You are right, cousin; perhaps Skyfather did will us to meet. I hope he will guide my hand for it will not be an easy shot.' He took an arrow, set it afire, jumped over the wall and ran towards the temple. I shouted: 'Beware javelins,' but I do not think he heard me. He ran for some twenty paces, turned at an angle and drew his bow to the shoulder[4] dropping his head to look along the arrow. There was what seemed a flash of light from the temple and he fell in a heap, his arrow skidding across the pavement. I found myself in the courtyard jinking like a hunted hare. As I reached him and stooped down a javelin struck the pavement beside me and slid like a striking snake over the stones, but they threw only the one; perhaps javelins were scarce. I caught his foot and dragged him back to the wall. I turned him over on to his back. The broken javelin shaft projected from his chest; there was a bloody froth on his lips; he was already dead. I closed his eyes, wished his spirit a safe journey and was again alone. They had killed my new-found and only friend.

I tested the bow; it was light and well made – I think the maker had fashioned it of yew – but the draw was somewhat heavier than that of my own. I have used a bow all my life, my father had one made and taught me to use it, so I am not without experience. There were three arrows left; they were true, made of ash tipped with iron and well flighted.

In the temple courtyard stood many statues both singly and in groups; most had been overturned and lay in fragments beside their pedestals. One, which was still standing, was about halfway between me and the temple plinth. From behind it, and looking at an angle, I should be able at least to glimpse the wooden ceiling. The statue was well within javelin range of the temple but it, and especially its pedestal, would afford some protection. In any event I must make the attempt; I had a clear duty to my dead comrade.

I prepared all three arrows with strips of cloth well soaked in oil, slung the bow on my left shoulder, took a piece of wood from the fire and poured oil on to it. I jumped the wall, and with the now blazing wood in my right hand, ran straight for the statue. I believed that I could get there before anyone in the temple could reach me with a javelin. Such was the case, but only just, since as I ducked below the pedestal I heard the ringing thud of a javelin strike the far side, and the metallic screech and chatter as it slid away upon the pavement.

I peered round the side of the pedestal and looked to my left along the length of the temple. The plinth and the tall columns which stood upon it reared up above me, towering into the sky like forest giants, and between the tops of three of them I could see, in the two gaps they spanned, the dull sheen of gold. Because of my angle of view, the columns which stood beyond the three appeared continuous, like a wall with huge bulges, whereas immediately in front the heavy cornice running the length of the eave blocked my view. Accordingly, the shot, although difficult, was not impossible even with a strange bow.

My first arrow was too high and this I sensed almost before it left the string. It struck the lower edge of the cornice, glanced off and fell into the far end of the temple courtyard. I ducked down behind my guardian statue, a javelin hummed above my head and others struck pedestal, statue and pavement. Clearly the Romans understood their danger and held javelins poised, ready to throw immediately when any part of my body was exposed to them.

I took my second shot with legs crooked, almost crouching, so as to keep my head below the top of the pedestal. It was better directed than the first, skimmed up and past the top of a column into the dark and glistening shadow beneath the ceiling. I saw the sudden flash of flame as it struck; it hung there for a moment of time and fell, leaving neither smoke nor flame to mark its lodgement.

I notched my third arrow to the string, drew the bow, then stood slowly upright and as I straightened, let the arrow go. I ducked quickly and although my body moved fast I was not quite fast enough; certainly they had good javelin men; one parted my hair and a second took a bite from my neck. Perhaps Skyfather was watching, protected me and guided my arrow. It stuck fast and I watched as a red flower of flame began to blossom on the gilded ceiling. I believe my friend's spirit was watching for I seemed to hear a gentle whisper in my ear: 'Well shot,' and then a faint chuckle. To this day I know neither his name, nor from which part of our tribe he came, but I do know that his shade has peace.

The Romans were now quite without hope; either they must come out and be butchered, or stay and be burned or crushed to death when the massive roof crashed down upon them. Suddenly I was very tired and sick of the whole matter. That the magistrate who had unjustly condemned me, that the woman who had falsely accused me, that the landlord who was foresworn, that a drunken ex-soldier who had mistreated my friend might be among those trapped in the temple, was no longer of any great import. I had done my part and could now return home.

I slung my bow, turned my back on the temple and walked, very slowly as if in a dream, to the courtyard wall whence I had come. It was very strange; because of the danger of javelins, all my senses urged me to run and dodge this way and that as I had done before, but my body denied me. Perhaps Skyfather still held me in his protective hand and, in his wisdom, felt that were I to run I would, all unwittingly, mock him and this he could not stomach.

The watchers beyond the wall had seen the fire and now smelled blood. They roared like a pack of hungry wolves; there was lightning above their heads as their brandished weapons flashed in the sunlight. They sought to take my hand or clap me on the shoulder, but something in my face restrained them; perhaps Skyfather looked upon them through my eyes, and they suffered me to pass. So I left Camulodunum to return to my own people.

Once clear of the town and the temple standing near its edge, I made for the shelter of the great forest which lay to the west. I passed farms, all burned; saw no one but was conscious of hidden eyes which followed me, some fearful, some questioning and some which mirrored greed. I reached the forest edge at dusk, the distance was not great but I could walk but slowly. I passed that night in the fork of a great tree; a money belt well filled with gold makes cowards of us all.

I awoke at dawn and followed a well trodden track which led westwards. Soon I wished that I had not. There was a lightening ahead in the darkness of the forest, and a hum as of a myriad flies beat upon my ears. I found myself in a forest glade; in the centre there was a standing stone, wreathed with dying flowers, and set about it, impaled on stakes, were a score of what had been women, resembling the one I had chanced upon in the town, but with a difference. The heads of all hung forward upon cupped hands as if eating, and resting in their hands, their severed breasts. About each stake a cloud of flies buzzed angrily. This glade it seemed was sacred to Andrasta,[5] known to some as 'the High One' and to others as 'Queen of Nightmares'. I thought of my mother and my knees turned to water; I fell on my face and vomited, retching on an empty stomach. Then I rose, turned and ran from that awful place of torment with, it seemed, screams of eerie, mocking laughter ringing in my ears. Even now I am still dream-haunted and know that that cruel goddess is most aptly named.

There is but little left to tell. All men know that, after much bloodshed, Rome restored her power and the Iceni, Trinovantes and Catuvellauni, under the bloody hands of Suetonius Paulinus, paid a bitter price in blood and fire and agony. As news and rumour filtered through to us we were in two minds. Whereas some rejoiced, their fellows were in sorrow. Looking back through the thickening mists of passing years we were fortunate that the outcome was so ordained. Had the Romans been overthrown, my people, and I with them, would have been crushed to nothing by our more powerful neighbours. Now we have peace – the Roman peace – but I philosophise, a vice to which the old are often prone. In the aftermath of that great rebellion, we of the Coritani fared better than many of our fellows, for nothing could be proved against us, indeed we suffered losses at the hands of the rebels. I confess that I did not sleep easily, and avoided all direct contact with Romans until Petronius Turpilianus, during his governorship, announced a near-amnesty, holding that thus should old wounds be healed and bitterness and fear assuaged.

Since then affairs have gone well for us. I now control the supply of remounts for the Roman Army in all Britain and, as a reward for my services during General Agricola's campaigns in Caledonia, I was granted citizenship. I live in a fine house near Ratae and am waited upon by strings of slaves. These I treat well, my friends tell me too well; I do this in the main as a mark of respect to my dead comrade. Nevertheless, I seldom free them for I hold that they are well content as they are and would become less so as freedmen, whom I distrust, despise and actively dislike as a breed.

I have a young and very lovely wife; we do very well together. She seems happy and is now the mother of two fine sons and of a daughter who has become a lovely replica of her mother, but with blue eyes; these she gets from me – those of her mother are dark like forest pools at dusk. We entertain and are entertained; landowners, merchants, officials, military commanders and on one occasion the governor himself are on our guest list. I am in no doubt that those among them who are Roman born laugh at us – although not unkindly – behind their hands. My wife and I laugh also – over them – when we are alone together. Our Roman friends, and they are friends, are shrewd enough to know this but here we have them at a disadvantage, for whereas we often smile and even laugh at ourselves, this they cannot compass – a factor making for success, no doubt, but not, I hold, for real contentment.

I speak the Latin tongue as if it were my own with scarce an accent, or so they tell me, although this perhaps is flattery. My horses are still my life; I ride for much of every day and have improved the breed with an admixture of strains from Gaul, Iberia and the east. My horses now stand two full hands taller at the shoulder, stay longer and gallop like the east wind. My clients express their pleasure in gold, so our benefit is mutual and my delight enhanced. Epona is my chosen goddess, I place her second only to Skyfather; she would not grudge him that distinction, and her shrine is ever decked with fresh-cut flowers. It would seem that, being a woman – albeit divine – this pleases her, as does the scent of incense which I burn for her.

In my study upon the wall there hangs a hunting bow. I confess, if only to myself, that it looks misplaced between the frescoes on the walls and above the mosaics on the floor. But then I too am so misplaced and so we are comrades. From time to time, but ever with a smile, my wife reminds me of my bow and where it hangs; when she smiles she looks even more enchanting, so I kiss her, and she forgets the bow – for a while.

Men say that Camulodunum and its temple have been rebuilt and stand more splendid even than before. I cannot speak of this for I have never returned thence and never shall. I have no love for ghosts; in Camulodunum there are many such, and there are some who could be angered should I now disturb them. For although it was not I who caused the deaths of any, yet it was my hand which aided the Destroyer more quickly to grasp them as his victims.

NOTES

[1] Charon rowed the boat which, it was believed, ferried the spirits of the dead across the river Styx into the Underworld. When Caradoc was condemned to death it is unlikely that he knew of 'the Boatman' but, having become Romanised, perhaps he broadened his religious beliefs and so Charon, as it were, entered his life and his memoir.

[2] Celtic did not become a written language until probably the 4th century AD.

[3] The Britons, in common with Celtic tribes in general, seem to have venerated a tribal god or goddess in addition to a pantheon of other deities such as Epona the Horse Goddess. Caradoc's Skyfather was, no doubt, the tribal god of the Coritani.

[4] The short bow, then used, seems often to have been drawn only to the waist, whereas the long bow – used at Crecy and Agincourt – was invariably drawn to the shoulder. Perhaps our unnamed archer was in advance of his time; certainly the shot was a difficult one.

[5] Andrasta is referred to by Cassius Dio as the tribal goddess of the Iceni. There is no reason to believe that the atrocities which he describes in detail – upon which the writer's account is based – did not take place. Tacitus is more laconic: 'The Britons had no thought of taking prisoners or selling them as slaves … but only of slaughter, the gibbet, fire and the cross.'

Corvio

I am named Corvio and am of the Brigantes. As all men know, we are a people of fifteen clans. The Lopocares, from which I am sprung, hold all the land in the far north-east of our country and our northern border marches with that of the Votadini. My father was chief of our clan and, according to the custom of our nation, when I was become a man I came to Queen Cartimandua's hall to join her royal bodyguard. I was just turned eighteen, and had inherited my blue eyes from my father, whereas my fair skin and red-gold hair came to me from my mother. Barefoot I topped six and a half feet; I wore no beard but a moustache, which I combed most carefully, and of which I was so foolish as to be proud.

In my father's hall I had learned to wield a sword and cast a javelin, and he himself had taught me the use of a bow. I had been reared with horses and prided myself that there was no horse foaled which I could not ride. From my mother I had learned good manners both at meat, in speech and when about my everyday affairs, she being anxious that I should do her credit in the eyes of another woman, who was also a queen.

My mother warned me of this queen, as mothers will, saying that in her private life she was notorious for having lain with many lovers, including Ostorious Scapula, a former Roman governor, and with at least one other of those Romans who had followed him. As she spoke of this she averted her eyes from me and the colour rose on her cheek. I kissed her hand hoping thus to allay her fears and respect her modesty, but my father laughed; he warned me never to believe what any woman said of another, especially were that other a queen, and still laughing said that in his belief Queen Cartimandua did well and, because of this, was the butt of much slanderous gossip. In any event, and his eyes twinkled, should the queen look with favour on his son it would be discourteous to gainsay her, and he for one would not wish to deny his son the pleasure of her body. His words angered my mother; she blushed scarlet, stamped her foot, but as she opened her mouth to speak my father took her in his arms and kissed her, at which I too laughed, and she forgot her anger.

Looking back over the years, I was somewhat puffed up with my own importance, was overconfident to the point of rashness, but was not wholly bad for I prized loyalty, courage and the truth above all other virtues. I attempted, moreover, in my conduct, to reflect these beliefs. Nevertheless, having no sisters but only my mother, although to me and also I believe to my father, she was near perfect, I knew little of women. I was to find that this would be to my disadvantage.

The queen's hall lay three days' hard riding to the south. It stood in the heart of what I then considered to be a town but what was in truth a poor village, surrounded by a triple bank and ditch. The royal domain was circled by a further ditch and earth rampart surmounted by a timber palisade and parapet walk; there was but one narrow gateway, approached by causeway, offset to deny direct attack. Within the rampart stood stables, cattle byres, a rest house for guests, huts for storage, slave quarters and the like, built about the hall which stood in the form of an open square with buildings making up three sides. That in the centre comprised the great hall of the place, all of one hundred feet long and some forty feet from one wall to its fellow, with trunks of trees set in two rows lengthwise along the hall so as to bear the heavy roof. The floor was of puddled clay beaten hard. At one end was a raised platform approached by a flight of steps extending the full width of the platform. Here the queen held audience, and here she and her household sat down to meat, she and those of higher rank raised upon the platform for all to see, and we lesser folk at her feet, in the body of the hall. In a side wing were the living quarters of the household; a series of small, bare rooms divided one from the other and astride a narrow passageway running the whole length. The third wing of the hall composed the queen's private apartments and those of her women. Both these wings led into the two ends of the great hall and so faced each other across a yard which, although roughly cobbled, was ever dusty when dry and likewise deep in mud when it rained.

The three wings stood on one level and were fashioned of timber, wattle and daub with thatching for roof, save only the queen's apartments, which were of dressed stone and thus a wonder to us all. Roman engineers had designed and overseen the work of building, furnishing also the skilled stonemasons for the task. These 'invaders' also installed the means of bathing, both cold and hot, for the queen's pleasure and that of her women. To my astonishment, and all but indignation, I learned that the queen's nose was oversensitive and her tongue was only too apt, openly and without shame, to lash any member of her household, man or woman, whose smell offended her. Accordingly, all of us, even the slaves, to our distress found it needful to wash all of our bodies and even to wear clothes freshly laundered, yet it seemed that no one died or became sick because of it. Indeed one of the customs of Queen Boudicca which my queen found most abhorrent, lay in her natural and not unusual neglect of bathing and the consequent powerful reek which ever accompanied her.[1] It is even possible that had Boudicca bathed her body more often, my queen might have become her ally and so changed the course of history, for had she done so, and had Paulinus been defeated as would then have been certain, the Romans would have quit Britain never to return; but I run ahead of my tale.

At the time of which I speak, Cartimandua had been queen of our nation for nigh-on twenty years. Her father had died the year before the Romans came. He had no son and so, as was customary, our council, upon which sat men from every clan, chose her to be our ruler. She was then turned sixteen so when I came to her hall she was in her mid thirties. It would not be seemly to be more precise, for women, whether or not they be queens, are, I have learned, apt to be less than frank over the matter of their age; even my mother suffered from this woman's vanity.

Following her father's wish, the queen took for her husband a man named Venutius, bore him two sons but had little joy of him or them, for both her sons died in infancy. Her marriage was unhappy; perhaps the queen was too demanding, perhaps Venutius could not stomach the spectacle of his wife as queen, while he ruled only in name and by her leave. They quarrelled long and bitterly and at length she drove him from her side into exile in Caledonia. In his stead she took another man for husband, Vellocatus, who had been Venutius' comrade in arms.[2]

The ill luck which attended her first marriage was, I believe, ordained by the gods, but was finally occasioned by the Roman presence in Britain. The queen was allied to Rome by treaty made with the emperor himself. Faithful to her oath, she seized the person of Caratacus, King of the Catuvellauni, who had fought the Romans for eight years and then sought refuge in her lands. Having seized him she delivered him bound into the hands of his enemies. Here it should be said that they took him to Rome and treated him well, but he never returned to Britain. In her action I hold that not only was the queen true to her oath, but also wise.

The Catuvellauni, before the Romans came, had won dominion over all the tribes in south-eastern Britain and their ever-growing power began even to threaten us. With no Caratacus to lead them this threat withered; Venutius, however, opposed the queen openly and urged our nation to avenge Caratacus against the Romans. Even in exile he never ceased his plotting, aiming to overthrow his one-time wife, become king in her place, deny the treaty and make war upon the Romans. To this end he sought often to contrive her death so it behoved us of the bodyguard to be ever watchful for her safety.

It was for us to guard, both day and night, the gateway leading to the hall and check all who entered; it was for us to guard the queen's apartments and with her women carry out a nightly search of these before she retired to her couch. Should she hold audience we kept the doorway into the hall and stood by her chair; when she left her private apartments not less than two of us were ever with her.

Vellocatus was captain of the guard; this, it seemed, was his only duty except to bed with the queen when so summoned. It was plain that this more pleasurable task he performed but seldom, for the guard lay on straw in the great hall; he lay with us and his place was rarely empty. I held him in contempt for he was a glutton and a drunkard, was boastful beyond belief, and his arrogance as the queen's husband was insufferable, although it was plain to us all that he was in fear of her. Moreover, because of his mode of living, he had become as soft as a woman's breast and enjoyed neither the respect nor loyalty of the guard.

The queen had a great love of horses, and hunting was her abiding passion, although I was to learn that the quarry she sought was not always to be found in the forest. She was often abroad in her chariot, it being her custom herself to drive the horses, but when hunting she went mounted and showed herself to be a skilled rider, and quite without fear. I had been in her service for some sixty days when it fell to me to go out hunting as her escort. Beside me rode Comux, a veteran of the guard. We were followed by a group of Brigantes nobles, some of whom attended the queen at her hall whereas others came only for the sport. Comux and I, as members of her guard, wore winged helmets of bronze, with beasts embossed upon them, scale tunics of iron rings sewn upon leather, white trousers cross-gartered in scarlet, and scarlet cloaks secured at the shoulder with a heavy bronze and enamel brooch bearing the royal insignia. We each carried our long, straight swords and two light javelins, and I carried my hunting bow and quiver slung upon my shoulder. The queen, as was her custom when hunting, was attired as if she were a man in white trousers cross-gartered as ours, a loose white tunic with a golden girdle from which hung her dagger, the hilt fashioned like a naked man. From her shoulders hung a scarlet cloak, the twin of ours, secured with a brooch of gold and enamel. Her dark hair was plaited, the plaits coiled about her head and secured with a scarlet band low on her forehead. She too carried a light hunting bow and two light javelins; in truth these were but poorly balanced and were little more than children's playthings, but this I forbore to tell her.

It was warm for early spring; the sun shone brightly from a sky of deepest blue; the forest was cold but sweet and it was good to be alive. We took pleasure in our sport; two deer, one well shot by the queen herself, greatly to her pleasure, and one wild boar which, having been wounded by others of our company, had come at me boldly in its rage. The God Cernunnos, Lord of the Beasts,[3] was with me since, before we set out, as was ever my custom, I had invoked his aid with ritual and an offering, and it was he who guided my javelin to the beast's heart. Having thus assured meat for the hall and enjoyed good sport among ourselves, we made for home and neared the forest's edge following the same path by which we had entered. Until now Comux and I had ridden knee to knee like good comrades, a full horse's length behind the queen. Beside her had been others of our company who rode with her for a time and were then dismissed to make way for another. Vellocatus, who rode with us, was not summoned by the queen. She now turned her head, smiled upon me and said: 'Come, Corvio; I must know who taught you to cast a javelin and perhaps could learn something to my profit.' I felt the colour rise on my cheek and my heartbeat quickened – I was very young – as I urged my horse forward to come up with her.

As I did so I saw a hare break from a thicket, dark and tangled, which lay to my right, some thirty paces distant from the path we followed. The beast ran towards us; I thought, that is strange, were that hare in fear of us he would scarce run towards his fear. I felt a chill, as if some spirit touched me, and suddenly I feared for the queen's life. Urgently I drove my heels into the flanks of my horse and felt the beast leap forward under me. I shouted: 'Ware ambush,' and pointed from whence the hare had run. I was now drawn level with the queen and so rode between her and the thicket; I was conscious that her eyes were open wide as she gazed at me in some dismay. There was a whisper like the rustle of a snake in dry leaves; I felt a sudden, sharp pain in my right arm and looking down saw it shot through with an arrow.

I wheeled my horse from the path and galloped at the thicket, plunged through the tangled branches and saw, beyond, a man in the act of mounting a horse, a bow grasped in his hand. With my javelin serving as a lance, for with the arrow fast in my arm I could scarce throw it, I rode at him, the point taking him in the back. He fell, wrenching the javelin from my hand; his horse screamed in fear and was gone among the trees. I leaped from my horse, hitched his bridle to a tree, withdrew the javelin – the head being unbarbed – and saw that the man was dead, the javelin head having passed clear through his body. I looked up at Comux and the queen and said: 'The gods, through their messenger the hare, keep good watch over you, my queen; they merit our thanks.'[4] With my left hand I took the head of the arrow, clenched my teeth, and drew it steadily through my arm; my head swam and I all but lost my senses, the pain was so great. Anyone but a young fool would have cut off the head and drawn it out by the flight, but my action served, and I heard Comux cursing me for a fool under his breath. I looked closely at the iron tip but it seemed clean and I doubted that it might be poisoned. The queen and Comux were now on their feet beside me. Comux with his dagger cut a strip from my cloak and bound up my arm; it was spurting blood and for this I was glad, believing that thus would it overcome any poison or infection.

The queen looked at the body; her eyes were like flints and her voice was thick with rage; she said: 'Another of my former husband's hirelings; will they never cease coming. I wonder how much this beast was paid for my head.' She spurned the body with her foot, then turned to me, smiled, and with her eyes bright and her voice a little shrill, said: 'My thanks, Corvio; under the gods you saved my life and could have lost yours because of it; you will not lack the favour of a queen.'

That evening as I sat in the hall playing, left-handed for the wound pained me, at chess[5] with a companion, a cup of wine at my elbow – we drank wine not mead in the hall – a slave summoned me to the queen's apartments. As I walked the length of the hall I sensed Vellocatus' eyes upon me and it seemed that they were angry. A man laughed and Vellocatus cursed him roundly. I passed the two sentries at the queen's door, who averted their eyes, as if they had not seen my coming, and strove to keep their faces without expression. Against my expectation the queen's antechamber, where she was wont to talk privately with those whose ear she sought or who sought hers, was empty. The slave motioned me forward and I passed on, through a doorway masked by a scarlet curtain, into her bedchamber.

I knew this room well because of our nightly searches. A wide couch stood along the centre of one wall. There was a long, low table upon which were set the tools of a woman's trade: jars, pots, phials, combs, tweezers, a large hand mirror of polished bronze and the like. There were two chairs with skins covering them, and here and there a stool. Heavy chests stood about the room. Much of the smooth stone of the walls was covered with scarlet hangings; the floor was of stone patterned black and white. Two charcoal braziers glowed warmly in the corners; lamps burned by the couch, upon the table and in a cluster, on bronze chains, hung from the ceiling.

The queen stood by the table. She was dressed in a plain white mantle which covered her body from throat to toe; it was gathered at the waist with a scarlet girdle. She wore no jewellery save for her eyes of violet blue, which sparkled as they met mine, and a golden fillet about her forehead. Her dark hair hung loose and shining to her hips, she looked radiant and very lovely in the soft and tender lamplight which caressed her. I gazed upon her beauty from the doorway, scarce daring to approach her. She stared at me in silence, as if appraising me to her pleasure, then gave a slow smile, her lashes low on her cheek, and beckoned me forward with her hand.

Beside the queen stood the youngest of her women, so young, indeed, that she was scarce become a woman. Men said that she was orphan, her father having died of a wound received in battle and her mother dead in childbirth. She was, they said, of the royal house and looked upon the queen as her foster-mother. I saw that her face looked old beyond her years and that her eyes, which matched the colour of her dark green mantle, were sad. She was called Gwynnach, which in our tongue means happiness, and so seemed ill-suited to her nature. She was staring at me and I knew pity in my heart. Her eyes never left my face as slowly she raised her right hand and gave to the queen a heavy golden torque, chased, enamelled and bearing the royal device. I went down on one knee and the queen, with her own hands, placed the torque about my neck. She said: 'You will wear forever with honour the scar you took for me; this torque perhaps could be its good comrade.' I bent my head, kissed her hand, stammered my thanks, rose to my feet and made as if to go from her. She said: 'Stay, Corvio.' She turned to Gwynnach and although her lips smiled, her eyes, it seemed, were cold. She said: 'Go to your couch, child, should I seek further service of you I will call.' To my disquiet I saw Gwynnach bite her lip; then she bent her head and without a word almost ran from the room, her sandals chattering on the stone floor like the bill of a woodpecker. My eyes met those of the queen and I saw that hers were angry. She tapped her foot as she said: 'She is very young and life has brought her but little joy, poor child.'

She began to move swiftly about the room snuffing the lamps. She looked up at those hanging from the ceiling and turned to me with the words: 'you are taller than I', so I reached up and snuffed them for her. When all the lamps were out save one, she moved back to the table and stood facing me. Very slowly, as if she were dreaming, she unclasped her scarlet girdle and laid it flat upon the table, then she said: 'You will forget that I am a queen; you see only a woman, and now you will love me.' Her hands leaped to her throat, fumbled for an instant and her white robe slid to the floor leaving her naked. Very slowly she raised both hands to her head, lifted the fillet, placed it with her girdle and stood with her elbows spread wide and her hands clasped behind her neck. Her long, dark hair fell about her body like a shining veil, but in the dim light I saw her gently rounded shoulders above pale breasts upon which her nipples stood proud and erect like wild plums. I saw her smooth belly sliding into darkness between long, straight thighs, her full lips were moist and slightly parted and between them I could see the tip of her tongue. I fell on my knees at her feet, threw my arms about her thighs and drew her body to my face; desire rose hot within me. I felt her body quiver like a taut bow string and heard her panting breath as she rested her hand on my head and ran her fingers through my hair. She gave a little, breathless laugh and said: 'If you will rise and bow your body towards me, as is but fitting, I will help you draw off your mail shirt.' As we struggled together to pull the mail over my head I thought, I have but tumbled some of the slave girls in my father's hall; it seemed that I gave them pleasure for they were ever eager, but she may look for greater skill than I can offer. When I too was naked she moved quickly to the couch and I at her heels, eager for her body, but in doubt.

After we had lain together she kissed me again, with passion, full on the mouth, turned on her side, rested her head on my shoulder and said: 'Corvio, I have known many men, have taken pleasure of them and they of me. My body as now you know is tender and fashioned for love, but must not be hurt lest desire dies. In truth you hurt me – a little; you must be more gentle in your loving, and not act as does a stag in rut. One day, your wife, should she learn of what we do together, will thank me for my good teaching.' She laughed softly, gave a little sigh, and came to me again, put her arms about me, pressed all of herself against my body and I felt her tongue between my lips as she pressed her mouth on mine. So again we loved and thus we passed the night loving, sleeping and loving again. I learned the soft pressure of her lips, sensed her thrusting tongue, the flutter of long eyelashes on my skin, her questing fingers on my body and the eager, demanding pressure of her soft flesh upon mine.

There was a glimmer of light behind closed shutters when once again we loved. She whispered: 'Now you must go from me and I am become queen again. In my arms you have learned to give me pleasure and my weariness tells me that you have taken pleasure also. Because of this you could even better the magic of your javelin.' I felt her body shake and heard her soft laughter in my ear.

I saw her eyes upon me as I dressed, but she slept before I left her room. I felt utterly weary, as if after a long day in the saddle; I smiled to myself as I thought that never before had I taken so much pleasure from such a ride. When I entered the great hall it seemed that Vellocatus lay awake for he half sat up, and I sensed the black hatred which flowed about me. I found that I lacked the strength even to doff my mail shirt; I slept and dreamed of a woman with long dark hair, questing fingers and a soft and eager body, but her face was that of Gwynnach.

The day following I saw crowning the stakes, which stood before the gateway leading to the hall, two heads newly severed.[6] One was that of the would-be assassin whom I had killed, the other was of a man I had seen about the household, who had done me a small service when I was yet a stranger in the hall. His eyes had been put out with fire, for the empty sockets were but blackened pits, and the open mouth, set in a soundless scream, showed that death had been long in coming. This was done, I thought, by the queen's command, slowly and in torment as we lay together; I shuddered and vomit rose sourly in my throat.

It was but two days later that a group of Iceni sought audience of the queen. Most were small, dark men, but all had tight mouths and quick, fierce eyes. With them were two Trinovantes and this I found strange, for Iceni and

Trinovantes have long been enemies. They wore no body armour save bronze helmets; they carried swords and daggers which, with an ill grace, they suffered us to take from them, it being forbidden for any save the bodyguard to go armed to the queen. They talked with her in the privacy of her antechamber, ate in our company, spoke little, slept together in the hall and were gone before sunrise, their weapons having been restored to them.

Soon after they were gone Vellocatus summoned me with Comux and two others of the guard. He said: 'The queen, my most devoted wife' – his voice was heavy with irony – 'sends Ceredig, her councillor, to the Iceni. He rides on the morrow at sunrise and looks to return within twelve days. You will go with him.' His gaze fell upon me and upon the torque about my neck; his eyes met mine and I saw murder in their depths.

In the half light between dawn and sunrise I sprang upon my horse and settled myself for a long day's riding. One of the shutters covering a window of the queen's apartments was half open, and in the gloom beyond I caught the shimmer of a woman's hair; the colour of it was auburn. All the women, save one, were dark and that one was Gwynnach. With a tight rein I goaded my horse with my heels so that he fretted, pranced, reared up and danced prettily on his heels. My scarlet cloak floated from my shoulders like the wings of a great bird in flight; I waved my left hand towards the window, eased the pressure on the reins and my horse darted like an arrow for the gate. As I passed through I looked back, waved for the second time, and saw the shutter close.

We rode for two days striking ever further south and at the same time veering towards the east. The land was strange to me but was known to Ceredig and Comux, whose clan dwelt in the southern part of our country. One night we passed in the hall of a kinsman of Ceredig and the other in the forest, wrapped in our cloaks about a fire, taking it by turns to keep watch. On the first night Ceredig told us that he had been at the queen's side when she had spoken with the Iceni. They had told her that their tribe, the Trinovantes and others were now in open rebellion against the Romans; that they planned to destroy first Camulodunum, next Londinium and then, having gathered all their strength, strike at Paulinus. Queen Boudicca herself, they said, was already in the field. Under the gods they were assured of victory but this success would become doubly sure were our queen to set aside her treaty with the Romans, join Queen Boudicca, and throw the whole might of armed Brigantia into the scales. This action they had urged most vehemently upon the queen. To gain time, she had assured them that so important a matter must needs be discussed in full council and that, accordingly, they could expect no swift reply since to assemble the council must bring delay. Ceredig's task was to gauge the strength of the rebels in the field, assess how far they enjoyed the armed support of other tribes, determine the extent to which tribal feuding had been put aside and report back with all possible haste. The queen doubted whether Ceredig would be able fully to report without having obtained speech with Boudicca herself, but in this he was free to use his own judgement. In the light of Ceredig's report the queen would give her answer. Ceredig appointed Comux as our leader should he himself meet with some misfortune.

Early on the third day we crossed a great river into the land of the Coritani, and after a further hour's riding came to one of the great roads which the Romans had built. I marvelled at the sight of it. This road struck through the forest straight as an arrow, with a gravel surface as smooth as the floor of the queen's great hall; there was, moreover, a ditch on either side to carry away the rain.[7] We crossed in haste for now the eye of Rome herself lay heavily upon us, and we had no wish to awaken its vigilance. Nevertheless the road was empty and no man hindered nor spied our crossing. We rode ready for war, javelin in the right hand, shield on the left arm and our swords loose in our scabbards, but we found the land at peace. We saw men working in the fields while others herded cattle; these looked upon us with angry, hostile eyes, since we and the Coritani are ancient foes, but they bore no weapons and attempted naught against us. We passed two villages, mean and dirty, smelling of smoke, sweat and dung; we saw half-naked women, crouching like animals among the huts, who screamed at their children to come to them and beware of Brigantes raiders.

On the evening of the third day, as the shadows lengthened, and the great trees of the forest towered into the darkening gloom about us, we sought a stream by which to pass the night. To our front a dog fox barked and was answered by the scream of a vixen deep in the forest to our left; behind us another fox barked and to our right yet another. I know foxes and their ways; the notes rang not wholly true. I shouted: 'Those are not beasts, they are men!' I poised my javelin ready to throw.

Ceredig reined in his horse, held up both his hands to show that he carried no weapon and called out: 'We are friends; we come in peace.' I lowered my javelin and suddenly the forest was alive with men, some with bows each with an arrow notched to the string, some whirled slings, some with raised spears or heavy clubs and others with swords or daggers gleaming in their hands. Most were naked to the waist with loin cloths or ragged trousers fashioned from the skins of beasts. Faces and bodies were painted in great whirls, twists and spirals of colour which flowed about them like coiling snakes. Their fierce, darting eyes above tight-lipped mouths were set upon us. From behind a huge tree, beside the path we followed, stepped a man who wore a close-fitting iron cap; a cloak hung from his shoulders to cover his nakedness. Ceredig said: 'We are sent by Cartimandua, Queen of the Brigantes. I am Ceredig of her council; we seek Boudicca, your queen, for I see that you are of the Iceni.'

The man replied: 'It is peace; I will take you to our chief.' He sheathed his sword, put his hands to his mouth and called like a wolf howling at the rising moon. Suddenly the forest was empty for the tribesmen were gone, vanished into nothing, as if they had never been. He motioned us to follow and we walked our horses at his heels.

We came to a place of many fires and a myriad figures. Among them I saw women and children, for when these people make war they take with them their wives and children. A little apart from the throng we came upon a rough shelter, fashioned of branches, and saw in the dancing, ruddy glare of a huge fire which burned before it, a group of men. Among them was one who wore a winged helmet, such as ours, a blue cloak and tunic with a golden torque about his throat. He bade us welcome; Ceredig sat down beside him, and three of us crouched together behind Ceredig leaving one to watch our horses. Ceredig and the chief spoke in low tones and I could hear little of what passed between them.

After what seemed a long time Ceredig rose to his feet, motioned us to follow and we went with him to a place apart where stood our horses. Ceredig said: 'This war band is of the Iceni. Foilan, the chief with whom I spoke, claims that he has eight thousand men with him. Queen Boudicca, with more than twice that number, is at Camulodunum which he swears now lies in ruins, utterly destroyed. Romans, hastening south from about Lindum and seeking to bring relief to Camulodunum, now lie in camp some five miles distant. They have four cohorts of their IX Legion and one regiment of auxiliary cavalry, say two and a half thousand men. They march by their road which passes close by us, Foilan plans an ambush for the morrow and would welcome our aid. Whether we aid him or no, he will not suffer us to leave him until his battle is done, in case we contrive to betray his presence to the Romans. Were I him I would act likewise. To profit our task I believe we must aid him, for should we not, he is like to take our refusal as proof of treachery and kill us out of hand. Moreover, having fought, and having thus won, perhaps, their trust, we can better gain the knowledge which our queen seeks. How say you, do we fight?'

There was silence and in the darkness fear touched my heart with icy fingers for I had not witnessed a battle, still less had I fought in one. To regain my courage I said: 'We have no choice; we must fight else these savages will call us cowards, and we shame for ever our queen, our nation and ourselves.' There was laughter in the darkness and Comux thumped me on the shoulder.

Ceredig replied: 'So be it; we fight on foot by Foilan's side, but one of us must guard our horses. Comux, it will be for you to choose the one who does the guarding. Choose well; our allies on the morrow,' there was contempt in his voice, 'these Iceni, are noted horse thieves, so your man must keep good watch.'

Sunrise found us gathered near the forest's edge. Beyond stretched another of the great roads built by the Romans; this one, it was said, reached from Lindum to Londinium; beyond the road there lay yet more forest. On either side the trees had been felled to the distance of a thrown javelin, say forty paces, to guard against ambush. It was the custom of the Romans, being well versed in war, to march with cavalry screening not only front and rear but also spread wide to watch both flanks. Foilan, however, believed that since the forest where we lay was very dense, and since the Romans marched in haste to bring aid to their people in

Camulodunum, they would not stomach the delay which movement among the close-packed, tangled trees must occasion. We soon learned that he had judged wisely for thus was it done.

We heard hoof beats and glimpsed through the trees two score troopers, some upon the road, others riding on either side along the forest edge but just clear of the trees. We lay as if turned to stone, as did such few scouts as crouched within the forest's edge, and the horsemen continued on their way unaware of the myriad eyes that dwelt upon them. For a time there was silence and then a thunder of hoof beats as perhaps ten score cavalry, rank upon rank, with lance pennants fluttering, shields and armour gleaming in the sunlight, high-stepping horses with multicoloured saddle cloths and bridles streamed southwards under our eyes, and were gone. Next I heard a rhythmic beat as of distant thunder, saw a group of mounted men in brightly coloured cloaks, shining cuirasses and sparkling greaves and at their heels men on foot in ranks of six, each rank hard on the heels of that in front. They were armoured; tall narrow shields hung upon their backs and they carried javelins sloped upon their shoulders. Short, straight swords swung in unison back and forth by the side of each, matching their steady, unhurried, never varying and unyielding pace. Among them passed groups of laden mules each led by a soldier, and light wagons drawn by teams of horses. Above the serried ranks, at the head of each group of marching men, I saw their standards set on tall pikes, gleaming in the bright sunshine, each one borne by a soldier who wore the head of a beast upon his helmet with the skin hanging from his shoulders. I thought that these must be their gods, which went with them into battle, and who we must also overthrow were we to achieve victory.[8] I found that my mouth was dry, my heart thumped like a smith's hammer and my body was as ice, so great was my fear.

All about me men moved, some crouching, some on hands and knees like beasts, towards the forest's edge. Some carried bows and well-stocked quivers, others slings with pouches heavy with sling stones. I saw Foilan tap the shoulder of the man who lay beside him. This other put a war horn to his lips and sounded one long blast which sang among the trees; the blast was echoed by other horns to left and right. Suddenly the forest's edge was alive with men who notched arrows to bows, whirled slings about their heads, and the air was filled with the twang of bow strings and whirr of slingshots. Upon the road, under the arrow storm and hail of stones, where there had been ordered movement there was now confusion: men fell singly and in heaps, horses and mules screamed in pain and fear, some broke loose and galloped wildly forward and back. Trumpets sounded urgently, men shouted orders; the column halted and faced towards us as the soldiers strove to unsling their shields and guard themselves against our stones and arrows. Foilan's horn sounded again, but this time three short blasts, which as before were echoed by other horns. A great rush of men surged forward from the forest and raced, screaming and brandishing their weapons, down the gentle slope towards the road. I saw that they faced a solid wall of shields above which rose lines of helmeted faces like strings of beads. There was a ripple of light and a wave of javelins rose from among the beads and was lost in the throng. There was a great crash as of a giant striking an anvil with a huge hammer, and then a tumult of noise which beat about my head like an army of smiths gone mad, and amid the clash of metal upon metal, a medley of shouting and screaming, rising and falling like the roar of a great river in spate.

I saw Foilan rise to his feet and move towards the edge of the forest; Ceredig was with him, and I followed at their heels. Comux strode forward beside me and I saw his lips move but could hear nothing above the clamour. We came to the forest's edge; the shield wall was unbroken and our men beat upon it but without avail, like waves of the sea challenging a great cliff. Foilan's horn, echoed by others, sounded. The shouting died; our men drew back, at first sullenly and then in haste, making for the comfort of the trees. As they ran javelins flashed about them, sank into backs, necks, legs: men fell in heaps and their fellows leaped over them as they raced for shelter.

About us I saw archers and slingers, sprung from nowhere, and again the air was filled with the harsh music of bow strings and the snarl of slingshots as an arrow storm and hail of stones broke upon the soldiers who faced us. Our bowmen and slingers, aware that they could achieve nothing against legionary shields, directed their arrows and sling stones at the faces which rose above the shields or at the naked, unprotected legs which showed beneath the lower shield rim. I saw soldiers fall but each sap was at once filled by a comrade from behind and so the shield wall was maintained. To my right and left I heard shouting, the thunder of wheels and the beat of horses' hooves. This sound seemed to come from beyond and behind the watching legionaries. I saw the unbroken line of shields begin to sway and over the heads of the soldiers I saw horses' heads, and behind them men in pairs darting back and forth, like birds in flight. Of each pair, one cast javelins while his comrade guided the horses. I understood that they were Iceni chariots which had lain hidden in the forest on the further side of the road and now assailed the Romans in their backs.

Foilan's horn sounded a series of short, sharp blasts like a dog barking but with each bark suddenly cut short. As before other horns brayed their sharp defiance and there was a throaty roar of shouting. Foilan and Ceredig broke from the trees and bounded forward down the slope. I found myself leaping at their heels, with Comux on my left hand, and about us a swarm of half-naked men waving swords, spears, knives and clubs, with staring eyes and gaping mouths.

Upon my left arm I wore my shield which was round, fashioned of leather, with rim and boss of bronze. I waved my long straight sword and shouted my father's war cry. I remembered his counsel: a Roman will strike at you with his shield and when you are off balance thrust for your belly, his sword point coming at you from beneath his shield rim or from your left. To counter this, he said, you must carry your shield low and as he drives his at you, sidestep and thrust for the knee. I found his counsel strange for when fighting other Britons, or among ourselves, we relied upon the edge of the blade and not the point. Nevertheless he and I practised together until I was heartily weary of it; he armed with a tall bowed shield and short straight staff, and I with my round shield and a long wooden sword. I fancied that I still wore the bruises from the blunt end of the staff with which he stabbed me, and from the raised boss which formed the centre of his shield and which came at me like a battering ram.

I chose my man. He was tall, dark and clean-shaven, with a smear of blood on his cheek. I saw his body sway forward to take the shock, for it seemed that he expected me to throw my body upon his shield. I checked, thrust and felt my sword point jar as I took him in the left knee. He made no attempt to strike with his shield but his sword point darted at me swiftly, like a striking snake, and I caught it upon my shield rim. His left leg crumpled beneath him and as he fell I thrust into his throat. The man behind him was slow, he had perhaps been wounded, for his shield rested upon a dead mule exposing head and chest; my thrust took him full in the face, it bit higher than I had intended and he fell backwards. On my right I glimpsed a man fighting

Ceredig. I drove my sword through his unprotected right shoulder and deep into his chest, his fall almost twisting the blade from my hand. There was now a press of yelling Iceni about me with spears lunging and swords slashing. I could see the further forest; a chariot passed at full gallop only a spear's length distant and it came to me that we had broken the shield wall. A tall man stood on my left, two Iceni lay at his feet. He wore a cuirass of silver and bronze, a scarlet cloak hung from his shoulders but he carried no shield. There was a sneer on his thin lips and I read contempt in his cold eyes as he looked at me. In anger I leaped at him; his thrust was like lightning, but I caught the point of his sword on my shield and lunged for his knee, missed and my right shoulder struck him full in the chest. He wound his left arm about my waist and struck me beneath the chin with the pommel of his sword. My head swam and there was thunder in my ears but I threw the full weight of my body upon his; his legs crumpled and I fell with him striving to trap his right hand beneath my left arm and shield. As we lay with, it seemed, the breath knocked out of him, I drew my sword slowly across his throat and blood spurted like a fountain into my face. I staggered to my feet, half blinded with his blood, my jaw on fire and my head swimming. I reeled forwards, stumbled into the ditch on the further side of the road, lurched forwards over it, heard the thunder of hooves and a man screaming in agony, and then something struck me as if it were a whirlwind; I was tossed into oblivion.

Where my head had once been there was now only throbbing agony. My whole body ached as if I had been savaged by a bear. I heard a man groaning and understood that I was that man; I clenched my teeth, opened my eyes and saw Comux's bearded face and anxious eyes. His lips twisted into a tight smile; he said: 'I feared that you were dead but it seems that our Goddess Mother – Brigantia, the

Great One – has ordained it otherwise. You have lain speechless and without movement for all of two days, I will call the Druid.' I knew darkness and the earth beneath me shook.

I saw a man so tall that his head seemed in the clouds. His white hair and beard flowed to his waist; a dark mantle covered his body and a gold chain hung down upon his chest, half hidden beneath his beard. I felt his hand on my forehead; there was soothing magic in the tips of his fingers and his eyes were bright and kind. He said: 'Very soon you will be well. Your jaw, which the Roman broke with his sword hilt, is mending, but for a time you must drink, not eat. You were struck by an Iceni chariot run wild, the driver dead and his comrade sore wounded. Your body is whole, if everywhere bruised, your head, saved by your helmet, is sound and, save for your jaw, you have no bones broken. Now you will sleep.' There was power in his fingers as they stroked my forehead; the pain left me and it seemed that I lay in a boat, which rocked gently upon deep waters, lulling me to sleep.

I lay in a round hut upon a couch of rush and bracken. Above my head the roof rose steeply narrowing to a square hole above the hearth upon which a bright fire burned. Comux sat beside me and beyond him, in the gloom, I glimpsed a black shape which seemed to hang above the fire. I raised myself upon an elbow; Comux placed his left arm about my shoulders, lifted me and propped my back with a bundled cloak against the hut wall. I saw that his right arm was bent across his chest, a strip of hide passed below his wrist and the ends were knotted about his neck. His upper arm was gone green and I saw that it was swathed in moss held fast with tied rushes. He grinned as he said: 'We make a fine pair of cripples, you and I. After the battle Ceredig rode south seeking Queen Boudicca and taking only Mael with him. When he returns he will come this way and, hopefully, we shall ride with him to our queen's hall. Dengel is dead and I looked to his burying…'

I broke in: 'What of the battle?'

Comux stared at me for a moment in silence, then he replied: 'We did well, and the ever-watchful spirits of our fathers should be content. The last man you killed before the chariot struck you, the one who wore a scarlet cloak, was, so they said, a noble who commanded one of their cohorts. I took his sword from the hands of a thieving Iceni believing that you had a better right to it. I have hidden it in my couch and will return it to you when you are well. The legion, or that part of it which we met, four cohorts so they said, was utterly destroyed. I doubt that one soldier escaped. Most of the wounded were killed where they lay and were thus fortunate; the others were offered as sacrifice to a goddess whom they call Andraste, and found slow death. In my dreams their faces haunt me and their screams ring in my ears.'

I saw his body shake; he moistened his lips and continued: 'The greater part of their horsemen escaped with their lives and it is likely that they galloped all the way to Lindum, whence they came.' A smile flickered and he went on: 'For this Foilan blames the Trinovantes, who he swears sought loot among the Roman baggage rather than hard knocks. It seems that there is neither love nor confidence between that tribe and the Iceni; they have warred too long with one another and have old scores to settle. It is for sure that I would trust neither.' He turned his head and spat with slow deliberation into the fire, then continued.

'When it was done, Foilan brought you and others of his wounded here, telling us that his uncle, who is also a Druid, of some standing it would seem, would attend you. This Druid is a good man, and very skilful; for this we are his warrant.' He glanced towards the fire, turned to me, and whispered: 'He is aided by a witch.' Suddenly, over his shoulder, I saw a face framed in matted grey hair which, it seemed, had never known comb nor teasel, a huge jutting nose, black sunken eyes above high cheekbones, a mouth like a sword cut and a deeply cleft chin upon which there was a stubble of black hair. Her scrawny throat rose from a long black robe which flowed about her body, ragged and mud stained. Comux, seeing fear dawning in my eyes, and sensing its cause, shot like a sling stone from the log upon which he sat. The woman's mouth, I sensed it was a woman, cracked for an instant; it seemed that this served her for a smile. Then she knelt beside me and handed me a heavy cup. Sensing that I doubted what it held, she took it from me, sipped at its contents, swallowed, for I saw her throat move, returned the cup to me and without a backward glance returned to her place by the fire. I tasted what was given, found it excellent and drained it dry, conscious of Comux's anxious eyes who clearly believed it poisoned.

During the following three days my strength returned to me, and the spark of life within my body crackled into bright flame. I talked much with the Druid and walked with him in the forest. He knew the name of every tree, herb and flower. He would stand not twenty paces from me and I watched the gentle deer, playful hares and once a wild boar, with mighty tusks, come to him while he spoke to them in some strange tongue, stroking their flanks and tugging gently at their ears, at which the deer licked his hand. He told me that fear was the true cause of evil. Banish fear, he said, and neither hatred nor cruelty could live. I asked him of Druid sacrifices and how such could march with his beliefs. I saw that he was troubled by my question, and as we walked in silence he sighed deeply; then he replied: 'Many of us are in doubt and ask ourselves whether Lug of the Long Hand, or Belenus, Lord of the Sun, can find pleasure in the stench of burning human flesh or the spectacle of men or women so tortured. Now it is done – sometimes – but those who suffer so are themselves criminal, their lives are forfeit, and their agony may dissuade others from their villainy, and thus from evil good may spring. In time I am assured that the truth will be made clear to us so that we may follow it.' On this matter he would suffer no further questioning saying that his oath as a Druid forbade it.

I grew to love that old man, and if we mortals can ever be assured of anything, I know that his spirit has peace and is beloved and honoured among the shades. I hope also that the Destroyer, when he came, treated him as gently as he deserved.

On the evening of the third day Ceredig, with a face like thunder and angry haunted eyes, returned with Mael at his back. They lodged in our hut and at sunrise, having taken leave of the Druid, we rode north.

For much of our journey we rode in silence and then, on our second night, as we lay by our fire in the forest Ceredig, who had scarce uttered one word, began to speak as if talking to himself.

'Camulodunum destroyed: its great temple a heap of scorched marble and tumbled stone; its priests buried alive. Fragments that had once been human stinking in the ruins. Ashes of great fires and the charred bones of men and women burned alive. Crosses and stakes, like grass in the field, and upon each a twisted body with swollen tongue, starting eyes and gaping mouth; some still living in their monstrous agony. Women among them, their severed breasts stuffed in their mouths with wine-sodden, filthy savages flaunting gold and fine cloth upon their bodies, laughing at the spectacle of their barbarity. Boudicca – how that woman stinks – preening herself, but ever among them, as if they were her equals, taunting our queen, whose slipper she is not fit to lick, as a friend of Romans and so unfitted to be a queen in Britain; scarce veiling her threats of what would follow when she, Boudicca, ruled this whole island. Surely it were better to suffer the Romans and not these savages.'

His voice died into silence; we eyed each other and then, in the same dull tone scarce above a whisper, he continued: 'She holds her own people in the hollow of her hand, rather they grovel at her feet since she is worshipped as their Red Goddess. The Trinovantes follow her – from fear. They and the Iceni have no love, the one for the other, and agree only in their Roman hatred. She claims that the Catuvellauni also are with her, and some I saw, so in this, perhaps, she spoke truth. I saw none other, but should we march, others would surely follow. Together we could smash the Roman power, but more blood would flow after as we warred among ourselves. Surely we do better to hold fast to the treaty, while guarding ourselves.' He looked at us in silence, wrapped himself in his cloak and lay back, his neck propped on a stone; only his eyes moved in the firelight. The day following we came to the queen's hall.

I found the place in some disorder. The queen had summoned the full council for the day following. Many of the councillors with their followers and escort had already arrived and more were expected. The guest quarters were overfilled and storage huts had been newly swept for yet more space. To add to the confusion it was rumoured that an embassy of Romans would come within the week.

It seemed that something was lacking and I found myself restless and ill at ease. It came to me that what I lacked was Gwynnach, since neither she, nor any of the queen's women, came out from the royal apartments. I told myself that they were doubtless hard-pressed to prepare the queen for the morrow. Nevertheless I had half hoped, even expected, that Gwynnach might contrive at least to make me welcome and perhaps enquire how we had fared on our journey.

The day following the full council met not, as was customary in the great hall, but in the queen's antechamber. Perhaps there was a need for greater privacy. I was among those who kept the door. When evening fell and the council ended it was said, at first in a whisper and then more openly, that our nation would keep the peace, hold fast to our Roman allies and deny Queen Boudicca's cry for aid. This hard decision was not to the liking of all and, with my face impassive, I saw some who came forth from the queen with black looks and angry eyes, some indeed who spoke bitter words alleging cravenness, betrayal, dishonour and the like, while I feigned deafness. That night there was feasting in the great hall but not for those, and I among them, who kept the gate.

It was, if my memory serves, but two days hence, the sun barely risen, that the Romans came. Two men wearing highly polished cuirasses of leather, bronze and silver, crossed by baldrics of red leather with bronze or silver studs, bronze helmets and greaves of the same bright metal but chased and embossed. From the shoulders of the one who seemed to be their leader floated a scarlet cloak, and I thought of the man I had killed. They were small, dark, black-eyed men who carried sword and dagger.

With them was an older, much taller man with hair the colour of ripe corn but shot with grey. He was clothed and armed as a noble of our nation, and I learned that he had been taken by the Romans as a hostage in the year of the treaty. His name was Esus, after some god, who had appeared to his mother in a dream the night before the birth pains came upon her. For escort I counted thirty horsemen, all armed with lance and sword and all heavily armoured; unlike the two, these men bore shields. All were mud spattered, their horses foam covered, wild eyed and blowing through distended nostrils, so it was plain that they had ridden long and hard.

The two were clean-shaven and hawk faced with tight-lipped mouths; their eyes were uneasy and flickered this way and that. It seemed that something had angered them and that this anger, which they strove to keep pent within their hearts, grappled with their fear. I saw also that the escort, although weary, ever kept half their number mounted, while those upon their feet stood to their horses alert for scent of danger; their eyes looked all ways as if they feared attack. The two, and Esus, having passed but one short hour with the queen, took their leave, mounted, and they and their escort were gone.

A slave summoned me to the queen's apartments; I thought of when before I had been so bidden and hoped that I might see Gwynnach. I found neither queen nor Gwynnach but only Ceredig, and he alone. He stared at me in silence for a full minute and his voice shook with anger as he said: 'Corvio, where lies the sword which you took from that Roman?'

I was astonished at his question and his anger; I replied: 'It lies in the great hall with such things as I have here, and thus it has lain since our return.'

There was again silence as I looked him in the eye; his voice was steadier as he said: 'I believe you speak truth, and I assured the queen that this was not your doing. Tell me, who knows of this sword?'

I replied: 'Most, perhaps all, the guard. Comux and Mael spoke of it and some have asked to view it. There are stones, precious I believe, set in the hilt; the blade is chased and finely tempered. The scabbard is of scarlet leather with silver beaten into it.'

He said: 'Have you an enemy?' and I, becoming angered at his questioning which seemed without purpose, replied:

'That is more difficult to answer since we all, even you most noble Ceredig,' and I bent my head in mock humility, 'have enemies, but unless I know the reason for your question I am loath to answer, as you would be, were I to demand that of you.'

He smiled, but his eyes were as ice as he said: 'That sword now hangs upon one of the stakes which stand before the gate and above it is set a head, so mistreated as to be scarce human, and which could thus be Roman.'[9] Again he smiled, and I wished that he had not for his smile was like that of a demon. He continued: 'Our queen learned of the presence of the head, and its comrade the sword, from her Roman guests. Even you, young as you are, may understand that she was not well pleased, since it smacks of broken faith and so touches her honour. At first she was minded to match that head with another – yours – but since you saved her life she thinks to spare yours. Nevertheless, so great is her anger that she commands you to leave her hall and return to your father, lest she, being not only a queen but also a woman, could change her mind.'

His voice was smooth like a silken robe but full of menace. Although my heart felt like a lump of ice within my body, and I shivered, yet my shivering was not from fear but from black rage which boiled within me like a cauldron overheated upon a great fire.

Ceredig saw my rage and his voice softened as he continued: 'You are angered, my friend, and rightly, but this you must curb. I should not be astonished,' he spoke very slowly, as if choosing his words with care, 'were I to learn that not only did you save the queen's life, but that you also performed for her another, even more personal service – as others have done before you. Vellocatus, small wonder, has no love for such and despite the contempt which I, and perhaps you, feel for that puffy and puffed-up windbag, nevertheless as her husband, he has some reason, right even, for his fury. I see his hand in this but am no clearer-sighted than is the queen. Revenge, if we may call it that, lies in her hands should she see fit and is not for you. You will leave one hour from now. Comux and Mael will ride with you to your father's hall, and I will see to it that Vellocatus has other matters to attend to until after your going.'

He walked towards me, across the room, and now there was warmth in his tight-lipped smile. He clapped me on the shoulder and said: 'In time all this will be forgotten. The queen knows well that you are among the most devoted of our nation, and I am proud to call you friend. It could be that, because of what they saw this day, those Roman dogs, our allies, may learn better manners. Nevertheless, when you pass the gate take that sword with you and guard it well lest it strike at you more subtly anew.'

It was high summer; the cattle were fat, the herdsmen waved to us and the women, squatting beside their huts in the warm sunshine pounding grain, smiled as their children ran to greet us. Comux and Mael were joyful and, after a time, I shook the black dog from off my shoulders and joined in their laughter. We spent six whole days on our journey, for they would neither hasten nor suffer me to leave their company, and so we came to my father's hall.

I was troubled in my mind for I was uncertain as to the welcome I might receive. My father dispelled my doubts coming himself to greet us at our threshold, embracing me and making much of Comux and Mael, as good comrades all. We sat together at the high table in the great hall, each with a flagon of mead and a cup at his elbow. My father bade me tell of all that had passed since I had ridden southwards to join the queen's bodyguard. I told him all, omitting only the matter of lying with the queen, for I believed that to speak of this in the hearing of Comux and Mael would not be fitting. When I spoke but briefly of our battle with the Romans Comux broke in, praising what I had done and assuring us that, were he a bard, he would contrive a ballad and so preserve the deed for ever. At this, my father laughed but I could see that he was glad of it, whereas I sought refuge in my cup. When I had done my father wished to see the sword and, with his own hands, he set it among the other trophies which hung on the wall behind his chair, and above the chest wherein lay the heads of old enemies.[10] I saw, however, that he did not hang it by the baldric but bound it fast to the wall, perhaps to guard us all from further misfortune. When he had done he looked at me smiling, and with his blue eyes a-twinkle said: 'Comux, Mael and I have matters to discuss; your mother would be pleased should you care to wait upon her. She has, moreover, something to show you which could be to your liking.'

I came upon my mother sitting in her room, her distaff in her hand, and at her feet her hound, whose tail thumped when he saw me. She dismissed her women; I knelt beside her and kissed away her tears which she assured me were those of joy rather than of grief. She would not be content until I recounted anew all that I had told my father, which I did, omitting only the tales of blood, which I held unfitting for a woman's ears. She wept over the arrow scar on my arm and ran her fingers over the lump on my jaw. She asked me of the queen, wishing to hear how she was attired, how she bore herself, whether I found her as fair as other men held her to be and, was I fallen in love with her, or with another. The tone of her voice when she set me this last question was, perhaps, over shrill and I saw her lip tremble. I kissed her anew assuring her that, under Brigantia – the Great One – she was my mother and my guardian goddess. Then I told her of Gwynnach, that I felt pity for her, and perhaps something warmer than pity, but now could scarce hope to see her again. I bent my head to hide from her my sorrow lest such should cause her pain.

I heard her call softly: 'Come, child.' I looked up and saw Gwynnach standing beside her chair. I sprang to my feet with thoughts of magic, and was ashamed, understanding that doubtless she had stood hidden in my mother's bedchamber of which the doorway gaped at her back. At this I asked myself how much Gwynnach had heard of what was said. She seemed taller than I remembered her, perhaps because of the long white robe which covered her from throat to toe, girdled in gold beneath the gentle swell of her breasts. Her auburn hair fell to her waist and was held by a narrow fillet, also of gold, set low on her brow. There was a sparkle in her green eyes, beneath long lashes, and her lips were full and tender, parted in a smile. I stared at her, stammering like a tongueless mute, saw the colour rise upon her high cheekbones, as she bent her head, and saw the grip of her clasped hands tighten over the folds of her mantle.

My mother broke the silence with a half laugh and said: 'Gwynnach comes from the queen, who believes that you may have a question to put to her. The queen does not command this but believes that you could be well suited, and that Gwynnach would bear you fine sons, who could enter the bodyguard and continue our line. She brings as her dowry neither land nor cattle but gold, a chestful of it, the gift of the queen. Nevertheless, the queen is steadfast in her belief that those two who are most concerned must order their own lives, it being for the man to seek, should he be so minded, and for the woman to give herself, should she be willing to suffer him.' My mother smiled at Gwynnach and added: 'Is there aught I have forgotten?' Gwynnach slowly shook her head, looked directly at me and then blushed scarlet.

I was in no doubt and found that, all unwittingly, I had approached her closely, and that the top of her head brushed my chin. She looked up, a question in her eyes, and I kissed her full on the mouth, drew back and said: 'With all my heart I seek you as wife.'

She replied: 'I loved you when first I saw you at the

queen's hall and could know no greater happiness,' and then, with a dimple forming in her cheek, she asked: 'Will you love me more even than the queen?' I saw my mother start in her chair and to hide my confusion I kissed Gwynnach again.

We were wed within the week and knew eight years of true happiness, living together as man and wife in a part of my father's hall. Gwynnach bore me two sons and a daughter and thus, perhaps, I profited from the queen's good teaching.

Then came the year of the four emperors, when Rome was divided against herself, and the legions in Britain were uncertain, even mutinous.[11] Venutius rebelled and brought a great army out of the north. I rode south with a war band of Lopocares to join the queen. The passage of years had dealt but gently with her; there were lines on her cheek and about her mouth where there had been none before, but her eyes were as clear, her chin as softly rounded, her forehead as proud, her hair as lustrous and her lips as full as I remembered. While holding herself as queen she greeted me as an old friend and loyal comrade, and despite the ill fortune which beset her, I listened anew to the magic of her laughter. With eyes half closed, and her long lashes low on her cheek, she expressed her pleasure that I wore her torque at my throat; with a half smile she sought news of Gwynnach and of our sons. When I assured her that we were ever in her debt I saw her eyes brighten and the colour rise on her pale cheek.

We fought Venutius and his army of savages and renegade Brigantes; Ceredig died bravely and Comux coughed away his life in my arms; we were beaten and the remnant of the queen's army melted away like snow in summer. Much against her wish, for she was ever steadfast and courageous, but fearing what Venutius in his rage might do to her body, I took her to the Romans. They received her courteously and with all the respect which befitted her rank and fortune, for I saw to it that she carried with her the royal treasure. Leaving her in safety I rode north to find our hall burned, my father and mother dead and Gwynnach and my children lying hidden. Having lodged my family at Lindum I again rode north, raised a further war band and offered our swords to the Roman governor, Petilius Cerealis, who as the one-time legate of IX Hispana, had escaped Foilan's ambush upon the road from Lindum to Camulodunum. Perhaps a god laughed at the irony he had thus contrived.

We fought three campaigns, expelled Venutius, reduced his once-great army to a handful and all but destroyed my nation, crushed to powder in the warring as is corn between the mill stones of a quern. For what was done I was accorded citizenship, a string of Latin names and appointed prefect of the 4th Cohort of Britons – thus they dignified what was in truth my war band.

It being the Roman custom not to employ auxiliaries in the land of their birth, a custom whose reason I understand but cannot love, I now find myself and my cohort in garrison on the banks of the Rhine. My family is with me; my wife grows ever lovelier; my children wax sturdy; we live in a fine house; we have many friends. I take pleasure in my chosen trade as a soldier and my cohort is envied by Romans, and feared by Germans, whom we quell when they grow restless. Nevertheless I am as much an exile as is Venutius, for whom I cherish naught but bitter hatred, and as is the queen herself whom I respect, honour and in my own fashion still love. In all this I find the last great irony, and hear ringing in my ears the mocking laughter of the gods.

NOTES

[1] Britons of the nobility, in common with those of Celtic tribes in general, seem to have paid some attention to personal hygiene partly, perhaps, because of their love of finery and ostentation.

Indeed it would seem that they used both soap and perfume. It is, however, very doubtful whether their standards could match those of the Romans or even those of Queen Cartimandua who was a Romanophile. It is possible, moreover, that Queen Boudicca went rather to the opposite extreme since it seems that she regarded Roman bathing habits as effete.

[2] Vellocatus is described as having been Venutius' 'armour bearer' and could thus be expected to fight by his side. No doubt this is the basis for Corvio's description of him as 'comrade in arms'.

[3] Cernunnos is also known as 'the Horned One' since he wears stag's antlers. He was worshipped throughout the Celtic world. It is possible that the Christians later identified him with the devil, which hints at his importance in Celtic religion.

[4] The hare was widely regarded as being sacred and so, in the mind of Corvio, was a fitting instrument for the god or gods who had wished to save the queen's life.

[5] Board games were played and one of these, called 'Wooden Wisdom', may have resembled chess. It seems to have comprised two sets of men which were pegged into position on a board.

[6] The Celts were headhunters and displayed severed heads as trophies before their gateways. These served not only as proof of valour but the power which was thought to rest within each head would, it was believed, protect the home or fortress which displayed it.

[7] No doubt this road was the Fosse Way upon which was based the frontier defences of what was then the Roman Province of Britain.

[8] Standards in the Roman Army performed a similar function to the colours of a British infantry regiment, serving as a recognition and a rallying emblem. Very like British colours they were also objects of veneration, playing an important part in religious festivals which the Roman Army observed most scrupulously; so Corvio was not all that wide of the mark in regarding them as gods. Unlike British Army colours which are carried regimentally, Roman standards were carried not only by legions but also by each company.

[9] There is evidence that the victim's sword was, on occasion, hung upon the stake below his severed head.

[10] Severed heads were not only displayed outside a house or fortress but were preserved in oil and kept as family heirlooms.

[11] Nero committed suicide in AD 68. He was succeeded by Galba. In the following year Galba was overthrown by Otho, Otho by Vitellius and Vitellius by Vespasian. The Roman Army in Britain was divided in its loyalty and there were mutinies.

Lucius

Letter from Lucius Aemilianus Silvanus – tribune on the staff of Caius Suetonius Paulinus – to Julius Poraponius Atticus, senator.

Greetings,

I take the liberty of addressing you, first because I was proud to enjoy the friendship of Marcus, your son, and second, because my general so commanded me, believing that the heaviness of your grief could in some degree be lightened were I to recount the circumstances which attended your son's service in Britain, and which in the end brought about his hero's death. Overtly the second of these reasons would seem the more compelling, nevertheless I write, in truth, not because I have been so ordered, but because of my one-time friendship with Marcus, and of the joy I had of it. As his father you are able, in some degree, to temper your sorrow at his loss with pride at having sired so noble a son, whereas I am now but the shell of a man, my true and better self being with him for ever in the shades.

The general, his staff and I among them, had been landed upon the island of Mona but two days when Marcus joined us to take up his appointment. Unlike some commanders, our general, when in the field, lived like a Spartan of old. His tent, although somewhat larger, resembled closely those lived in by the legionaries; indeed it could be distinguished more from its location beside the Praetorium[1] in the centre of our camp, and from the presence of his personal standard hung upon a lance set at the door, than from any sign of ostentation in colour, ornament, texture or design. The general, moreover, brought with him only his orderly, being attended by neither slaves nor cooks; he ate legionary rations in common with his whole army, which it was the task of his personal bodyguard to prepare and serve in the same manner as they contrived their own. It followed that his staff shared in his austerity, indeed we took pride in it, since we believed that it enhanced our standing among the legionaries when they understood that we shared, in great measure, the full rigours of their way of life. I lay in a legionary tent adjacent to that of the general, and it was my good fortune that Marcus was assigned to the empty space within it, which formerly had been that of another tribune killed in the landing.

The general made it very clear that he expected of us as high or higher standards of physical fitness, endurance and skill-at-arms as those displayed by the legionaries and auxiliaries of his army. Accordingly, at sunrise daily, and for the hour that followed it, save only when the headquarters was on the march, all of us, except those on other duty, exercised with the bodyguard, taking orders from their centurion. You could find it strange that, for this one hour, tribunes, whether they wore the broad or narrow stripe,[2] should become subject to a centurion; but even the general, when his burden of command permitted, joined us and so humbled himself, thus we felt no shame. All but naked we ran, leaped, wrestled, vaulted, cast javelins and practised swordsmanship at times on foot and on occasion mounted. To better our swordplay we used for 'enemy' stakes planted in the earth, or armed ourselves with dummy swords, skilfully fashioned and balanced to resemble what they portrayed, and fought each other. Marcus, for the most part, was my chosen opponent although his skill with a sword outshone mine, and often he left me panting like a near-foundered horse, with my body covered with dark blotches from the blunted point of his dummy sword. Even the centurion, who, in common with many of his like, was a sardonic, insensitive machine rather than a man, chuckled at Marcus' skill, strength, exertion and inexhaustible fount of good humour. I remember that on one occasion, when I was on other duty, Marcus paired for swordplay with that centurion, matched him thrust for thrust and parry for parry and left him gasping, whereas he breathed easily as if he had just risen from his couch. He was, indeed, a wonder to us all but was never puffed up with his own outstanding merit. The bodyguard, tough veterans all, took him to their hearts and nicknamed him 'Young Lightning', so great was their regard for him.

When Marcus joined us all serious fighting was done and we were engaged in rounding up fugitive rebels and Druid priests. Additionally we cut down and burned the trees which had formed their sacred groves, so as to stamp out their vile religion with all its foul cruelty and dark sorcery. Druid priests and their attendant witches we killed out of hand, holding them guilty of burning alive Romans so unfortunate as to fall into their bloody hands. Armed rebels we killed or enslaved, and any village in which such men lay hidden we burned, seizing as slaves the peasants who dwelt there. By express order of the general the women, generally, were left unharmed save those, and these were but few, who fought against us. From these we took the younger and less ill-favoured for the soldiers' brothels; those not so taken we crucified as a warning to others. Thus was loyalty, good order and the Roman peace established in the island of Mona where, hitherto, no Roman had ever set foot. In all this Marcus performed his duty as should a tribune of the headquarters staff, and I at his side, as his guide and even mentor at the outset of his military service.

I was duty tribune on the day we received the news of Boudicca's rebellion. I was seated at a table in the rude shelter which served as our Praetorium, dictating orders to a clerk; orders as I remember designed to exploit a mine in the north of the island which, as our surveyors had learned, would give us copper so adding to the revenues of the province. It was raining and I had just moved my stool so as to avoid water dripping down my back when, having heard a sentry challenge, I raised my head and saw a courier, who looked like a corpse, stagger in through the open doorway. He saw the general hunched over a table at the back of the shelter, straightened, saluted and said in a voice so weak as to be little above a whisper: 'Sir, I am come from Londinium. The Iceni and Trinovantes with Queen Boudicca as their leader are in armed rebellion. Five days since they destroyed Camulodunum. Your prefect sent me to you, and my comrade to IX Hispana at Lindum. I was to bring you this tablet.' He reached under his cloak; the tablet fell from his hand; his knees suddenly buckled and he fell in a heap. I thought, allowing one day for news to reach Londinium, that man has ridden two hundred and fifty miles in four days, he must be near death; and then the purport of his message exploded within my head. My eyes fell upon the general and I saw his face a mask.

In truth his situation was cruel. In Mona our business was all but accomplished, but prudence dictated that at least auxiliary infantry and cavalry should remain, lest much of what we had achieved must need be done again. Deva lay sixty miles to the east and the way across wild, mist covered, mountain country was subject to raids by Ordovices. Even now we were building forts along the road and these required garrisons, both horse and foot, if raids were to be denied. Of his legions he had XIV Gemina with him, and vexillations[3] of II Augusta and XX Valeria. The greater part of both these legions lay in Deva, along the road which led east from it, and on the frontiers of the province facing Silures on the west and Brigantes to the north. IX Hispana lay in and about Lindum also facing the Brigantes and with, perhaps, a vexillation already marching south against the rebels. XIV Gemina could not reach Londinium in fewer than twelve days and even now, as we sat, Boudicca's army could be firing its thatch.

The day following, taking only four regiments of cavalry, our general, and we with him, left Mona and reached Londinium on the evening of the fifth day. I shall never forget the sharp agony and abiding misery of that wild ride, thighs and knees rubbed raw, back – it seemed – broken and no part of my body which neither ached nor cried out for relief. We were fortunate that at the posting stations along the great road[4] lay small vexillations of auxiliary cavalry, many of whose horses we took, leaving our own poor beasts, when they were recovered, for their use. To add to the utter misery of that ride it rained without respite, so we were ever soaked through like fish in the sea. Too long riding on the hard surface of the road lamed our horses and often we took to the verges which, deep in mud, covered men and horses from helmet to hooves in an ever-thickening veil of slime. Each night, having dismounted weary unto death, and having looked to our exhausted horses, we must establish a marching camp with ditch and rampart, before throwing our weary bodies upon the soaking earth to sleep as best we might. Again we were fortunate that on three nights we could use what remained of former marching camps, the wrack of earlier campaigning, and direct our labour to their improvement rather than be forced to build anew. It is not customary for cavalry to be put to such work but the ride was so perilous that we had no choice. Yet of those who left Mona, which were two thousand and fifteen – I know the figure for it was I who prepared the march table – but twenty-two were left on the way, and so we came to Londinium to find no rebels, as yet, but the town in turmoil.

The place stank of fear. Terror was writ plain on the faces of such few members of the town council as met us when we reached the borders of their city. Indeed, they must have found but scant comfort in our near-foundered horses and their exhausted riders, as we stared with dull eyes at these fat and fearful magistrates, merchants and the like. When the general asked why they were so few they replied that their fellows had already fled the town, taking ship to Gaul or seeking safety among the Cantii or Regni whose lands lay to the south. Among those who had fled by ship, so they told us, was the Procurator, Catus Decianus, who had taken with him his household and enough treasure to fill a ship, leaving his staff and the citizens of Londinium to find refuge as best they might. The streets were largely empty; such as ventured abroad moved swiftly with backward glances, as if fearful of pursuit, with barred doors and shuttered windows on every side to add to their fears and speed them on their way. Only the wharves were busy, thronged with jostling, shouting citizens and their frightened families, bargaining with such ship's captains as remained, offering them ever greater sums in gold for passage from the town which all believed was doomed. Nevertheless, there was life of a kind in the poorer quarters where men lurked in alleyways and dark places, peered round corners only to vanish at the sight of our helmets and drawn swords. Burned and burning houses; litter strewn in the street; broken debris scattered from shops and warehouses; chests forced open, broken furnishings, smashed pots, torn cloth and fine linen trampled in the mud; here and there a corpse crumpled in the gutter and most stripped for the clothes or rags that once were theirs; doors once barred now hanging awry, half open. Such sights showed where looters had been at work. Rumour was rife and the horrors of what was done at Camulodunum, and the manner of death inflicted by the rebels upon those who had lived in and about that town was on the lips, and frozen in the frightened eyes, of all.

We assigned a full regiment to the town to restore order and enforce a nightly curfew. We assigned a second to guard the wharves and warehouses and to furnish soldiers to hold such ships as remained. Our general put some heart into the poor fragments of the council and bade them give what comfort they could to the citizens, for he still hoped that Londinium might yet be saved. Given seven days, and XIV Gemina, with much of II Augusta, together with auxiliaries, could reach the town, so bringing fifteen thousand soldiers to face Boudicca's rebels, of whom we still had no more word despite our cavalry patrols which screened Londinium being widely spread, and some fifteen miles distant, to east and north. There was, moreover IX Hispana which had, perhaps, already met the rebels in battle and hopefully destroyed their army. Nevertheless, it was, I believe the gods who, being as yet unsatisfied with the blood already spilled, misery and fear suffered and agony endured, ordained matters otherwise, decreeing that our nightmare must plumb new depths of horror and despair.

We had been in Londinium but two days when the first blow fell. The general was out upon the wharves, leaving Marcus on duty, when a courier arrived from Glevum bearing a tablet from the acting legate of II Augusta. Marcus broke the seal and read: 'It seems that you are not aware of the true situation confronting this legion. Should I despatch to your aid but one weak cohort of auxiliaries, the Silures and Dobunni, will surely rise. Only by the unceasing toil of every man I have can I hope to keep them in check and stay this rebellion. It irks me to disobey your order but, by the gods, I can do naught else. Only if our affairs mend, and this I do not foresee, can II Augusta or any part of it come to you.'

That same evening a cavalry patrol brought a Tungrian trooper with sombre news of IX Hispana. This man had ridden with Petilius Cerealis, the legate of that legion, four cohorts and two regiments of auxiliary cavalry, seeking the rebels at Camulodunum. Their march had been over hasty and three days since had fallen into ambush laid by an immense host of rebels with bowmen, slingers and chariots, who had swarmed upon the column out of the forest. The infantry had been totally overwhelmed and the same fate had overtaken the advanced guard cavalry. The Tungrian, trapped beneath the weight of his dying horse, had been left for dead by the rebels; as evidence the whole of the left side of his head – he had lost his helmet – was caked with dried blood and his left arm hung useless from the shoulder. He had been fortunate, when darkness fell, to drag his body clear, steal a loose horse he had found wandering in the edge of the forest, and riding only by night had headed south for Londinium; on his way he had ridden into one of our patrols. He thought it possible that some of the rearguard cavalry could have escaped to the north and found safety in Lindum. As to the fate of the legate, he knew nothing.

I should be speaking less than the truth were I not to confess that now I knew fear. Fear, indeed, which I believe touched us all, perhaps even the general himself, although of this he gave no sign, being in truth a most gallant soldier and a commander of genius with a will of iron.

During these anxious days of never-ending toil, hard riding and harsh living, Marcus bore himself most nobly, performed his full share and more of duty, and was ever in high humour making light of hardship, ever confident of victory and scoffing at rumour. I learned later, from a decurion commanding a troop of our cavalry screen, that Marcus, who had come bearing an order from the general, rode with him against a band of marauding rebels. As our cavalry approached more closely, further rebels, sprung seemingly from nowhere, joined the band. The decurion, seeing himself greatly outnumbered, was in doubt whether or not to press home his attack, but Marcus rode on boldly, and so for very shame the troop followed at his heels killing a number and causing the rebels to flee to the comfort of the forest. At which Marcus, the general's order delivered, wiped his sword and rode back to Londinium praising the decurion and his troop and reporting, as a good staff officer should, the place, hour and nature of the fighting, but saying not one word of the part which he himself had played.

We could delay no longer. To remain in Londinium would not save the town; indeed, not only would further delay engulf us in its ruin but drag the whole province to complete destruction. Couriers galloped north with orders to halt XIV Gemina, and bid that legion fortify a camp at

Letocetum with space enough to hold its own legionaries and auxiliaries, together with our four regiments.

In the early morning of the day following, our general met the town council and informed them that he would withdraw from the city at sunrise on the morrow. He would take with him such citizens as were well enough mounted to ride with cavalry. These could bring only such baggage as their mounts could carry together with food for themselves and fodder for horses, for we had none to spare. Such other citizens as sought safety in the south must be across the river by sunrise for at that hour he would fire the bridge. Throughout the day, moreover, he would destroy every boat to be found on the north bank, the destruction of which, together with that of the bridge, would add to the safety of those who had already crossed to the south. He reminded the council that a number of ships still lay at anchor in the river, or were moored alongside the wharves, and that these could take upwards of one thousand refugees. It was for the council to decide who these might be; perhaps they should include the old, the sick and the very young. In any event embarkation must be completed by midnight to catch the tide, at which hour the soldiers on board the ships would be withdrawn, and such small craft as had served them in the matter of embarkation would be destroyed. He would continue to maintain order in the town up to the moment of his departure, from which time any citizens who remained behind must look to themselves for safety.

During the day, which seemed unending, our cavalry screen drew back slowly and sullenly towards the town reporting increasing pressure from rebels, some mounted but most on foot, flooding in from east and north-east. Our regiments lost both men and horses but in their bitter anger struck back savagely at the barbarians that swarmed upon them; they took no prisoners.

Together Marcus and I spent much of the night at the bridge. It was guarded by two troops of Asturians who had prepared bundles of brushwood, soaked them in oil, and secured them beneath the decking and thickly about the heads of the timber piles which carried the bridge. Throughout the night there was a never-ending stream of ghost-like figures making for the south, some mounted on heavily laden mules or donkeys, some riding upon carts drawn by oxen and piled high with household goods, shop wares, sacks of grain, furnishings, huge storage jars for oil or grain, couches, stools and the like. Most, however, were on foot in sad, bedraggled groups already swaying beneath the load of such poor possessions as they strove to carry on their backs. From these people, and seemingly from the whole unhappy town, there rose a dull, throbbing murmur rising and falling like the sigh of the south wind as it blows over the Alban Hills.[5] I can still hear that sound. As dawn came up and the eastern sky was shot with rays of rosy pink, brightening first to scarlet and then to gold, the throng increased. The decurion in command looked at me and said; 'Sir, it is time; do I stop those still coming and apply fire?' I thought, the sun is risen, we have our orders, further delay would endanger the lives of these soldiers.

Marcus broke in: 'These people trusted Rome and because of it have lost all that they had save only their lives. We are soldiers not murderers.' This was, I believe, the first occasion upon which I had ever known him angered.

I looked at the decurion and said; 'You have your answer; we shall wait a little.' And I saw smiles flicker on the lips of the soldiers, flaring torches in their hands, who stood at his back, though their eyes were uneasy.

We delayed all but one hour, until none more came. We fired the bridge, ensured that it was well alight and then hastened westwards, our hoof beats echoing through deserted streets, and came out of the city. Once clear, we took the road which turned north and caught up with our rearguard, who had given us up for lost, some five miles beyond the town. As we rode we looked over the flat land to the east where smoke columns rose one by one from burning farms and hamlets and crept ever further south. We saw movement and in the movement there was an unceasing ripple of flashes as of fire, where the sun caught helmets and spear points, as Boudicca's army swept out of north and east eager to grasp Londinium.

We rode through Verulamium and found a town all but empty, since of the townsfolk most had earlier fled to Londinium or into the west. We glimpsed frightened faces which peered at us through gaps in closed shutters or barred door grilles. We tarried long enough to urge these to flee to the west while there was yet time. We rode on, passing sad groups staggering up the road: most of these stared at us with blank, sullen faces, but there were those who shook their fists, spat at our horses' hooves and cried aloud in anger that Rome had abandoned them.

Every posting station on the road was empty, their small garrisons withdrawn to join our regiments. Where these had been infantry they either mounted spare horses or rode bareback, each behind a trooper, with arms clutching the rider's waist. Their obvious distress and clear dismay brought smiles, and I had seen but few since we came to Londinium. Hard by each posting station stood a clutter of poor huts. All were deserted, their owners fled, most to escape from, some perhaps to join, the rebels. We saw two such clusters which, it would seem, had been raided for the huts were burned and about them lay corpses and dead cattle. Thus we came to Letocetum.

Our general now had under his hand XIV Gemina and with that legion two cohorts of auxiliary infantry – Gauls if my memory serves – together with the four regiments of cavalry which had been with him in Londinium. The losses which they had suffered, at least in numbers, had been offset by the troopers of the posting station garrisons. In all this gave him a little less than eight thousand men. Elsewhere in the province there was the greater part of II Augusta, in and about Glevum, and what remained of IX Hispana; but from neither of these could he look for aught. There remained a vexillation of II Augusta which held the road between Deva and Mona, and XX Valeria which held Deva and forts to east and north, watching the border with Brigantia. If the general could be assured that the Brigantes would not join the rebels but honour their treaty with Rome, he could withdraw part or all of XX Valeria, leaving certain of their auxiliaries in the abandoned forts, while withdrawing others, and so greatly strengthen his army to face Boudicca. He determined, therefore, to send an embassy to Queen Cartimandua's court – she is queen of the Brigantes – to read her mind and hopefully stiffen her loyalty.

The general sent his chief of staff to head the mission, so important was its task, and with him rode Marcus. The embassy took as escort a cavalry troop, and with them as their guide rode Esus, a Brigantes noble and one-time hostage, who had served successive governors of Britain as a member of their staffs, becoming almost Roman in his outlook and manner of life. This man, however, was well known to Queen Cartimandua having formerly attended her court; he knew, moreover, how best she might be reached.

Marcus himself, on his return, told me something of how they had fared, but from Esus I learned more. They had covered but ten miles of their journey when they were attacked, not by Brigantes, whose land lay still further to the north, but by a band of Coritani. They killed seven and paid the score with the lives of two troopers of the escort. It was Marcus who unhorsed and killed with his own hand the Coritani chieftain who led the band, and whose death caused his followers to flee for their lives. They crossed a river and Esus was again among his own people. He led them by secret ways through the forest and over wild moorland, for although the queen, perhaps, would keep faith, her people were often restless and had but little love for Romans. As they rode they saw on occasion men, some single and some in groups, but always armed, for Brigantia lies without the province and so to bear arms is not to break our law. Esus shouted that they sought the queen, but none answered; each stood, or sat astride his pony, as if fashioned of stone; only their eyes moved, but they sought neither to aid nor hinder those they watched. Esus gave it as his opinion that there was doubt in the land concerning the treaty, that none knew whether it was peace or war, and so all waited and watched until word came and they knew their duty.

On the fourth day, with the sun scarce risen, they came to a place set within a triple girdle of earth ramparts with deep ditches between each. With Esus leading, bareheaded to show his hair, yellow as a cornfield but shot with grey, clothed in barbaric splendour with white tunic, scarlet cloak, long white trousers cross-gartered in saffron with gold ornaments about his throat and wrists, they rode through a narrow gateway and threaded their way past a huddle of round, thatched huts, among which stood men and women who watched in silence. They came to an open space beyond which was yet another great ditch fronting an earth rampart, but this one crowned with a timber palisade, and above the timber moved the helmets of armed men. This rampart was pierced by a narrow timbered gateway, approached by causeway, so affording passage over the ditch. Set beside the causeway were sharpened stakes, some crowned with the severed heads – many reduced to mere skulls – of enemies slain in battle, and others with those of men put to death as traitors. Beneath each of the heads there hung a sword once wielded, it would seem, by the man whose sightless eyes stared into eternity from the summit of the stake. One of these swords was Roman and the head above it new severed. This, whispered Esus, could herald the queen's answer and so their peril could be mortal.

You have been guest at a banquet where the first dish was superb, so contrived as to excite, with the delicacy of its flavour and magnificent manner of serving, the most jaded pallet, whereas the dishes which followed could not attain such a measure of excellence. Thus it was at Queen Cartimandua's court, where nothing chanced which could match the shock of the welcome offered at her gate. The queen was very gracious, permitting her guests even to retain their weapons which, it would seem, was not customary in her court. Marcus, as he told me, was impressed with her dark beauty, high courage, natural dignity and strength of will. She reminded him, so he said, of a black panther he had once seen at the games, beautiful in her lithe grace, and with menace in her latent ferocity. She was very frank, asserting quite openly that Queen Boudicca had, indeed, sought her aid, that so important a matter had been discussed in her full council and that, after long debate, it had been decided, to the indignation of some, to deny aid and uphold her treaty with our divine emperor, whose equal she clearly believed herself to be. She regretted the sword at her gate of which she had no knowledge and which thus could signify nothing. She assured our embassy that she would look into the affair, which she found as insulting to her honour and royal dignity as to her Roman guests. She enquired after the health of our general, expressed her regrets at the misfortunes which had been suffered by his army, although she was assured that the extent of these had, no doubt, grown in the telling; she wished them a safe journey and withdrew leaving them open-mouthed and looking, as Marcus said, like peasants gaping at their first sight of the Palatine.

They returned by a different route. Esus, despite the queen's assurances which, as he made plain, he fully accepted, deemed this to be only prudent and he was not gainsaid. They came to Letocetum on the evening of the eighth day, weary and mud spattered. I was with the general when his chief of staff came to him and made his report. For a moment he was silent and then I saw him smile; it was his first since many days and that night couriers rode from our camp into the west.

Next morning we set about the work of extending our camp and during the ensuing ten days our army grew. An auxiliary cohort marched in from Viroconium and was followed a day later by a further two coming from the north. Hard on their heels came a regiment of auxiliary cavalry, also from the north, their tall lances resembling a forest of young saplings rising from a garden in spring, so gaily coloured were their shields and horse furniture. The last to come upon us was the greater part of XX Valeria which poured out of the west, with the rhythmic thunder of nearly eight thousand nailed boots, each man in step with his comrade, so that the great road itself seemed to shake beneath their unhurried, never-varying beat. Above their heads, set boldly on its pike, floated the legion's eagle, brilliant gold flashing in the rays of the dying sun, its jewelled eyes and cruel beak contemptuous in its lofty, godlike loneliness. I know of nothing on this earth which can match the majesty of a legion on the march, and the hearts of all who watched the coming of Valeria, even the legionaries of Gemina, beat the faster for the spectacle.

During these days of waiting, we of the general's staff received, examined, probed and sifted news of Boudicca and her army. Reports came in by courier from cavalry patrols deployed astride the road along which we had come from Londinium. Agents slipped through the forest into the camp, reported and were gone. Rebel and suspected rebel scouts captured by patrols screamed or whimpered what they knew as their bodies writhed and jerked beneath the knives, hooks, twisting cords and hot irons of the torturers. We learned that, having destroyed Londinium and butchered the sad remnant of its people, the rebel army, or much of it, had moved slowly north to the sack of Verulamium. That accomplished with blood and fire the rebels tarried, perhaps because of the immense task of procuring food for so great a host. Now the army was again flooding steadily north with its van already past Bannaventa and Queen Boudicca with it. We could not gauge its number but all men said that this was the greatest army ever seen in Britain.

That Boudicca was on the move brought comfort to our general for our own supply problem was now serious. Our foragers had swept the land bare and we could take no more from our granaries in Viroconium and Deva. Should

Boudicca not come to us then surely we must go to her; this would have irked our general for not only had he planned in what manner he would fight his battle, but had chosen the ground to fit his plan.

Some miles east of Letocetum[6] the road runs through a flat plain, much of which is tilled. All but one mile south of the road the plain ends in a gentle upward slope reaching to the summit of a low, grass-covered ridge beyond which lies forest. This ridge, in its centre, is shaped like a bow, the tips approaching the road more closely than its handgrip. The distance from one tip to its fellow is, perhaps, one thousand paces.

When he knew that the rebel van was approaching Venonae we marched from our camp in fighting order, but with our cloaks on our backs, leaving only an auxiliary cohort to hold it and so guard our sick, baggage and such supplies as remained. We took with us five days' food for men and three for horses, and deployed the army upon the general's chosen ground. In the centre of the bow in the ridge was posted XIV Gemina and four cohorts of XX Valeria. Upon each flank stood auxiliary infantry and beyond them our general posted cavalry, two regiments upon either flank, so forming an unbroken line between the tips of the bow. As a further defence against any attempt by the rebels to turn one or both our flanks, we posted the last of our auxiliary infantry among the trees of the forest, intermingled with, and on the outer flanks of, our cavalry. The two legions deployed half the number of their cohorts in the main battle line, with the remainder forming a second line on the higher ground some fifty paces in rear; but behind where stood the auxiliaries we lacked cohorts for a second line. As his reserve the general retained, upon the summit of the ridge and in the centre of the bow, two cohorts of XX Valeria and one regiment of Pannonian horse.

The army was deployed in this manner by early afternoon. The general rode along the ranks to ensure that all had been accomplished as he had ordered. When he was so assured his trumpeter sounded the 'stand fast' and the soldiers, although they remained where they had been posted, sat or lay upon the earth eating their dinner and once finished, as is the custom of soldiers, sleeping, talking, jesting, telling stories and playing at dice; thus we waited in the warm sunlight.

Marcus and I sat together on the top of the ridge close enough to hear the general's voice, should he summon us, but not so close as to disturb him with our noise. At our feet lay some twelve thousand soldiers sprawled in ordered confusion, the murmur of their voices rising about our ears like a hive of well-contented bees. Beyond them the flat plain was a patchwork of yellow and green, with dark lines upon it where our soldiers had marched. Beyond lay the ribbon of the road and then more plain melting into the further forest, which stretched unbroken right and left. It was warm and we were weary, for we had been at work before dawn. I remember that we spoke of Rome and of our families, of baths and banquets which had, or had not, given us pleasure; we spoke of women as young men will, of rosy dawns and of whispers, caresses and soft laughter in the gentle moonlight. Marcus was more serious than I and this I found strange; perhaps he knew what was ordained for him, but of the battle to come we spoke no word.

I was perhaps half asleep when I became uncomfortably aware of a new sound which swelled upon us out of the east. The rising clamour awoke an echo in my mind and suddenly, I thought, it is like the sound of the crowd at the circus before the games begin. I roused myself, sat up, looked and saw movements upon the road and upon the plain before the road, men in masses drifting in from the east, like a tide rising upon a gentle beach, with tongues of water thrusting their way forward along the lower levels. Some were mounted but most were on foot, there were chariots, two-wheeled carts and heavy wagons, and everywhere there were flashes as the sun caught helmets and spear points. The murmur of bees at my feet had grown shrill and it seemed that our quiet hive was now disturbed, even angry. The throng upon the plain grew, flowed towards us, and halted perhaps three hundred paces beyond our line, forming a solid wall of men who stared at us, some shouting but most in silence. I heard the general say: 'It will be dark within the hour; they will not come at us before sunrise by which time their whole army should be gathered. Our men will sleep where they now rest, but with double sentries posted a javelin's throw in advance. We stand-to half an hour before dawn.'

As darkness fell the whole plain before us twinkled with a myriad fires; as the night wore on the fires multiplied as the rebel host increased. The air was filled with shouting and singing, but we lit no fires and lay in the darkness wrapped in our cloaks; our thoughts were broken only by the snores of men asleep, by the stamp and neigh of horses and by the harsh bray of a trumpet recording every hour as it passed, bringing those marked for death one hour nearer to the moment of it.

It is hard to be brave during stand-to with knowledge of a battle beating in a man's heart. For the first half hour the darkness seems absolute. Speech is not permitted, since if the enemy approaches, a man's ears will serve him better than his eyes, and so all men wait, standing in silence, while their thoughts bring but scant comfort. It is ever cold; the stomach feels empty, lips are dry and there is a sour taste in the mouth. Perhaps the darkness is, in truth, an understanding comrade for he veils the fear in men's eyes. Then, as time passes, you chew the dried dates in your hand, the sky lightens, the gloom lifts, eyes can see once more, fear withers, dies, is gone and courage once again is reborn. Thus it was with me, and I believe with Marcus also, as we stood together in silence upon that ridge.

When the light served, the general and his augurs, under the eyes of the two legates, the tribunes and prefects commanding cohorts and the more senior centurions, took the auspices and pronounced them more than usually favourable. In common with most rational men I believe in a supreme being or beings, whom men call gods, but am in doubt whether they reveal themselves at the auspices. Had these been favourable or no, still we must fight; should they be adjudged unfavourable would the augurs have disclosed as much to the general or the general to his army? This the gods, in their all-seeing wisdom, must know and I doubt they would wish thus to be mocked.

The auspices taken for good or ill, the general spoke, and as in all he does, he acquitted himself well. The commanders returned to their soldiers. Marcus turned to me, and smiling said: 'All of us are, indeed, most fortunate for we now fight one of the greatest battles in Rome's long history. The fate of this whole province lies in our hands, and how we conduct ourselves will be on men's lips until the end of time. Moreover, those of us who fall this day will be honoured and held in awe for ever among the shades.' There was a note almost of triumph in his voice; I believe he knew.

We stood with hands clasped and looked down from the ridge. At our feet, and some fifty paces from us, was ranged the second line of legionary cohorts formed in six ranks. A further fifty paces forward and our eyes rested upon the first line, again formed in six ranks with on both flanks cavalry melting into the trees. The soldiers stood at ease each with his shield resting upright at his feet, and his javelins also upright, their butts set fast in the earth. Beyond our foremost soldiers was a space of perhaps three hundred paces and there was gathered the greatest throng which I have ever seen. Its ragged edges extended widely beyond the two flanks of our army and in depth it touched the road. It seemed that the rearmost were raised above their fellows; this I found strange until I understood that what I saw were men – later I found they were women – standing upon their wagons and so commanding a view of the battle. Deep in the crowd we saw movement like an eddy in the centre of a great lake; the eddy was approaching with a great roar of voices. We saw a chariot drawn by two white horses bearing a figure draped in red and holding a spear, for its point twinkled in the sunlight. The chariot broke through the foremost barbarians and wheeled; the horses tossed their heads and quickened their pace to a full gallop, continued past our left flank, wheeled about, and galloped the full extent of their army; the cheering followed it like the roar of the crowd at the hippodrome. War horns blared; a great roar beat upon our ears like thunder overhead and the crowd surged towards us.

There was a ripple of movement among our leading cohorts as the soldiers raised shields and grasped javelins. They waited until the leading barbarians had closed to perhaps forty paces; there was a flash of light as the sun caught javelin heads cast in unison, then a continuing ripple as the soldiers cast independently each of the other, the second rank passing through the first to cast more freely. A trumpet blared urgently; there was a harsh whisper as a blaze of swords leaped from scabbards, rank upon rank, and the whole army thrust forward; then all was bedlam as if a myriad smiths beat upon a multitude of anvils.

The legionaries forced their way forward, now standing, now gaining one pace or two, then standing again. The unbroken line of shields became ragged since some companies and cohorts advanced more swiftly than their comrades. In some measure this had been planned since enemy, where our line tarries, can, to their confusion, thus be assailed both in front and flank. From where we stood the advance seemed slow and painful but after a time I saw the second line of cohorts, while maintaining their distance of fifty paces behind the first, stepping over heaps of dead and wounded barbarians, so giving the measure of our advance. I saw also that their swords, as they passed, were busy among the heaps.

After yet more time I saw the general pointing with his sword, looked in the direction he thus indicated, and saw that the auxiliary cohort on the right of XIV Gemina was bowed inwards and there was clear danger of its breaking.

To add to our peril our second line of cohorts did not extend thus far with a wide gap between their right flank and the trees. Led by his bodyguard, the general trotted his horse towards the point of danger, his chief of staff riding at his right knee and Marcus some twenty paces at their backs. They were followed by one of the reserve cohorts of XX Valeria who moved forward at a steady trot. Lacking orders I hesitated and then urged my horse to follow the general, in case I could be of service. I saw a tall barbarian leap from the midst of a pile of corpses; he carried a long spear in his hand and ran, somewhat from the left, at the general's back, he and his bodyguard being quite unaware of the danger. I saw Marcus urge his horse into the fast-closing gap between the general's back and the point of the spear. I saw the barbarian lunge and Marcus take the point in his left side as he strove, awkwardly because of the angle, to parry the lunge with his sword. I rode the man down, leaped from my horse and as he staggered to his feet thrust deep into his belly and then, as he lay, cut his throat. Marcus was quite dead, the spear still fast in his body. I closed his eyes and wished his shade safe journey. I saw the centurion leading the first company of XX Valeria salute with his sword, and as he passed me heard him say: 'Your comrade did well; but for him Paulinus would lie there.'

It was late afternoon before the barbarians in the end broke and the battle became but slaughter. Their wagons bore their women and these they sought to save, but to no purpose, for we killed them and their women also and thus appeased the unquiet shades of those other women whom they had impaled, crucified or burned alive at and about Camulodunum, Londinium, Verulamium and elsewhere in the province.

We lost upwards of a thousand dead and the barbarians perhaps twenty times that number, although some say there were more.[7] We burned our dead on ten great pyres with Marcus among them. The general and I together laid him on the faggots. I placed the coin[8] between his lips and the general poured the libation. When the fire was spent, together we gathered ashes and these I know he has sent to you.

Now we fight a centurion's war in the land where the Iceni once dwelt. The orders we obey are to burn every dwelling, destroy every patch of tilled land, seize every beast, kill every man and boy and bind for slavery every woman save the old, whom we kill; thus will the Iceni become as if they had never been. It seems that Boudicca cheated us for men say that she died by her own hand, and none know where they laid her body.

So my task is done and I hope that I have not wearied you with so much writing. Marcus was in truth a man. He lived as a good soldier should, was beloved beyond all others and threw away his life to save his general and with it this whole province, for had the general fallen, the battle could in truth have turned against us. When my time comes, I would be glad for the tenth part of his honour.

NOTES

A number of specific auxiliary units feature in the story. The Tungrians came originally from Belgium, the Asturians from north-west Spain, the Gauls from France and the Pannonians from Hungary. All these units are attested as having been in Britain not later than AD 122. When Aulus Plautius invaded in AD 43 his army included some twenty thousand auxiliaries. Few are likely to have been withdrawn during the ensuing seventeen years of virtually continuous fighting. It is, therefore, not unreasonable to assume that all the units mentioned were with Paulinus.

[1] The Praetorium was the headquarters of a Roman military camp where stood the general's tent.

[2] The 'Broad Stripe' signified senatorial rank and the 'Narrow Stripe' that the wearer was of equestrian family.

[3] Vexillation means detachment.

[4] The 'great road' was Watling Street but there is doubt whether, by AD 60, it had been completed as far north as Chester.

[5] The Alban Hills are close to Rome and served as a refuge for the wealthy from the summer heat of the city.

⁶ Near the village of Mancetter there is some rising ground which overlooks Watling Street. It is indented by a number of defiles and, since it consists of older rock than that of the plain below, might well, in Roman times, have been thickly wooded whereas the plain would have been scrub covered or even cultivated. It seems to fit Tacitus' description: 'He (Paulinus) chose a position in a narrow defile, protected from behind by a forest. Here he could be sure that there would be no enemy except in front, where an open plain gave no cover for ambushers.'

⁷ Tacitus tells us that the Romans lost 400 against British losses of 80,000. With due respect to him, I doubt that we need take either figure very seriously; perhaps Lucius' estimates are nearer the mark.

⁸ The coin which Lucius put into Marcus' mouth would pay Charon's fee and so win, for his spirit, unhindered passage into the Underworld.

Rufinus

In truth it was never much of a village, nevertheless it was home to a dozen families, the only home that some, at least, had ever known. Now there was nothing standing except a few short lengths of what had been a cattle fence surrounding the place. Of the dwellings there remained but a dozen heaps of glowing, smouldering, smoking ashes, from the edges of which rose charred timber uprights which glowed, flamed and glowed once more, fanned by a gentle breeze out of the west.

It seemed that mounted raiders had struck out of the night in the half light before sunrise. Fire arrows into the thatch of the huts had heralded their onset and the whole affair was done in a matter of minutes. Of a score or so of men and boys two only were alive; both were wounded, one seriously. Three of the younger women had been taken, five were dead, and of those who remained, all, even the old, had been raped not once but often. Some still lay as the raiders had left them and looked at us through dull eyes, others crouched singly and in groups seeking to cover themselves in their torn rags; they rocked their bodies back and forth like the slow oar beats of a galley at sea. The air was filled with a sobbing murmur from which at times there broke a higher-pitched screaming as of grief too heavy to be borne. Children, huddled among the women, cringed out of sight and pressed their thin bellies to the earth in fear when their eyes met ours.

Every beast within the compound had been slaughtered, and to complete the bitterness of destruction, the raiders, in savage fury, had galloped their ponies back and forth across the few poor patches of sown crops which had once stood about the village.

Our medical orderly knelt on the ground tending with careful hands the two wounded men. I could see that my officer was with him so I tethered his horse, and mine, to what had once been the cattle fence, beckoned to a Thracian trooper[1] to watch both horses, and approached more closely in case my officer sought something of me. I heard the orderly say: 'Sir, should we leave this one here he will die; should we take him to Glevum he could mend. I have seen to the other; he suffered only a scratch; I have cleansed it and he will be well within the week.'

My officer replied: 'Prepare your men for the journey to the legion's hospital; secure him to one of our led horses; ride back with him. Should he recover, one day he may thank us.'

The lightly wounded man broke in; he spoke in the lilting Celtic tongue; his hands were tightly clenched and his eyes were red with anger. He said: 'He is my father, headman of this village; my mother lies dead; my sister is stolen. This is Rome's doing; Rome offers us no defence and denies us weapons to defend ourselves against the Silures, who have long been our enemies and are now Rome's. The Silures prosper, we die and Rome speaks of thanks. When the Destroyer comes for me he has a right to look for courage, but not for thanks. Rome is our Destroyer.' He spat on the ground.

I was angered by his words and at the insult to my officer; I dropped my hand to my sword hilt. My officer stared at the barbarian and in careful Celtic replied: 'My friend, you have a point. We will do what we can to mend your father. We will follow the raiders, and our forts beyond the river are being alerted to deny their crossing. You may see your sister again.' He turned to me and said, in Latin;

'Were you or I he, I would hope that we had the courage to speak as he did. Bring my horse; now we ride.'

I am called Rufinus and am a soldier of II Legion Augusta. I was orderly to Poenius Postumus, camp prefect of the legion. I was born in the high mountains which divide Gaul from Hispania where our Goddess Pyrene has power. I never knew my real father, but my mother, whom I loved, took another man for husband when I was but a boy. This other treated her cruelly and often beat her with a great staff until she lost her senses; I feared him, for he beat me too, but as I grew towards manhood my fear of him withered as my hatred flowered. One evening I came down from the high hills and found my mother dead; he had beaten her into a bloody pulp and, in his madness, was still striking at her body. My hatred blossomed into scarlet rage. He came at me swinging his staff; there was murder in his eyes. I tripped him and, as he fell, struck him with my clenched hand on the back of the neck. He fell on his face, his head in the fire. I dragged him out by the feet, took him by his burning hair and beat out his brains upon the hearthstone.

I went to the headman of our village and told him what had passed. He said: 'Under our law one who kills his father is put to death. In my heart I pardon you, as would many in the village, but the law allows no mercy so, should you remain here, I may show you none.' He paused, looked at me kindly, and continued: 'The Romans always seek men for their legions. Tell their recruiting officer that I sent you, now go; you must never return. We will do honour to what was your mother.' Thus I joined the Eagles and became an exile from my own people.

For a time I greatly feared the anger of our goddess since in my own eyes, and perhaps in hers, I was in truth a patricide and so accursed, meriting death. I hoped she would think of my mother, knew that I had truly loved her, and knew also that to avenge her murder was indeed my duty. Moreover, being a woman, albeit divine, she was thought to favour women above men and, since what I had done was done for a woman, this could stand to my credit. In time my fears grew less for I did not hear her soft footstep, smell her hot breath on my neck or feel her claws upon my flesh; even my dreams were untroubled.

In my new life I found a clean, well ordered world where food was abundant, the roof kept out the weather, I had fresh straw for a bed, good clothing for my back and coins in my hand. For this they had the use of my body, to mould as they thought fit, and I revelled in the moulding of it, all of me except my feet which for a time rebelled, for I had never known boots. I was the best recruit in my squad and even my instructor, who was not a man at all but a monster fashioned of bronze, iron and leather, praised me and swore a great oath that I did him credit. He then cuffed me soundly to remind me of my duty.

We were to join a Gallic auxiliary cohort, for only Roman citizens could enter a legion, and we were as far removed from citizenship as one of my goddess' bears. It seemed, however, that II Legion Augusta needed men, so they contrived citizenship for me and others;[2] thus we became legionaries and came to Britain with Plautius as our general and Vespasianus – later to achieve the purple – as my legate. My centurion was Poenius Postumus. In time I became his orderly; marched in his service as he advanced through the centurionate; won his trust and confidence and in some measure – when we were alone – his friendship. In the main it was because of him that I learned to read and write the Latin tongue. I owe him much, and although many besmirch his memory I do not, but am assured that his spirit has peace and is honoured and respected among the shades, not least for the manner and courage of his dying.

My officer, Poenius Postumus, at the time of which I speak, was approaching sixty years. He was a short man, very square with huge shoulders, a barrel chest and was more hairy, like a bear, than any man I have known. He had served just forty years having joined the Eagles when Tiberius was emperor. His strength was legendary throughout the army, and among his decorations he had been awarded the Crown with Battlements not, as is customary, for being first over a defended wall, but for his feat of plucking out single-handed the heavy timbers which formed a German palisade, and then fighting his way into and through the breach which he had thus made. He had won the Oak Leaves, two torques, the armlets and upon his breastplate hung nine silver discs; all this regalia he had gained for bravery. Those who now call him coward have but short memories. Having, again through personal gallantry, won promotion in the field to the rank of centurion, he worked his way up to become chief centurion of II Augusta, and thence became camp prefect in the place of Longinus who died in battle against the Silures.[3]

It has often been said that no officer is a hero to his orderly. My officer was and ever will be a hero to me but, being mortal, he was not without blemish. He was too merciful and to be ruthless was not in his nature; he often told me that in his long service he had seen too much blood, agony and grief and had become sickened by it; accordingly, he now sought to cherish rather than squander men's lives; he sought to command by example and not through fear of punishment. He was, moreover, a man who met difficulty in making a decision. This I found strange but believe that it was born from his habit of mercy; he was apt to seek a way round, to lay siege, as it were, to his intention, rather than to achieve it through direct assault. In another man in another age these faults could yet be virtues. To him in our time they brought death and in the eyes of many, but not I believe in his, disgrace.

Most of II Augusta was in garrison in Glevum. Four legionary cohorts and all our auxiliaries, save the Thracians, occupied forts and fortlets for the most part on and beyond the great river – the Severn. Our task was to overthrow the power of the Silures while holding the loyalty of the Dobunni, whose tribal lands extended widely about Glevum. To this end successive governors of Britain had campaigned against the Silures for upwards of ten years with scant success. Because we had killed so many of them they now feared to meet us in battle in the open field; now they attacked our forts but seldom. Nevertheless they raided us without respite whenever they saw fit, were always eager and alert to ambush any patrol or supply train and, if hard-pressed, would seek safety in their wild mountain country where we could scarce follow and, when we did so, seldom catch them. It was war without end, war, moreover, without glory or achievement, indeed it was war almost without hope. The whole legion and our auxiliaries were heartily weary of it but could hope for no relief.

Looking back over the years I now believe that we rated them too highly; they were neither gods nor supermen, nevertheless they knew their land far better than did we. Being unencumbered with armour they could ever outdistance us, even when on foot; moreover, their raiding parties rode rough ponies and seemed never to rest.

Although they could use both sword and spear, they were skilled archers,[4] and thus could strike at us from a distance and were gone before our ballistae could redress the balance. I have never met the horse archers of the Parthians but have spoken with soldiers who have fought them. In Parthia, it would seem, our legions faced difficulties similar to those of II Augusta, but whereas the Silures are now tamed, the Parthians are not, so perhaps we have no great cause for shame.

What I must now record smells of disloyalty to my

legion. This gives me pain for should a soldier lose his loyalty he loses his reason for living, and were better dead. Nevertheless I owe a still greater loyalty to my officer and to his memory; thus to be true to the one I must, with sorrow, betray the other.

II Augusta suffered at the hands of our legate and he was ill-served by his tribunes, although here too he was not without blame since the appointments of some, at least, he had himself contrived – or so it was said. This legate was perhaps an able magistrate but he was no soldier, and neither understood nor had any feeling for us whom he commanded.[5] The tribunes aped their legate and their activity, or rather their lack of it, infected the cohort commanders. It followed, as night follows day, that real authority fell to the centurions and they, being human and unchecked, abused it. Good men were flogged for no good reason; irksome duties were performed by the few and shirked by the many; discharges were not properly completed by due date; sleeping-out passes were improperly withheld and pay accounts dishonestly entered. In short, should a soldier hope for justice and fair treatment he had to buy it, by payment to his centurion. Of course I would not claim that in any legion bribery is unknown. There are venal centurions as there are venal magistrates, dishonest tax gatherers and the like, but the practices which flourished in II Augusta were almost beyond believing and worse than that, were almost beyond enduring.[6]

My officer was well aware of all this and of the true and shameful condition of II Augusta; he was utterly revolted by it. Many times, to my knowledge, sometimes even in my hearing, he complained, but to no purpose. As camp prefect he was without the necessary authority, being responsible only for stores, arms, equipment, buildings, defence works and our hospital. He commanded none save his own staff. We could liken ourselves to a well ordered barrack room within a disorderly hut, and the condition of the hut worsened.

On an evening in March I went to him, as was customary, to learn the routine for the day following, and what he sought of me. I pushed aside the door-curtain, entered his room, saluted and stood at attention. He had a room in the headquarters building which served as his office and in which he also slept. It was a bleak, cheerless, unheated place. Not even in midwinter would he permit himself the comfort of a brazier. He slept on the floor upon a legionary paillasse stuffed with straw stretched in one corner under his cloak, and the warmth of a bearskin covering. When first I saw those skins I was in fear, for bears are sacred to my goddess, and mortals touch them at their peril. Even today I am in doubt. Britain is far distant from my land and yet, could the goddess have known, and in her bitter rage contrived, over the years, the destruction of my officer? Such riddles are beyond my poor understanding and to dwell on such is to walk with peril.

He had a table, some stools and three iron-bound chests, one for his few possessions and the others for his duty. The one unglazed window was never shuttered and the rough timber walls were bare save for a long straight sword which hung behind his table. This sword had once been that of a German chieftain whom my officer had killed in single combat. It was the only adornment in that bare and simple room.

He had never married, believing that a wife could turn a soldier from his duty. When he had need of a woman, and this was seldom, he would go to the officers' brothel, where he was known and greatly respected and where any woman was honoured, should he care to lie with her.

As I had expected, I found him seated at his table upon which lay disordered heaps of tablets and scrolls. Spread upon them I could see a large map which depicted the land held by II Augusta. He looked up, smiled and said: 'Rufinus, I am but just returned from the legate.' I knew this was so since, as his orderly, I kept myself informed of his movements; he was still speaking: 'Since you watch over me like a mother hen this will not be news to you.' I remained impassive, and as a good soldier should, stared at a spot on the wall just above his head where my eyes found comfort in a knothole and in the many whirls and twists which contrived it. He laughed and continued; 'But, I have other news. Our legate with two cohorts and all the auxiliary cavalry, save only the Thracians, is ordered to join the governor at Deva. He marches two days hence and thinks to be gone four months. He takes with him the senior tribune and leaves in my hands what remains of II Augusta and the auxiliaries. I grudge him the cavalry but, if I could, would add to the four months. Nevertheless in that time between us, you and I should make something of II Augusta. Go, summon the senior quartermaster – for together we must plan the legate's move and make provision for his march.'

The following three months were, I believe, among the happiest that my officer had ever known. He could feel the pulse beat of the legion quicken and grow strong under his hand. It was as if he placed his arms beneath a useless carcass and, using his great strength, lifted it bodily from the ooze into which it had sunk so deeply and then, like some god, breathed life into the pallid corpse. He visited every outlying fort and fortlet not once but often and, for the most part, unheralded. Good discipline with justice returned to the companies; military crime, formerly widespread, all but ceased; soldiers sang on the line of march and walked erect with eyes alert and jesting mouths; joy in living and pride and purpose in soldiering returned. The cohort commanders set about their duty, each attempting to outshine his fellow; only the centurions grumbled, but never in the hearing of my officer. In all my service I have never seen so much accomplished in so short a time, or have sensed such an uplifting of spirit.

Despite our almost complete lack of cavalry we enjoyed some success against the Silures. During all this time we suffered but five raids; one war band was ambushed west of the river and destroyed to a man, having achieved nothing; of the other four, three were intercepted on their return, were badly mauled and their prisoners – all women – freed, although in truth some had had their throats cut before their bonds were loosed. Spring became summer and the sun shone bright and warm upon the bold spirit, gleaming arms and bright armour of II Augusta.

It was in early June that the commander of our secret police sought a meeting with my officer. He was a freedman named Constantius; doubtless he was clever but with close-set tawny eyes utterly without warmth, expression or humanity, like beads of coloured glass set on a string. I was in fear of him for he had once asked me many questions about my officer, which I had answered honestly and as well as I was able. He then put it to me that I should become his spy. At this I flew into a rage, told him that I would not stomach his impertinence, that I despised him and his like, and would beat him unless he took himself off, which, with an ill grace, he did. My officer laughed when I told him what had passed. He said: 'Most faithful Rufinus, never despise any man, not even the most humble slave, because of the nature of the work he does, whether he uses head or hands. Save your contempt for the manner in which that work is done, should it be but poorly accomplished. This policeman does well and merits our approval, both yours and mine. I doubt whether you or I would be as diligent.' He looked at me smiling and continued: 'Have no fear, I will see to it that he does not trouble you again.'

I took the man to my officer and stood behind his chair.

The policeman stared at me, saying that his news was for my officer's ears alone. I made to go but my officer restrained me saying that from me he had no secrets; this I believe was the truth for he honoured me with his confidence. The policeman spoke for upwards of an hour. There were rumours in Glevum and among the Dobunni that Rome was falling. This had been foretold by the Druids who had great power in all Britain, and against whom the governor was even now campaigning. These rumours were supported by information given by police headquarters to all senior police commanders, such as himself, within the province. It was believed that the Iceni and Trinovantes were plotting rebellion. It was known agents from these tribes were abroad among the Catuvellauni, Coritani, Cornovii, Dobunni and perhaps others. It was believed that these men were attempting to spread the rebellion. He himself, it seemed, could confirm this belief in that two Iceni had been arrested in Corinium. They could give no good reason for their presence in the town and both had died under interrogation, but not before disclosing the names of a number of Dobunni chiefs and headmen with whom they had spoken. These chiefs and headmen were now being hunted. The policeman spoke much else besides, being puffed up with his own importance like most freedmen, but what more he said added nothing to our understanding.

When the man had left my officer sought my opinion. I said: 'Sir, there is fear in Glevum. The usurers are calling in their loans, and are pressing such soldiers as have been foolish enough to become indebted to them. To obtain credit is all but impossible; certain even of our contractors, I am told, have become anxious for their gold. Such men, it seems, know more than we. Brawling in the town has become more frequent. Were times normal much of the blame could fairly be laid upon the soldiers; not so now.

Discipline is better almost than I have ever known it; our men are attacked without cause. I believe that the soldiers would favour increasing the numbers and scope of our town patrols. I believe also that they would accept, without grumbling overmuch, that certain of the more disreputable wine shops and brothels, certainly those where there has been brawling, should be denied to them, provided the reason for such denial is made known. Such action, moreover, could encourage the owners of similar establishments to mend their manners, restrain their other customers, and so guard their livelihood. We could, perhaps, impress upon the Dobunni that we are here, and intend to remain here, by undertaking further training exercises over their land and inviting their chiefs to witness the spectacle; thus they could sweep away their doubts and clear the cobwebs from their thick heads. The Silures, no doubt, will look for profit; we should press them harder and so make them work and hopefully die, to our benefit.'

My officer chuckled and in mock humility said; 'Well said, legate, all this and more we will accomplish.' He grew serious, looked at me hard and said: 'I hope our governor completes his campaign soon; he may find good use for his army elsewhere in the province. Meanwhile it is for us, while giving the appearance of truly Roman unconcern, to bestir ourselves to the advantage of all Britain. You will admit that policeman, immediately he seeks me, ignoring all other business. In the meantime, as always, I have confidence in your sharp eyes, keen ears and wise judgement. See to it.'

The sun still shone but it seemed to me that its brightness had dimmed and that its warmth had cooled. It seemed also that a cold wind was blowing out of the east, and that the wind was rising.

Among my officer's duties was to meet with the town council of Glevum. This council comprised a dozen of the more influential citizens; there were landowners, merchants, shipowners – for the river port was a busy one – the chief magistrate, a banker and others. The council met in mid-June and, as was both customary and fitting, my officer presided. I stood behind his chair; two sentries kept the door. We were fully armed and armoured and dressed as for ceremonial purposes; thus we wore the purple helmet plume which distinguished II Augusta.[7] I had seen to it that my officer wore his best cuirass, which was of highly polished and decorated bronze, moulded to resemble a naked chest. His insignia sparkled at his throat, wrists and upon his cuirass. He wore also his best leather baldric, the one with the silver studs. He looked magnificent and the council members, as we had intended, were visibly impressed.

These meetings were often lengthy, since most of the councillors felt impelled to speak on every matter raised so as to signify to their fellows, and to my officer, their own importance and wide knowledge as men of affairs. From the outset I sensed that this meeting could be different. The councillors seemed uneasy, even anxious; they were wont to avert their eyes from my officer and even from each other; instead they stared at the table and seemed to busy themselves with the tablets and scrolls which most carried.

My officer welcomed them all individually and by name, dwelt at some length upon the success of the campaign being waged by the governor, and upon the certainty that it would soon, and successfully, be brought to an end. He spoke of our operations against the Silures and gave details of the numbers of raiders killed, stressing that the figures he gave were not assessments but dead raiders counted where they lay. He pointed out that because of our success, and of certain other measures which were being taken, it would seem that the number of raids had lessened. He had hopes that this decline might set the pattern for the future. An essential part in our success, he said, lay as always in the high standard of training of the soldiers concerned; as a means to this end members of the council would be aware that the incidence, spread and rigour of training exercises were increasing. All subordinate commanders had been made aware that they must prevent, as far as possible, damage to growing crops. He, personally, would investigate any claims alleging damage. Finally he drew attention to the increase in the number of town patrols and the fact that soldiers no longer frequented certain less reputable establishments. He was sure that the council would understand that this was to the benefit of all law-abiding citizens, and afforded continuing and convincing proof of Rome's good intentions towards all such.

I sensed a slight easing of the tension, and the council moved on to discuss more routine matters. These included the possible extension of the port, water supply in the town, a serious brawl involving soldiers in which two citizens had been killed, and whether military assistance could be invoked in the recapture of certain runaway slaves.

My officer was about to end the meeting, when one of the landowners asked leave to raise another matter which was concerning the citizens. He was a small, dark, clean-shaven man with a nervous twitch, soberly dressed in a dark brown tunic and white trousers cross-gartered in red. He stood with folded hands staring at the table. Without raising his eyes he said; 'There are rumours of rebellion in the east. The slaves who work my land are unsettled; they dared even to mistreat one of my overseers telling him that when they were free they would first cut his throat and then mine. Thereupon, I hanged the two ringleaders and the remainder are now quiet. Can our acting legate give us any information on such matters and can he also assure us of his protection? I for one, would welcome most warmly, soldiers on training exercises on my land.' He resumed his seat with obvious relief and frightened eyes dwelt upon my officer.

There was dead silence in the room. I could see the two sentries standing like statues at the door and, beyond, the pale and dusty sunlight. It seemed that there was a faint chill in the room; my officer smiled and said: 'I know of this. It could be but idle rumour or it could be smoke heralding a fire. You will be, perhaps, as aware as I am that we have a full legion, together with auxiliaries in and about Lindum, say ten thousand men. That should be ample to handle any madmen who dare to conceive rebellion. In that event, should more soldiers be needed, then, as I have stated, the governor's campaign nears its end and his great army will be in readiness. Glevum and its citizens are safe; on that you have my oath.' He looked at the little landowner and added: 'Your invitation is accepted. I find it strange...' – he chuckled – 'that we are not always made so welcome.'

Whispers of rebellion and slaughter were already rife in Glevum before an exhausted courier, riding a near-foundered horse, rode in from the east with the sombre message of disaster. The colonia at Camulodunum had been utterly destroyed by massed Iceni, Trinovantes and others. Now the rebels were marching on Londinium which, as my officer and I well knew, lacked both walls and soldiers for its defence. There was news neither of the governor nor of IX Hispana, which lay in and about Lindum.

At dusk of the day upon which the courier reached us, I was summoned by the duty centurion whose company furnished the guard on the east gate of our fortress at Glevum. He said that a barbarian had sought to pass the gate alleging that he had word for the camp prefect. The guard commander had very properly detained the barbarian, and informed his centurion, who now led me to the guard room. I recognised the man as the wounded headman, whose hurts had been healed in our hospital. I remembered that my officer had several times visited him before he had returned to his people. He grinned when he saw me and said: 'I remember you with the officer who saved my life when you came to my village. I am come to repay the debt.'

I examined him for hidden weapons, and again he grinned. I found none and took him to my officer. They met like good comrades of long acquaintance. The man said: 'I owe you my life and could, under the gods, save yours. Our young men are restless believing that Rome falls. There are tales of rebellion, of Rome's soldiers overthrown and their slaves and women butchered, of farms and hamlets burned and great towns and temples destroyed. It is said even that the Goddess Andrasta, who all men fear,[8] having overthrown the gods of Rome, now leads the war bands of all the tribes of the east against the might of Rome. We older men are wiser than our sons and urge restraint upon our young warriors, having been deceived by such tales before, but we are mocked and our power grows less. Should your soldiers remain in Glevum, strike at Silures raiders and keep their strength among our people, I have good hope that the fathers can restrain their sons from battle; but should you loosen your grip even a little our sons, and mine among them, will rise and then much blood would flow to little purpose. Guard yourself, my friend, retain here your strength where all can witness it, and in so doing you could spare my son's life as you spared mine.'

Another long day passed and then Constantius brought further word. IX Hispana had been destroyed, their eagle had been lost and their legate killed; none but a handful of auxiliary cavalry had escaped to bear the news. My officer and I believed his tale, not understanding that although it held the truth, nevertheless much of what he said was false. He also told us in a hushed whisper of the manner of death which the barbarians had brought upon the men, women and children of Camulodunum: burning or burying alive, crucifixion or impalement. These cruelties, he said, had been witnessed by police informers who, hardened as they were, had vomited when they spoke of what they had seen. Constantius spoke also of his disquiet regarding the Dobunni. He gave it as his firm opinion that should my officer relax his endeavours and reduce the extent or incidence of the legion's presence throughout the tribal lands, the Dobunni would join the rebels and rise against us. He was assured, moreover, that they possessed hidden arms in plenty to further such rebellion.

In truth it seemed that the cold and bitter wind blowing from the east had now become a raging tempest, carrying with it black darkness, the smell of blood, the acrid reek of smoke, the screams of the tortured and the sobs of the dying; a storm, moreover, which threatened soon to blow us all into oblivion.

That same day my officer summoned me. He carried in his hand a despatch from Army headquarters in the field, and there was bitterness in his voice when he spoke. 'Our governor has ended his campaign and now understands that the province at his back is afire. He rides for Londinium and bids me bring II Augusta to Letocetum. Do I obey?'

I was astonished; a soldier's duty is always to obey. I said: 'Sir, the governor commands; you obey, as you expect obedience from all who serve you. When you have given an order you brook neither question nor delay, nor should the governor. Should you not go, and should the governor stamp out this rebellion, you are shamed for ever and men will call you coward for all eternity. Should you not go and the governor be overwhelmed, the province falls, and with it falls your honour also, since men will say that the province fell through you, since had you gone the governor would have mastered this rebellion. You have no choice. You can but obey, to do otherwise would condemn you utterly.'

There was a long silence then, in a flat voice as if he were weary unto death, he replied: 'You are a good soldier,

Rufinus, and are fortunate that no more is demanded of you. I bear the burden not only of a soldier's duty but also hold in my hand the lives of all those thousands yet loyal to Rome, who dwell in and about Glevum. Should I obey the governor, then assuredly the Silures will raid and the Dobunni will rise, for there would be naught but auxiliaries to restrain them. My people must then suffer the fate of those in Camulodunum. Moreover, I should be foresworn, having assured the council of Glevum that the citizens were safe. Should the governor succeed I should return to a desert – haunted, screaming – and be pursued forever by the shades of those whom I had condemned to a vile death. Should the governor fail I should not return, but this would not restore life to the dead nor bring peace to their unquiet ghosts. By remaining I may save lives, by marching I would most surely sacrifice them. You, at least, will understand that my honour, forfeit although it must be, cannot be permitted to sway this hard decision.' He lifted his head and looked at me. I saw death in his face, his eyes were tortured and II Augusta did not march.

Everywhere there was an all-pervading fear. In the streets men hastened about their business, spoke seldom, laughed never, started at a careless footfall, anxious not to be too long absent from the shelter and comfort of their homes. The fields were seemingly empty, farms deserted, but when riding abroad with my officer I was ever conscious of unseen eyes upon my back. Windows were shuttered; doors were stoutly barred. Women endlessly sought assurance, and reassurance, that their men would themselves kill them so that they would not fall alive into the bloodied, fire-blackened hands of the rebels. Children wailed unceasingly and hid themselves away, ever fearful of a monster shaped like a woman with flaming hair, sharp teeth and claws of bronze which gorged its huge belly on human flesh.

We lived each day as if it were our last, ate when we

could and slept in the saddle or upright upon our feet. My officer was everywhere; should there be difficulty he was there to resolve it; where there was doubt he inspired certainty; where men were fearful he gave them courage; if they were weary he brought them strength.

We threw up a rampart and dug a ditch about Glevum to deter attack, or should such be made, to deny it.[9] Much of the work was performed by the citizens, their numbers swollen by refugees fled in fear from the land. They relished neither their aching backs nor bleeding hands, but when the task was done slept more soundly in their beds. The rampart built, we guarded the gates, checking all who entered and left the town. We enforced a nightly curfew to guard the law-abiding and deter those who were criminal or disloyal. We were ever active throughout the forested and settled areas of the Dobunni. Our patrols were ever on the move, guided by men still loyal and often aided with police informers. We found arms caches and arrested rebel spies and agents; these men under torture gave further information for our patrols to follow. It was a covert, cruel war which cost us much sweat but little blood. Its gain was that the Dobunni kept the peace and none but a handful were active against us.

We harried the Silures, were ever watchful at the mouths of the valleys which entered their land, ambushed intending raiders and intercepted others as they galloped for home. They achieved but little against us and paid a heavy price in blood for scant success. Our losses too were heavy and the strength of our cohorts beyond the river melted like snow beneath the sun.

On the day it was said that the governor had won a great victory, and the rebel army in the field had been destroyed, hope, at first but a spark, flamed into certainty and fear was forgotten. It seemed that the great tempest which had raged for so long was suddenly stilled, and that the sun shone once more upon a stricken world. All men rejoiced, save our soldiers, who grumbled that they had little but hard knocks, weariness and the scars of old wounds to show for all their unceasing labour. The centurions complained, moreover, that their honour and that of II Augusta was forfeit and – this being their true grievance – they had lost their share of the spoil.

I was sick at heart and very weary when, one evening, I went to my officer for orders. I entered his bleak, sad room and found him lying upon his face in a great sea of blood. Holding against his body the point of the long German sword, which had hung upon the wall, he had wedged the pommel between the floor and the edge of his upturned table, and then, leaned forward over the blade and fallen upon it. Very gently I turned his body over and saw his face. It came to me that he was suddenly grown old, his forehead deeply lined, his cheeks sunken and his hair streaked with white. I closed his eyes, wished his brave spirit a safe journey and, for the first time since I became a man, I wept.

II Augusta, albeit grudgingly, gave him the funeral due to his rank, but none would have marked the place, or accorded him any memorial, had not the citizens of Glevum and the chiefs of the Dobunni erected a funerary stone as a token of the love and respect they bore my officer. In very truth he gave his life, and threw away his honour, that they might live.[10]

NOTES

[1] The VI Cohort of Thracians are attested at Gloucester.

[2] It seems not to have been all that unusual to get round the regulation which stipulated that legionary recruits had to be Roman citizens.

[3] In AD 51 the camp prefect of II Legion and eight centurions were killed when attempting to build forts in Silures territory.

⁴ The writer knows of no evidence which would indicate that the Silures were skilled archers whereas, in later years, the Welsh most certainly were. It is, however, by no means impossible that Welsh skill with the bow dates back into pre-recorded history.

⁵ The commander of a legion was designated 'legate' and the appointment was in the hands of the emperor himself. Legates were usually senators who had served the state in a number of appointments including that of senior magistrate. The appointment as legate was usually but a stage in a man's career and so military ability varied greatly.

⁶ Rufinus may well have been unfair to II Legion in his description of the state of that legion in AD 60. It is certain, however, that the legion had endured a very tough ten years of unrewarding fighting, and that it failed to come to Paulinus' aid when so ordered. This suggests that all may not have been well within its ranks.

⁷ Helmet plumes were worn only on ceremonial occasions. It is doubtful whether a meeting of the town council would normally qualify as 'ceremonial', but conditions were not normal and military splendour can do something to put heart into frightened men.

⁸ The god or goddess particular to a tribe was seldom well known beyond the borders of his/her people. Normally, therefore, Andrasta would inspire neither fear nor worship much beyond Iceni frontiers. Conditions, however, were far from normal. Moreover, the Iceni were led by a woman, who could be Andrasta in the flesh, it being not all that unusual for deities to appear as mortals. Small wonder, therefore, that the man whose life Poenius Postumus had saved should refer to her as 'whom all men fear'.

⁹ One of the surprising things about the Great Rebellion is that Colchester, London and St Albans, probably the three most important towns in Roman Britain, were all unwalled and so fell, a comparatively easy prey, to the rebels. At Gloucester there was certainly a legionary fortress, and since some three months were to elapse between the destruction of Colchester and Boudicca's

defeat, it is not unreasonable to assume that some defensive measures were taken to safeguard the town.

[10] Tacitus tells us: 'As for Poenius Postumus ... he fell on his sword when he heard of the honours won by the XIV and XX (Legions), for he had cheated his own men of a like distinction and disobeyed his commander's orders, in defiance of army regulations.' As a result he is known in history for cowardice and suicide. Tacitus could, of course, be right but his unbending judgement is difficult to accept; after all he was certainly wrong in lauding Paulinus' vengeance against Classicianus' clemency. It is just possible that Rufinus might be a fairer judge.

AILIS

My name is Ailis and now I am ugly and bent; my bones ache and I feel very old. Some of the more foolish are in fear of me for they say that I have the evil eye. When I walk abroad, leaning on my staff, the children run from me believing that I am a witch and could curse them. This grieves me for I have ever loved children. I am lonely, but not often hungry, for the women of this place are kind and give me food even when times are bad and the harvest a poor one. I do not believe that I shall long be a burden to them, forever in my ears I sense the soft footsteps of the Destroyer, as he treads yet more closely upon my heels. As others I have known, I have no savour for his coming, but am not wholly in fear of him. The length of the lifespan of all of us is preordained, and there is naught that any can do to take from or add to it. Nevertheless, I hope that when my time comes, he will be quick and not, as a man would, botch his task; that he will cut my life thread cleanly, not leaving it to stink and smoulder like an ill-kept lamp but poorly snuffed.

In my life I have known more sorrow than joy but I have truly lived. Because of how I was made and the task which the gods laid upon me, I have played my part in the unfolding chronicle of human fate. That I am quite unknown is of no import for I can preen myself that had it not been for me the story of women, and that of men also, would be the poorer.

I am of the Parisii. My grandfather's grandfather came over the Great Sea with others of our people and with their bright swords took this land. Those who were here before them they killed, enslaved or drove into the west. My father was a lesser chief who held his land from another who was yet greater than he. He was of true Parisii stock, loud-mouthed, tall, red haired, blue eyed and fair of skin, whereas my mother's blood was tainted with that of the people who once had called this land their own; from them, I believe, came her gentleness, and they contrived her black hair and dark eyes although, like my father, she also was fair of skin. I scarce remember her for she died when I was yet an infant but I do know that she truly loved me, whereas my father did not; indeed, I remember him more for the beatings he gave me than for any tenderness at his hands or warmth in his nature. Looking back, with in my ears the whispers of those long dead, I believe that he loved my mother and was ever true to her and to her memory. I believe also that his grief weighed heavy when her gentle spirit left him for the shades, and since I was fashioned all too closely in her image, he had but to look upon me to recall her memory and so awake anew his sorrow. It was, perhaps, because of this that he ever mistreated me and I had cause and more for tears, but none for laughter. Men ever claim that women are gifted neither with logic nor reason, whereas I have more of both in my little finger than lay in the whole of my father's handsome, empty head.

His comrade had a son but five years older than I. He was called Oisc, after my father, and could have been his son since – although in truth there was no blood link – they were as much alike as two grains of wheat in the same ear. When I was turned fifteen we were wed, to my joy, since I knew no happiness in my father's house and hoped that as a wife my life could become less burdensome. I took as my dowry a stallion, two brood mares, ten fat cattle and much of the jewellery which had been my mother's.

Lacking a woman's counsel I knew doubt as to how my

body could best serve a man, but my husband soon resolved my dismay in his own fashion. Naked, he entered our bridal chamber and set two torches about the couch where I lay. He stripped the covers from off me and struck me, when with hands and hair I sought to cover my nakedness from his greedy eyes. Then he threw himself down upon me and took my body with violence like a stallion ruts with a mare in season, not once but often, taking pleasure in the pain he occasioned and in my shuddering loathing of the manner of his lechery. When it was again day he left me, my body bruised and bleeding, my belly and thighs raw and between them pain as from a dagger thrust. Thus he served me throughout our marriage, never seeking to awaken any desire in me, but only to pleasure himself.

Having thus suffered I found I was with child, and so looked for relief from him. This, indeed, I found to the solace of my body, if not of my mind, since he took my slave woman to his couch, quite without shame, saying openly that since I could not satisfy his desire he must bed with another. When I was in the eighth month of carrying my child, he came to me, being full of mead and, despite my pleading, because of the peril to my child, he took me again with his accustomed violence; I found I was in labour and after a night and a day of agony gave birth to a son – dead – at which, with fear writ large in his eyes, he upbraided me for my wantonness in destroying his child. In truth it was not until then that I understood how much I truly hated him.

Knowing that I could look for neither aid nor comfort from my father I crept, with but a cloak to hide my shame, to the hall of our chief. I found the place in some confusion for his wife also was in labour. Perhaps my coming gave him some relief from fear as to how she would fare for he received me kindly, was attentive to my tale, and swore that he would himself judge my husband, since it is against our law that a woman, near her time, should be known by a man, whether or not that man be her husband.

My case was heard and my slave woman herself supported my tale, under torture, for it is our custom that no slave may bear witness except under torture, lest that slave should dare to lie. Indeed, she had no love for my husband who had mistreated her body as he had used mine. His crime was judged well proven and he paid the score in full, for in that very place they cut away his manhood and I watched, taking pleasure in what was done and in his anguished screaming. The wound became infected; he was dead within three days and I found myself a widow.

It seemed that the chief had good reason for his fear, for his wife died giving birth to their first child, a daughter, whom almost with her dying breath she named Boudicca, which in our tongue signifies 'Daughter of Victory'. With my son dead, my breasts' milk swollen without relief, I became Boudicca's wet nurse and then, in some measure, her foster mother, for even when she was weaned she would not willingly suffer another woman to attend her. She would scream mightily, beat with her tiny fists and kick unceasingly until I came to her, at which she sighed like a gentle breeze in growing corn, smiled her pleasure and immediately slept.

A woman who is without love is like a tree without roots: both wither and die. For nigh-on sixteen years I had been such a tree, but with Boudicca at my breast, my life began anew, indeed, I blossomed as a flower in spring and knew true happiness; she could have been child of my body and I in truth her mother. In the beginning I knew the pain of my dead son but this faded and in Boudicca I found myself, knew my destiny and in some measure hers also, which was disclosed to me in this fashion. While it was yet dark, except for the dim light of one poor lamp, I held Boudicca in my arms and she noisily at my breast; I was very weary for she had been fretful and I had scarce slept for nights. Indeed, my head was nodding when I heard a woman speak. I raised my head and looked, thinking that one of the slaves had come to my aid, but saw in the half dark not a slave but my mother. I knew that it was she for in her I could see myself, and set about her throat a necklace of gold which she had loved – or so my father had told me – and which now was mine. She was smiling; her eyes were very bright and I knew no fear of her spirit. She said: 'Ailis, my daughter, guard this child well for she will be great in this land. She is named most fittingly for she will win great fame and victory, and because of it her name will live in honour for all eternity.' I said: 'Mother'; heard a long-drawn sigh like the wind at evening and knew that, save for Boudicca, I was again alone, at which I wept – but only a little. I told no one of what I had seen and heard, not even her father, for I feared their mocking laughter at a woman's idle dreaming.

When Boudicca was aged two years the chief married anew and I could not find it in my heart to chide him. He was alone; I could offer him but scant comfort and would not share his couch although he, I knew, would have welcomed me, but not as his wife. He was, moreover, save for Boudicca, childless. His new wife, Aelwen, had a shapely body but an empty head. She was nobly born but her father was both a fool and a cuckold, whereas her mother was a whore. Aelwen was young, but turned sixteen, with flaxen hair so pale as to be all but white. Her eyes were dark and lustrous, her lips full and moist but ever slightly parted as if in wonder at the world which flowed about her. Her breasts were full and her hips broad; I guessed that her body could be eager for a man, like that of her mother, and it seemed that this was the truth for in six years she bore her husband as many children, and of these, two sons and a daughter passed safely through their infancy. Until her coming the chief had found much pleasure in Boudicca, had held her on his knee, fretted were she sick and came often to her nursery, which was also my bedchamber. After he was wed, the demands made of him by his wife and her ever-growing litter enforced a change in his way of life. I am assured that he still loved his eldest daughter, but since he saw but little of her his fondness faded. It followed that the ongoing task of turning her from infant to child and thence to woman was left to me, in all but its entirety, and I gloried in my task.

Almost from the moment of birth she was grave beyond her years; there were ever questions upon her lips which I answered truthfully and as well as I was able. I taught her always to speak truth, since a liar is ever despised; to keep faith, since upon faith is built the whole fabric of life within a family, a nation and between nations; and ever to have courage, for a woman or man who lacks for courage is a poor thing, without honour and fit only to be mocked. I taught her of our gods and goddesses; of how they may best be honoured in ritual and sacrifice, of spirits and demons, of nymphs and sprites, of witchcraft and magical arts and of the ever-watchful shades of our fathers and our fathers' fathers. I taught her also the folklore of our people and spoke what I knew of the nations whose borders marched with ours, and of those others, more shadowy, who dwelt in the wilder parts of Britain. At my knee she learned the trade of a woman, how to hold and use a distaff and, once the thread was spun, how to fashion it. As daughter of a great chief I doubted that she would need often to practise such skills, but having herself achieved dexterity, I believed that she should then be more fitted to oversee her women at their work. I taught her the command of a great hall, as its mistress, and in my teaching sought the aid of the chief men among our household slaves. As she grew older I taught her of the blending of colour in her attire, of the wearing of jewellery, and how to match both to her fair skin, blue eyes and hair of flaming fire. Looking back on my own sad lack of knowledge, and what it cost me, I taught her also of her body, of its union with that of a man, of childbirth, of suckling and of the ills of infancy.

At other times, I fear, that I spoke of men but seldom, and much of what I said would scarce have brought them comfort. She lacked the company of children of her own age for Aelwen was ever jealous of her own, and flew into a rage should she find them with Boudicca. She saw but little of her father and so learned, although in very truth I did not teach her this, to hold men in some contempt, seeing in them creatures who took much but gave little, who ever boasted of their strength and courage, but whose deeds seldom matched their words, and who were only too ready to mistreat the weak, such as a woman, to her sorrow and their shame.

With her father's leave I saw to it that she was taught to ride, calling upon the aid of one of the older men among the chief's own company. In this fashion she acquired a great love of horses which became, I believe, the greatest joy of her life, and at which she excelled. However, I was careful to keep her ever mindful of her duty to Epona – the Horse Goddess – and daily, when the season served, to deck her altar with fresh-plucked flowers. Having learned not only to ride, but also to school a horse, there came a day when, in a crashing fall, she broke an arm. Between us, a slave and I set the broken bone and applied both stay to grip the bone and covering to guard the wound. Despite her agony she made no sound, shrugged us away from her, remounted and with her one good arm continued her riding while I, sick with the pain of her body and with fear beating in my heart, besought Epona to guard her from further ill fortune. She learned also to drive a chariot,[1] first with two horses and then with four, and in time outdrove all others in her father's hall.

Her teacher was wont to take her hunting so as to profit her riding but this too became a joy to her, although she took but little pleasure in the ending, and sought ever a clean kill, as she herself spoke of it, with the least suffering occasioned to the quarry whether it were gentle deer, courageous boar proudly at bay or slinking, snarling wolf. She ever practised with her bow to this same end, for she seldom shot live quarry unless she felt assured that she would kill rather than wound. With her bow, indeed, as with her chariot, there were but few who could match her.

She was turned twelve when the Moon Goddess touched her body; she became a woman and her father's thoughts turned to the matter of her wedding. In this I know that he was ever pressed by his wife, who desired greatly that Boudicca's face should be seen no longer in the hall since, whereas she was loved and honoured by all, her own spoiled children were not, and even her sons could not match Boudicca's art with a bow, her mastery of horses or skill and daring in her chariot.

There was no lack of suitors among the Parisii for her father was wealthy, a rich dowry was assured, and so many came who, to obtain what she would surely bring, would, without shame, have married their own mothers. Perhaps the day will come when a woman is taken by a man not because of what he can win from her father, but because of what she is and, doubtless, on that same day the sun will rise in the west and men will bear children, such is a woman's servitude in a world fashioned for men.

Boudicca looked upon each suitor in turn, both old and young, some handsome, others ill-favoured, some boasting, others discreet, almost humble; she read the greed in their eyes, marked their grasping hands, listened to their smooth words and her lip curled in contempt. Her father, to his credit, asked her opinion, which she gave him shortly like a whiplash, and did not seek to force her, but sent the man away with honeyed words and waited for the next until, at last, no more came and, to my knowledge, his wife raged at him. Then it was said that the wife of one Prasutagus was dead, and that her lord looked for another woman to share his couch – and his throne – for he was a king, and ruled a nation called the Iceni.

It is not the custom of kings to seek, rather they demand. Prasutagus did neither. The Parisii are not ruled by a king but by a council of the greater chiefs, Boudicca's father among them. To this council Prasutagus sent an embassy, empowered by him to build an alliance against the Coritani, who dwell in the lands which lie between his borders and ours. The alliance made, so said the king, our two nations would war against the Coritani, kill or enslave such as were so foolish as to guard their lands, drive their fellows into the great forests of the west and divide between themselves the land so stolen. As all men know, such alliances are often sealed by marriage. By chance, so said his embassy, their king sought a wife who would give him sons, and when her first was safely born, he would honour the alliance and make war upon the Coritani. Moreover, since King Prasutagus was rich and so lacked for nothing, and as a further proof of his good faith, he sought no dowry with his bride. Thus was Boudicca sold to Prasutagus, her price assessed in lands stolen, blood spilled, tears shed and slavery or exile for the many. Thus do men, under the gods, trifle with the lives of those whom they rule and those whom they seek to oppress, so great is their greed for the goods of others. That Prasutagus was old enough to be Boudicca's father was a trifle, unworthy to be considered. Nevertheless, as doubtless he had foreseen, for he was crafty, the council could not stomach the giving of a dowerless bride which must arouse the mocking laughter of the many who would deem the Parisii mean and shameless. Indeed, it is said that never before has so rich a dowry accompanied a bride of the Parisii to her husband's domain.

The wedding was occasioned in King Prasutagus' great hall and was witnessed by a throng of Iceni nobles, Druid priests, priestesses of a Goddess Andraste whom I came greatly to fear, soothsayers and Parisii chiefs. Boudicca's father was not among them for he claimed that he was too sick to make the journey. This claim, perhaps, was just, but such sickness as may have plagued him lay not in his body but in his mind for he had no love for the marriage, his dismay being overborne by the anger of the council, greedy for Coritani land, and also by his wife's vehement urging.

The wedding done, there was feasting in the great hall with wine and mead in plenty for those who supped. All that great company were men save two only: Boudicca, seated next her husband, and I standing behind her chair. With the king's leave, and with the lustful eyes of all upon her body, she withdrew early from the feast to seek her marriage couch, and I went with her.

Together her women and I stripped her naked save only for the golden fillet upon her brow which signified her rank and which, by Iceni custom, it was for her lord to doff since it was he who had placed it so. She was very calm and her blue eyes were unclouded as she stood in the soft and tender lamplight. She was tall and about her body hung her mane of well-combed, flaming hair which touched her knees. Having dismissed her women she lay down upon the couch and I drew with loving care the covers of fine linen about her. I thought, in truth she is not beautiful, her nose straight but overlong, her face too full, her chin too proud, her lips thin – some might say cruel, her eyes over large; but her body is well fashioned and so should bear kings, thus aiding her husband to keep his bargain and so destroy the Coritani. The sour taste of bitterness rose in my throat and I felt the prick of tears in my eyes. She looked upon me in silence, smiled and said: 'Dearest Ailis, you are far more distressed than I. Marriage is a time for joy and not for sorrow. Take my hand and aid my courage until he comes. I hope he will not keep us overlong. He is older than I would wish; he is not as tall as I am and I doubt that he is a bold warrior, but there is a kindness in his face which belies the craft in his eyes, which ever wander as if he plans new guile. I believe that he will be gentle with me; hope that I shall be a good wife to him this night and always and, if he is man enough, that I will bear him sons.' I gripped her hand for my tongue felt swollen, my throat tight and no words came.[2]

We listened to the tumult in the hall, loud voices, singing and shouts of ribald laughter which flowed about us. I saw her shiver, pressed her hand, leaned forward and kissed her forehead, at which she smiled. I saw the door curtain snatched aside; watched a small, dark man with grey hair, sparse uncombed beard and twitching hands hasten into the room, his feet twinkling beneath him like those of a bird. Behind him, through the doorway, I glimpsed a throng of bearded faces and heard cries of bawdy laughter. I felt my cheeks burn for very shame and, with anger in my heart, stood and bowed low for it was the king. The door curtain fell back into its place. I heard her say, a little breathlessly: 'Thank you, Ailis, for making me what I am. Now you must leave us for my husband and I have need of each other.' I knelt, kissed her hand, saw the king smile and hastened from the room with tears hot on my cheek; there was a plea in my heart that the Mother Goddess would watch over her, and that her body would not be mistreated as mine had been.

It was the year before the Romans came to Britain.

At her husband's side Boudicca was to know full seventeen years contentment, if not true happiness. In her own fashion she grew to love him and, in so far as a man is capable of love, I believe that he loved her. She bore him two daughters; Sevira, of whom she was delivered a year after she was wed, and Vodicia, two years younger than her sister.[3] The gods did not see fit to give her a son although, in truth, the fault if fault there was, lay neither with the gods nor yet with her but with her husband, whose manhood could not match the desire of his wife's body which, for a time, grew ever more eager. Nevertheless she was true to him; no other man knew her and in time she overcame the burning flame of her desire which cooled to glowing embers. That no son was born of the marriage freed the king from his intent to ally himself with the Parisii and make war upon the Coritani. Nevertheless, since he was a man of peace, I know that this brought joy, not grief, to his heart and served to allay his sorrow that he could not father a son. Indeed, in some measure he was even glad of it and never once chided Boudicca, as many men would, since such are only too apt to lay the whole fault upon the woman, and thus absolve themselves from blame.

Sevira and Vodicia grew to womanhood, both fashioned closely in the image of their mother, having her red hair, blue eyes and fair skin; but neither, and especially Vodicia, who was little, could match her stature. They were worthy to be her daughters, being courageous, truthful, wise and virtuous; they truly loved their mother and she them. To my pleasure I found myself chief nurse to both, and schooled them as I had schooled Boudicca under her ever watchful eyes, and with the willing support of the king, who took much joy in them as a good father should. I revelled in my task and was honoured and delighted with their love.

During all this time the king ruled wisely, and both he and his people prospered. In many matters Boudicca was his councillor, for he learned to prize her wisdom, and although he did not always heed her voice he leaned increasingly upon her, especially when he began to feel that his life spark was growing dim. In only one matter were they ever at odds and that concerned the Romans.

It was but shortly after their army came to Britain that the king, and many of his fellow rulers, allied themselves with the emperor of Rome, who himself journeyed hither from over the sea, spoke fair words and sealed all such alliances with gold in abundance. The king believed that he should be true to his oath, which he had given freely, that the Romans would keep faith, and, since they ruled the world, was assured that it would profit neither himself nor his people to take up arms against them. All the news from Gaul, which the Romans ruled, was of peace, great prosperity and a manner of life less harsh than was ever known. The king believed that as it was in Gaul so it would be in Britain. He was ever gracious to such Romans as came to his hall and urged his people to act as he did, to build fine houses and paved roads in the Roman fashion and mould their way of life in the Roman manner. There were some who, more to honour the king than because they wished to ape the Romans, acted as they were bidden and, being pressed for gold, foolishly sought the aid of moneylenders – Romans or their lackeys.

Boudicca, however, had no love for Romans and in this her woman's wit was wiser than that of her husband. She was angered by the contempt which she read in their cold eyes and by the disdain which seemed never far from their thin lips. Her hatred was matched only by her distrust of their true intent, and although she spoke them fair, out of duty to her husband, her hatred and distrust grew ever keener and more bitter.[4] Indeed, she would permit nothing Roman in the women's quarters, save only wine, which she drank but sparingly having no love for mead which, in truth, is fit only for men, being both rough and coarse. Many of her people, most I believe, shared her view and there were some, led by a young, hot-headed chief named Foilan, who rebelled.[5] These were swiftly overborne, and although many were killed in the warring, the Romans did not deal harshly with them; few were enslaved and even Foilan was pardoned – after a while. Nevertheless, because of the rebellion, our Roman masters commanded the king to disarm his people, greatly to their anger. This command was obeyed in as much as many weapons were surrendered and no man openly carried such. Nevertheless hidden arms were aplenty, and deep in the forests the smiths were busy fashioning more, against the day when, it could be, men would have sore need of them.

Many of the gods whom the Iceni hold in awe are honoured also by my own people. Among such are Lug of the Long Hand, Grannus, whom some call Belenus, Lord of the Sun, Epona the Horse Goddess and Matres the Goddess Mother, but they honour also men called Druids. These were strange to me since none dwelt among the Parisii. It seems that the Druids worship oak trees, or perhaps the oak is but a symbol for their god whose name cannot be spoken. They are wise, can read the stars and so foretell the future. Such men advised the king on Iceni law, custom and tradition and their memory reached back deep into the thickening mists of time. They are skilled also in healing and practise magic but for good rather than for ill. Boudicca, and I also, spoke much with them and profited greatly from their learning, their lore of healing and their wisdom in the affairs of men. Of their religion, however, they spoke but little since on such matters they are bound by most solemn vows of secrecy.

There is another goddess who has great power in the land; her name is Andraste and she I came to fear above all else, indeed even her name spoken in a whisper causes all who hear it to shiver and dart fearful glances into the shadows, as if they glimpse a demon. Andraste, it seems, bestows victory. It is she alone, moreover, who makes women fertile, causes crops to grow and cattle to breed. Without her aid the Iceni can look for naught but disaster and death. To gain her favour she demands blood and delights in the slow, anguished, screaming deaths of her victims. Andraste is served by women rather than by men and one of these was Boudicca, who was not only queen to the Iceni but also priestess to the goddess. It was but a little time after she was wed that she was initiated. I aided her to attire herself in a plain white mantle which covered her body from throat to toe. My hands shook, for I could feel the power of the goddess, as I placed a heavy bronze torque about her throat and bracelets of the same bright metal on her wrists. All were chased with strange designs and symbols which wound about them, evilly, like serpent's coils. She wore her hair loose save for a plain bronze fillet on her brow.

As the sun set two priestesses came to her apartments and I watched the three enter the forest which lay darkly behind the hall. Since I was in fear of what might befall, I sat upon a stool in her bedchamber and awaited her return. She came one hour before sunrise and at the sight of her I was in such fear that my knees shook and I could scarce rise to greet her. She looked like a corpse new risen from the grave: she was deathly pale, her hair awry, lank and drenched in sweat, her eyes open but seemingly sightless for she moved like one who walks but is yet asleep, her white robe was mud spattered and spotted evilly with great gouts of blood; there was blood also upon her face, hands and feet.

I led her to the couch, sat her on the edge of it and put a wine cup to her lips. When she had drunk of it her whole body shook as if she was sick of a fever; she threw her arms about me and wept while I embraced her cold, shivering body and soothed her with soft words as if she were still a child and I her nurse and comforter.

After what seemed an eternity she spoke in a whisper: 'We came to a forest clearing. It was lit by flaring torches set about the verge. In the centre was a great rock decked with flowers. There were many people of whom the most were women and among them were priestesses attired as I. We danced and chanted about the rock casting many flowers upon it seemingly for an eternity. Then priestesses brought a woman out of the forest; she was naked. They laid her on her back on a flat stone in the shadow of the rock and held her there without movement. They brought a sharpened stake and thrust it into her belly between her thighs and drove it ever deeper so that the tip came out of her right shoulder. They lifted the stake, with the woman impaled upon it, and set it in the earth so that she faced the rock. Then we came away and left her alone in her agony in that awful place. She still lived, for her head moved and her hands plucked at the stake but her strength had ebbed for she had ceased screaming. It was my hand that guided that cruel stake on its long slow journey the full length of her body. They said that the woman had mocked the goddess. They said also that unless I truly cherished her in my heart I would never bear sons. In this fashion we honour our goddess and give thanks for the harvest she has been pleased to bestow upon her people. Thus it has always been and should we not gain her favour in this fashion, my people wither and die.' Her whisper died in her throat and I sat with my arms about her until she slept.

In the eighteenth year after she was wed, Prasutagus fell sick of a fever, could not breathe and gasped away his life. His council met and chose Boudicca to be ruler of the Iceni against the day upon which one or other of her daughters was wed, when the matter of their ruler would again be weighed. The council was aware that their king had made a will in which he appointed the emperor of Rome co-heir with Sevira and Vodicia, but believed that their judgement would accord with the king's wishes since all doubted that the ruler of the world would concern himself in, for him, so small a matter. Boudicca accepted the council's judgement but, being in all things faithful to her husband, sent messengers to Camulodunum to inform the Roman Governor, Suetonius Paulinus, of the king's death, acquaint him of the nature of his will, and deliver into his hands a scroll upon which that will was penned.

King Prasutagus had seen fit to have his wishes written down in Latin, since we have no written language.[6] The matter of writing was accomplished by a chief, who attended at his hall and who to ape the Romans had not only built for himself a fine house in the Roman manner, but had also learned the Latin tongue. This man, having written down the king's words, was dismissed from the royal presence and another, who also knew that tongue, was commanded to read the will to the king, who thus ensured that he was not deceived. By making the emperor co-heir, I believe that the king hoped to further the safety of his people and the inheritance of his family, but his wisdom, if wisdom it was, served only to destroy both.

After a long time we learned that a Roman embassy was expected at the queen's hall; we believed that the governor himself, or perhaps his chief servant, a fat and vicious man named Catus Decianus known to and despised by the queen, would come to do her honour. Accordingly, Boudicca summoned all her greater chiefs to attend her, and prepared a great feast for the pleasure of her guests.

On the day the Romans came I attended Sevira and Vodicia in their bedchamber, which lay beyond that of the queen. We were debating how they should carry themselves at the feast which their mother had determined that they should attend. From the great hall came the sound of sudden tumult. Then, after a little time, we heard a woman scream with her cry suddenly cut short. We eyed one another in fear, wondering what such sounds should signify. We heard quick footsteps at the door; the curtain which masked it was roughly snatched aside and a Roman soldier, fully armoured with shield on his arm and naked sword in his hand, leaped into the room; two unarmed men followed and at their heels a second soldier.

The four darted quick glances about them and then stared at us with cold eyes as we stood in fear of what was to follow. One of the two who were unarmed, and who seemed to be their leader, spoke quickly in Latin. The two soldiers stepped across the room towards us while the leader and his fellow began a search, even opening the chests in which the princesses laid what they had, and snatching such jewellery and trinkets as they found therein. I was enraged at such insolence and shouted at them to mend their manners and restore what they had stolen. One of the soldiers, who had sheathed his sword sensing no danger for himself or his comrades from mere women, leaped at me and struck me in the face with his clenched hand. His blow was so heavy that I fell, struck my head against the wall, and lay in pain and all but insensible as the room whirled about me. Through the red mist which veiled my eyes I heard Sevira scream; there was the stamp of heavy boots; the thud of someone falling; a man laughed harshly and I heard the low sobbing of a woman.

The leader spoke; the red mist before my eyes faded and I saw him and his fellow go out through the doorway. One of the soldiers stood over me; I read lust in his eyes and understood what he intended. In terror I attempted to rise and drew my mantle more closely about my body. I felt his hand at my throat; he ripped first my robe and then my shift from neck to fringe exposing all of my body; he lay upon me and I felt his questing fingers between my thighs. I thought if my body can give first him and then his comrade pleasure they may spare the princesses, so I ceased to struggle and sought to do for them what, so long ago, I had striven so hard to do for Oisc. When first one and then the other had raped me I lay shuddering at what they had done to my body and in fear of what might yet follow. First there was silence and then I heard Sevira's and Vodicia's pleading voices, the sound of blows, tearing cloth, rude laughter and then panting movement upon the couches; in the heaving silence I heard sobbing and knew that my body had failed of its purpose, then I wept for my heart was breaking.

There was a footstep at the door. I opened my eyes and in my misery saw one of the two who had stolen the jewellery. I thought must we suffer him also; then I saw in his eyes compassion and anger. He spoke roughly to the soldiers and he and they left us alone with our grief and shame.

There was a water pot in the room and with it, and cloth from my torn mantle, I washed Sevira's and Vodicia's bruised and ravished bodies. I embraced them and gave assurance that no man would think the worse of them because they had been taken in violence by savage beasts against whom they had no defence. Then, together, we began to set the room to rights, I hoping that this would ease their misery and invoking in my heart every goddess I knew, even dreaded Andraste herself, to gainsay them bearing Roman bastards because of what they had suffered. It seemed that some goddess took pity on their ravished innocence for neither was gotten with child.

After a little while one of the queen's women came to us. From the blank horror in her face and the manner of her movement I knew that she also had been served as we had been. She said: 'Those beasts have whipped the queen and she is near death.' I answered: 'I will go to her, but comfort the princesses who have been mistreated as you were.' With fear and horror in my heart I hastened, almost ran, to the great hall, despite the pain in my belly and the black shame which lay upon me.

I found Boudicca seated in her chair, her body leaning forward resting upon her elbows. She had been stripped to the waist, her breasts hung naked for all to see and her back, from neck to buttocks, had been flogged into a bloody pulp; her two guards lay dead at her feet. The hall was filled with chiefs who stared at her in silence and uncertainty; the Romans had gone. I shouted: 'Is there a Druid in the hall?' and my heart leaped in my breast when an old man, whom I knew, stepped forward out of the throng. I said: 'Aid me lead her to her couch,' and together, one on either side with her arms about our necks, we supported her from the hall and laid her lying upon her face on her couch, she making no sound despite the agony of her torn back. The Druid took a pouch from under his robe and very gently shook what it held over her wounds, which he forbore to touch with his hands. At his bidding I poured wine into a cup; from a wooden phial at his girdle I saw him pour drops into the wine. We eased her on to her side, at which she bit her lip; she groaned aloud in her agony but shed no tear. I poured the wine into her mouth and saw her swallow.

The Druid said: 'In a little while, because of the drops, she will sleep. I will return before she wakes. Do not seek to cover her back, nor touch it; leave the powder which covers it free to do its work of healing; stay with her and drive away the flies lest her wounds become infected. She is strong and of high courage; were she not she would surely die. As it is, under the gods whose aid I will invoke, she will live.' Together, and with the aid of Sevira and Vodicia we attended her for many days but thanks to her brave spirit, the will of the gods, and the Druid's skill, her torn back mended and she became herself anew.

During all this time the queen would not rest. There were ever strangers in the hall seeking audience; most Iceni but I saw also Trinovantes and a handful of Catuvellauni. Foilan, the same who had been worsted by the Romans twelve years back, was ever with her. Foilan's presence with her, and the audiences she gave, caused me some disquiet for she could wear nothing which touched her back, indeed the Druid was hot against it, and yet I must contrive that her breasts be hidden; in this I succeeded albeit imperfectly, which troubled her not one whit. Should a man or men be with her I saw to it that I, myself, or a daughter was ever in attendance so as to scotch foul rumour at its root. During all this time there was but little laughter in the hall; brows were ever close knitted, mouths stern, eyes fierce and all, or nearly all, of such as came, tarried and went upon their separate ways, bore arms. Thus, as the days passed, I understood that the queen was bent on war.

There came a day when the hall was empty save only for those who dwelled therein: Foilan and the men of his company. Sevira summoned me to the queen, whom I found standing beside her couch attired in a robe of many hues, with red as their master, a blue coat upon her shoulders with a golden brooch as fastening, a torque about her throat and set on her head a winged bronze helmet surmounted by the image of a crouching wolf. In her hand she grasped a heavy spear tipped with iron.[7] She laughed at the wonder in my eyes and gaily asked: 'Do I seem to be a warrior?' I gazed at her in silence, saw her mane of flaming hair which streamed about her shoulders and hung to her knees, at her breasts which swelled beneath her robe, at her wide hips revealed and not hidden by her robe. I thought that were she a man she would be curling a moustache or combing a long beard, so smiling I slowly shook my head. I saw, for an instant, her foot tap upon the floor and it seemed that my answer displeased her; then she laughed and said: 'Most faithful Ailis, you ever speak truth and never seek to dissemble. In truth I seek not to be a man. Men chose me as their queen and so must be content to be led by a woman, even in war; for when in my chariot I drive hence on the morrow, I journey to our hosting where gather the war bands of every chieftain of the Iceni. At our hosting we shall welcome as allies Trinovantes, Catuvellauni and perhaps others.'

She laid her spear against the wall, doffed her helmet and set it upon her table. She looked at me and said: 'Now I am woman again for a little while. I have ever hated Romans but in my heart I have no wish to war against them. They whipped me, a queen, and this I neither forget nor forgive; from my daughters, who did them no ill, they stripped their virtue, the sole possession which every woman can truly call her own; for this they are shamed and accursed for all eternity. But were this all, and many would say that it is cause enough, I would not war. But they are bent on plundering this land and will destroy my people. Even now Romans and their lackeys harry our borders, seek by force the return of their gifts which now they hold were loans, steal our lambs and our cattle, despoil our farms and kill or enslave all whom they encounter. Thus it is that I have no choice. My people are already marked for death, but in our dying those who murder us will pay a price in blood, in grief, in agony for their broken faith, lust, greed and savagery.' She paused; the knuckles of her clasped hands were white from the power of her grip and her eyes flashed fire.

She continued speaking in a flat voice as if there was none to hear her: 'It could be, if Andraste wills it, that we shall overmatch them. Were they beset by but half the tribes in Britain, and were each war band staunch enough to set its teeth in Roman flesh and there lock its jaws, never to release them come wounds, come death, come agony, we could drag Paulinus down and with him smash his legions. This done, I doubt the Romans would return, not even to avenge their comrades. So this I must contrive with my woman's body and woman's wit; ever steadfast, ever courageous, never cast down, until it is done.' Her voice died to a whisper and it seemed that she again became aware that I was with her; she smiled upon me but I saw grief in her eyes. She said: 'Ailis, my mother, invoke the gods for us and especially for me, your daughter, who loves you and is ever in your debt. I wish you to remain here and keep this hall against my return. Now you must leave me for I have much to ponder.' She moved towards me, embraced me, kissed me on the mouth, turned and I saw that her shoulders shook; as I left her the tears streamed down my cheeks and I could not check them.

It seemed a whole lifetime that I waited upon her return. The hall was all but silent, peopled only by slaves and a handful of the queen's company too sick or too old to go with her to war. The hall, moreover, stood in an empty land, for not only had the men left for the hosting, but their wives and children journeyed with them. As in the hall, only the very old and the sick remained. Farms and hamlets stood empty and deserted, save for half-starved dogs howling in their loneliness and hunger. Fields were deserted and weeds grew long and lush for there were none to sow or till them and we could look for no harvest.[8]

I was in fear of thieves, and so from sunrise to sunset kept all doors barred save two only, and when the sun was down barred these two also. Moreover, I prevailed upon our old men, despite their grumbling, to keep watch of a sort.

We did not wholly lack for news although much of what came was naught but rumour. Men returned, most sick or hurt, seeking aid and comfort. I kept the Druid with me and for them we did as best we might and most again became well. When they were become whole men I drove them from the hall to return to the queen or to their homes, for I was fearful lest our food should be gone and those who followed starve. It was from the lips of such as these that we learned how the queen fared.

She had marched south, so they said, with her army, some mounted but most on foot, and with so many wagons that no man could number them. The throng was so great that it overmatched the multitude of stars in the sky; having watched from sunrise to sunset the passing of the host still more men came; the tumult of their passing was like that of a great storm as it echoes and re-echoes among the trees of the forest; never, since time began, had so great a host been assembled in all Britain and all hailed Boudicca as 'Daughter of Victory'.

Rumour came of the harrying and destruction of Camulodunum and of its great temple. We heard this from the lips of a man with a javelin head sunk deep in his shoulder. The wound stank of corruption; he babbled in delirium and we marvelled that he still lived. We tied his hands and feet and the Druid, with a knife, cut out the javelin head and cleansed the wound, while I pinned his body; he died in the night but what he told us was confirmed by a messenger sent by the queen herself. Then we learned of the ruin of the IX Legion, although this tale had gained in the telling for, in truth, it was but a part, not the whole, that was destroyed. We learned of the taking of Londinium and of the sack of Verulamium. We learned also of the sacrifices, and the manner of them, made to Andraste – the Nightmare Goddess – and my flesh crept. Then there was silence and the days passed one by one, each seeming like a year. Now there were more men, and women with them, in the land. These sought to hide themselves, should it seem that I espied them, when I walked abroad. This, I believed, ill-omened but told myself that in so great a host there must be some faint hearts, and that the queen would do well without such.

I awoke one morning to find myself alone, save only for the Druid. The slaves and even the remnant of the queen's company had fled. The Druid told me that in the night, while I yet slept, a band of mounted men had ridden out of the west crying that the queen's great army had been tumbled into ruin; that Romans, who spared neither man, woman nor child, were upon their heels. They had bidden us flee while there was yet time. Now I too was in great fear, but since the queen had charged me to keep the hall against her return, I could not flee; to his credit and my comfort the Druid remained with me.

She came in her chariot out of the setting sun and so, at first, I could not see her for the blood-red glare blinded me. I felt that Sevira and Vodicia were with her for I sensed their whispering voices. At her back rode mounted men for I heard the hooves and smelled the sweat of their horses. I stepped back into the shadows within the doorway of the hall so that I might see. One of her chariot horses wore a long streak of dried blood on its heaving flank; the harness had been roughly patched; a wheel was askew on the axle tree; the body of the chariot was splintered and none had sought to set it to rights. Her face was set as a mask; there was black desolation in her eyes and I knew that what we had heard was the truth. I ran to her but her voice was harsh as she said: 'They need food,' and I saw that but five men were with her, the poor remnant of her once-proud army.

I said: 'There is food in the hall but none to prepare it since all are fled.'

She looked upon me in anger, but then her eyes softened and she replied: 'Ailis, you are ever faithful and of high courage;' she turned to Sevira and Vodicia saying: 'Lead our guests into the hall and prepare such food for them as you may. Ailis will attend me to my apartments.' And so it was done.

I aided her to strip, save only her shift; we sat together on her couch. She said: 'It is finished; the army is destroyed beyond repair and Paulinus hunts without pity such as are yet alive. It would have been more fitting had I died, as did so many, but I could not bring myself to offer up my daughters' lives and so, when the battle was lost, I fled and now am shamed for ever. From my hands there drips the blood not of tens, nor hundreds but of tens of thousands; the blood of my warriors who looked to me and I brought them not victory but death; the blood of all those others who through me died, and yet will die, in this warring. My eyes are haunted forever by the spectacle, and my ears assailed into eternity by the screams of those I gave to Andraste for her cruel pleasure. Here too the fault lies upon me for I could never find it in my heart truly to serve or honour that goddess, as she well knew, and so I, and those others, pay the price of my having mocked her.'

She paused and looked upon me. In her eyes I saw a myriad sadnesses but no trace of fear. She continued: 'This night I die by my own hand; in very truth I can do naught else. You will pour me a cup of wine, most faithful Ailis, for the poison I hold is bitter. I wish none to watch me, lest my body struggles, and none must hear me, lest my mouth cries out, so you must keep my daughters from me. When he knows that I am dead it could be that Paulinus will lift his vengeance from my poor people and the killing could cease. Come to me at sunrise and, when you find me dead, fire the hall having a care that what remains of me is burned away to nothingness. The Romans mistreated my body when I was yet alive; were I to be buried they could, perhaps, learn the place and defile anew what remains of me, so nothing must remain. When all is burned take Sevira and Vodicia with you and seek safety among the Parisii but, as you journey, tell all whom you encounter that I am dead and that my body lies in an unmarked grave. Thus will Paulinus learn of it and the remnant of my people profit. Eliffer, leader of the five still true to me, knows my intent and will go with you to guard you on your journey.' I answered her not one word for I could not speak. I poured the wine, as she had bidden me, and proffered it kneeling at her feet. She leaned forward, kissed me full on my upturned lips and I ran from the room.

At sunrise we fired the hall, having built a great pyre of faggots beneath and about her body. We tarried a full day and a night, hiding in the forest lest the Romans should come, and then at sunrise I entered the place where her couch had been. The heat was still so great that I scorched my mantle and burned my feet, but I found not even a fragment of bone and so knew that the queen's desire had been fulfilled. Then we journeyed north; no man hindered our going and so we came to the Parisii, among whom Boudicca's memory was honoured and her deeds cherished, and where, free from the power of Andraste, we found pity, kindness and peace.

---

[1] The chariots of Boudicca's time bore little resemblance to that depicted upon her well-known monument at Westminster. They were very light and comprised two wooden wheels, upon which were shrunk iron tyres. The wheels were mounted upon an axle. This axle carried an open, wooded framework with wicker, perhaps wooden, sides. From the front of the wooden framework extended a long pole with a double yoke for two horses – we would call them ponies. The fittings were of bronze and the horse trappings and harness were often richly ornamented. Regrettably for the romantic, not a single chariot with scythes mounted upon the axle has been found in England.

[2] History tells us little of King Prasutagus, who is a shadowy figure compared with his wife. We do not know when his reign began but it is provable – not certain – that he was king in AD 43. It is fairly certain that he married Boudicca not later than AD 44 and perhaps some years earlier. He was also wealthy and, if for no other reason, may well have been cautious. Perhaps Ailis' description is not all that wide of the mark.

[3] We do not know the names of Boudicca's daughters. Since both were old enough to be raped early in AD 60 (or perhaps late in AD 59) one would hope that the younger was by then at least thirteen and so born not later than AD 46.

4 Perhaps another reason for Boudicca's dislike of Romans was the fact that Celtic women in general seem to have lived more emancipated lives than did most of their Roman sisters.

5 The Iceni rebelled against the Romans in AD 47 but with little success. As the price of failure the tribe was disarmed.

6 Until the Romans brought Latin to Britain there was no written language, although there is continental evidence of Celtic inscriptions written in Greek characters. The earliest written Celtic – using the Ogam script – dates from perhaps the end of the 4th century AD.

7 Cassius Dio describes Boudicca: 'She was huge of frame, terrifying of aspect, and with a harsh voice. A great mass of bright red hair fell to her knees; she wore a great twisted golden necklace, and a tunic of many colours, over which was a thick mantle, fastened by a brooch. Now she grasped a spear...'

8 Tacitus tells us: 'Famine was the worst of their hardships; they had omitted to sow the crops and brought every man into the army regardless of age expecting that they could secure our supplies for themselves.' A more likely reason for the lack of sown crops was that the timing of the hosting was such as to make spring sowing impossible.

Glossary

Bannaventa	Whilton Lodge (near Towcester)
Camulodunum	Colchester
Corinium	Cirencester
Deva	Chester
Gessoriacum	Boulogne
Glevum	Gloucester
Letocetum	Wall
Lindum	Lincoln
Londinium	London
Mona	Anglesea
Ratae	Leicester
Rutupiae	Richborough
Venonae	High Cross
Verulamium	St Albans
Viroconium	Wroxeter

Bibliography

Birley, Anthony, *Life in Roman Britain,* London, Batsford, 1964

Collingwood, RG and Myers, JNL, *Roman Britain and the English Settlements,* London, Oxford at the Clarendon Press, 1949

Dudley, Donald and Webster, Graham, *The Rebellion of Boudicca,* London, Routledge & Kegan Paul, 1963

Frere, Sheppard, *Britannia: History of Roman Britain,* London, Cardinal Books, 1974

Liversidge, Joan, *Britain in the Roman Empire,* New York, Frederick A Praeger, 1968

Mellersh, HEL, *Soldiers of Rome,* London, Robert Hale, 1964

Richmond, IA, *Roman Britain,* London, Penguin Books, 1955

Ross, Anne, *Everyday Life of the Pagan Celts,* London, Batsford, 1970

Scott, JM, *Boadicea,* London, Constable, 1975

Spence, Lewis, *Boadicea, Warrior Queen of the Britons,* London, Robert Hale, 1937

Webster, Graham, *The Roman Imperial Army,* London, Adam and Charles Black, 1974

MAJOR GENERAL PATRICK MAN, CB, CBE, DSO, MC, was educated at Rugby School and the Royal Military College, Sandhurst. His brilliant military career is attested by the honours awarded to him, and his many interests included wide reading and scholarship. He was a knowledgeable historian and an excellent judge of character.

He was born on 17 March 1913 and commissioned into the Royal Hampshire Regiment in February 1933; his first active service was in Palestine where he was Military Transport Officer (MTO) and then Company Commander, 1936–1938. When World War Two began, he was Transport Officer to the First Guards Brigade Headquarters and he entered the Staff College at Sandhurst in 1941.

On passing out, he joined the Headquarters Fourth Division as GSO 2 and Joint Planning Staff until 1942 when he returned to the Staff College as an instructor. He commanded two regiments in Burma in 1945, first the West Yorkshires and then the East Yorkshires. Finally, he commanded 2/4 Royal Hampshire Regiment in Greece.

Patrick Man achieved the appointment most coveted by all regimental officers – the command of the First Battalion Royal Hampshires, his own regiment, and he led them on perilous assignments in swamps and jungles against communist guerrillas from 1953–1956. He was awarded the Distinguished Service Order (DSO) and the Selangor Medal, which was presented to him in person by the Sultan of Selangor at a special Investiture.

Pat Man was known personally to every man in the battalion and throughout his service, the wellbeing of his men and of their families was his main concern, both as a Regimental Officer and as a Staff Officer.

He was GOC Aldershot Garrison and it was a most apt end to his career that he was appointed Director of Personnel Services for the Army at the Ministry of Defence. He died peacefully on 10 October, 1979 at his home at Quill Farm, Campsea Ashe, near Woodbridge in Suffolk, loved and respected by all who had known him.

Printed in the United Kingdom by
Lightning Source UK Ltd., Milton Keynes
138538UK00001B/10/P